Unconventional Lovers

Annette Mori

Unconventional Lovers

Annette Mori

Affinity
Rainbow Publications

2018

Unconventional Lovers
© 2018 by Annette Mori

Affinity E-Book Press NZ LTD
Canterbury, New Zealand

1st Edition

ISBN: 978-1-98-854908-8

Editor: CK King
Proof Editor: Alexis Smith
Cover Design: Irish Dragon Designs

ACKNOWLEDGMENTS

A huge thank you to all of my beta readers (Gosh I hope I remember them all – I sent this to a boatload of people): Gail Dodge, Cathie Williamson, Ali Spooner, Carrie Camp, Sue Fidler, Amy Herman-Pall, Ameliah Faith, Sue Rossman, Danna Micoletti, Dana Holmes, Elle Hyden, Darla Baker, Linda North, and my sister, who made great suggestions to improve the initial draft. Of course, once again, I have to acknowledge Erin O'Reilly, who is a constant support and encouragement to me. I am honored to call her a friend and have her support me in my journey. I would also like to express my gratitude to Affinity Rainbow Publications and the wonderful trio (JM Dragon, Erin O'Reilly, and Nancy Kaufman) who continue to provide feedback to tighten up manuscripts that need assistance and publish my unconventional work. This book, in particular, was very near and dear to me, and I am eternally grateful for the opportunities they give to let my stories see the light of day. My other family members, who are also very supportive, include my nephew and his wife, Aaron and Chelsea, my little sister, Kim, and my father, who struggles to read my books with one eye. I always enjoy working with beta editor, Nancy Kaufman, who helped tighten my story.
Thanks to CK King, aka Raven's Eye, for her magic as the final editor to tighten the story even further. Inevitably, there are those pesky final errors that slip through, and I am thankful that the final proof editor, Alexis Smith, caught those before the book went to print. Thanks to Nancy

Kaufman for the final cover. Nancy is also a promoter extraordinaire. A huge thanks to all the other readers and fellow writers who have sent personal e-mails, written reviews, and posted nice things on Facebook (you know who you are). The Affinity authors are an especially supportive group and often share posts or send words of encouragement. Finally, my wife, Jody, continues her support even when it interferes with our time.

DEDICATION

To my cousin, Dennis, who is in heaven sharing his love and light with everyone. To my wife, whom I love dearly for her patience and her ability to take care of me when I fail to do that myself.

TABLE OF CONTENTS

ALSO BY ANNETTE MORI

The Organization

Captivated

The Termination

The Review

The Ultimate Betrayal

Locked Inside

Out of This World

Asset Management

The Incredibly True Adventure of Two Elves in Love

(Affinity 2014 Christmas Collection)

Love Forever, Live Forever

The True Story of Valentine's Day

Vampire Pussy...Cat

Nicky's Christmas Miracle X3

(*It's in Her Kiss*, Affinity's Charity Anthology)

PROLOGUE

AUGUST 1990

Kathleen Kaufman could feel the sweat roll down her temple as it tickled the edges of her ear. Her husband, Jeremy, made cooing, supportive noises. She was done. If this damn baby didn't make her appearance soon, Kathleen vowed to tell the doctor she'd changed her mind about natural childbirth, and he should go ahead and give her the fucking drugs. She'd issued the eviction notice two days ago. With her hair plastered against her head, she was sure, right about then, she looked about as unattractive as she ever would.

"You're doing great, hon. I can see the head now," Jeremy cried out in excitement. He was stroking her arm in a loving gesture of encouragement.

1

"Okay…ready, Kathleen…give me another big push. We're almost there," Dr. Harding coaxed.

"Arghhh, that's what you said an hour ago." Kathleen grunted all her effort into the push. She was almost out of gas now. This had better do it. She was never having sex again if the end result was labor for thirty-six hours straight. When her contraction ended and still the baby hadn't arrived, Kathleen felt like screaming at every man, woman, and child anywhere near her bedside.

"It won't be long now, don't push until I tell you to, okay, Kathleen. I know you're going to feel like you need to push again, but hang on until we tell you to," Dr. Harding instructed.

"Easy for you to say, you don't have a fucking baby the size of a large watermelon coming out of a hole the size of a zucchini," Kathleen sniped.

Jeremy was holding her hand, and she crushed it when the next contraction came. "Oh hon, I think this is it. Can I get the camera?"

"No," Kathleen screamed and squeezed harder on his already squashed hand.

"Okay, one more push, Kathleen, push, push, push, that's great. You're doing great…" Dr. Harding encouraged.

With this last push, Kathleen could feel her baby slide right out. Finally, her daughter was making her entrance into the world.

Kathleen was a practical young woman. She'd opted for knowing the child's sex, because then she could properly plan for the nursery. Jeremy acquiesced to her wishes and went along with whatever his wife wanted. His role was to put together the crib and anything else that required his mechanical expertise.

Jeremy was also responsible for keeping the freezer stocked with various flavors of Ben & Jerry's ice cream, and a continual bowl of fried frog legs in the refrigerator she could microwave whenever she had the craving. Frog gigging was hard work, but he was happy to go out late at night and hunt the backwaters for the big bullfrogs to keep his wife content.

When Kathleen heard her daughter cry, it was music to her ears. She lifted her head to get a glimpse and noticed the furtive looks of the nurses and doctor. Jeremy didn't seem to notice, as the nurse laid the squirming bundle on Kathleen's chest. The other nurse handed Jeremy the scissors for him to cut the cord—like they'd talked about when creating their birthing plan. Kathleen could sense something was wrong, as she looked at the faces of the medical team. She knew the look of pity.

"What's wrong with my baby?" Kathleen asked.

Jeremy looked perplexed. "Nothing's wrong. She's kinda slimy right now, but I'm sure the nurses will wash her up in a minute. I count ten fingers and ten toes. She's perfect. Right, Doc?"

The doctor frowned as he looked down at their daughter and then turned back to Jeremy. "We should probably talk after the nurses have a chance to take care of your daughter. We can go over the Apgar score in a little bit."

Kathleen's heart sunk, as she looked at the crestfallen look on her husband's face. She could tell he was confused but had grasped the sudden realization something was drastically wrong with their first child. He was so excited at the prospect of becoming a father, and nothing short of a perfect child would do. His first reaction to the news left an indelible imprint on her mind, but this was something she

3

would never share with her daughter. That kind of emotional baggage was not something a mother should ever relay to her child.

CHAPTER ONE

JULY 2007

Deb rapped twice on the back door, then burst into her older sister's house, breathing heavily. Her niece, Siera, sat at the kitchen counter with her head propped on her hand and a little crinkle in her forehead. A thick textbook was laid out in front of her, and Siera's mouth moved as her eyes traveled back and forth along the page.

Kathleen kept shifting her attention to her daughter. Deb could tell her sister wanted to jump in and help, but that would end up placing more pressure on her niece. She'd been an outside observer of this, time and again. Kathleen pushed Siera and was vocal about not wanting anyone to treat her differently. She would refuse the additional services offered, stating flatly Siera did not require special consideration. That was the ironic part. Her stubborn sister never understood how her hovering and continued interference while Siera was

completing her homework was exactly the type of assistance the school officials tried to provide.

Deb was too excited to step in and save her niece from her overprotective sister. She wanted Kathleen's advice, even though she probably wasn't going to take it.

Kathleen finally shifted her attention away from Siera. "Where's the fire? Siera, why don't you take your homework to your room? I can already tell from Deb's vibrating body that she's going to disturb your concentration."

Siera looked up and gave Deb a toothy grin. "Hi, Aunt Deb. Are you staying for dinner?"

Deb smiled at her niece. "Nah, Carrie and I have dinner plans."

Siera frowned. "Carrie doesn't like having dinner with us because of me."

"That's not true," Deb answered.

Siera shrugged and gathered her books before rounding the corner and clomping up the stairs.

"Well, she might not dislike Siera, but she sure fidgets a lot when you bring her over for family barbecues." Kathleen folded her arms across her chest and frowned.

Deb ignored the comment. Although she had noticed Carrie's subtle shift whenever they came over, she assumed it had more to do with Carrie's discomfort with open displays of affection rather than her uneasiness around Siera. Deb never seemed to care who was around when she leaned in to kiss Carrie.

"I need your help." She pulled a small white box from her pocket and laid it on the counter. "I want to ask Carrie to marry me."

"What?" Kathleen raised her eyebrows. "It's not legal, so you mean you want to become registered domestic partners, right?"

Deb sighed. "Someday it will be legal. And don't give me that semantics shit. A registered domestic partnership is not the same as marriage. It's all bullshit if you ask me, but we have to take what we can get. At least the recent ruling is a step above what we have now. Just because this state thinks it's so magnanimous by extending benefits to domestic partners, does not mean we have all the same rights."

"Why are you even asking my opinion, if you're going to start an argument?" Kathleen asked.

"Ok, fine. Do you think it's cheesy to put this in her dessert or glass of wine? I need a good hook or something."

"Look, don't take this the wrong way, but I don't think you should ask at all. Carrie...well..."

"I knew this was a bad idea. Never mind. I should have asked Jeremy. When's he getting home?"

"He's not. He's at the firehouse tonight." Kathleen's jaw clenched.

"You're a narrow-minded homophobe." Deb grabbed the white box and stormed out of the house. She loved her sister, but Jeremy was always more supportive of her relationship with Carrie. It was just that sometimes she craved her sister's approval more than Jeremy's.

†

Deb's leg bounced up and down, as she waited for the waitress to bring the bottle of wine. A warm breeze kissed her skin, as they sat on the wrought iron chairs in the crowded, outdoor seating on the back deck. The porous black shades were pulled down to protect customers from the sun,

but they also blocked out the beautiful view of the lake. Deb wanted to ask the waitress to use the remote to raise the barrier to their view, but the old woman sitting in the next table had complained loudly. She preferred the shade. It probably didn't matter much. They were both locals, and maybe the beautiful lake view didn't make a difference to Carrie.

Deb had called in a favor and asked a friend to tie a ribbon around the stem of a wine glass and attach the ring.

"What's the matter with you tonight?" Carrie narrowed her eyes.

Deb turned her head and sighed in relief, as the smiling waitress approached with the bottle of wine and two glasses. She was "family." Knowing the waitress was rooting for her had made it a lot easier to set things up. The ring clinked against the glass as it was set on the table.

Carrie's eyes widened. "Deb..." she whispered.

Deb ignored the panicked look on Carrie's face and took her hand. "Look, I know it isn't legal yet, but it will be. We're so close. For now, the next best thing to marriage is this registered domestic partner thing, but I think we should have a ceremony and pretend it's a legal marriage and all. We can work out the kid thing."

Carrie was shaking her head. "I um...I wanted to tell you before tonight...a recruiter called, and I was offered a position at Sacred Heart. It's not far from Moses Lake, we could still see each other, but..." her voice trailed off.

Deb looked at the diamond sparkling in the dim candlelight, and her worst fear nearly choked the life out of her voice. "I guess that's a no."

"I love you Deb, but I'm not ready. There are still some major gaps in what each of us wants out of a relationship or our future. Can't we just..."

Deb grabbed the wineglass and pulled on the ribbon to release the ring. She jammed the diamond in her pocket. "No, we can't. Congratulations on your new job. I guess we can figure out what to do with the house..." Deb's voice hitched, "I can't do this now."

The loud scrape of the chair on the floor telegraphed her intention, as she tossed several twenties on the table and walked out of the restaurant with as much grace as she could muster.

†

The night was still warm, as Deb stepped into the fading sun. She heard several sirens in the distance and wondered if Jeremy was having a bad night. The flashing lights of two ambulances sped by, and Deb thought someone else was probably having an equally shitty evening. *Job security for Kathleen and Jeremy.* Dark humor was all she had left.

Deb pulled out her cell phone and called her sister. She was impossible sometimes, but when it mattered, Kathleen was always there for her family.

"I need you to come get me. I'm at Michael's on the Lake... Thanks, Sis."

Deb sat down on the curb and waited. She knew Carrie would give her the space and wait until Kathleen picked her up. Carrie didn't enjoy conflict. With her head in her hands, Deb allowed the tears to leak out of the corners of her eyes.

Two more police cars sped by, lights and sirens blazing. She looked up briefly and hoped the ruckus hadn't affected someone young enough to still have their whole life ahead of

9

them. She supposed there was always something worse happening in the world, and her heartbreak was probably insignificant in comparison.

†

Olivia paced her living room, stepping on and off the large cream rug with the subtle bamboo design. Irene had picked out the covering to protect the blonde maple floors after Sasha, Olivia's dog, had already managed to add character to the grainy swirls. The scratches in the glossy wood were only noticeable when the daylight streaked across the floor at the perfect angle.

Irene was like clockwork. Her longtime lover always came home around the same time every night. Three hours past her normal arrival, something was clearly wrong. When she heard the firm knock on her front door, a foreboding feeling traveled up and down her spine.

She opened the door hesitantly and met the apologetic eyes of the officer standing on her doorstep.

"I'm sorry to disturb you, ma'am. Does Irene Saunders live here?"

Olivia couldn't make the muscles in her mouth work, so she nodded instead.

"There's been an accident..."

CHAPTER TWO

Olivia stepped from one of the small rooms at her clinic and pulled the door closed. Standing in the middle of the waiting room with the sturdy, moss-colored chairs, she looked around feeling lost and alone. Brushing her hand against the vinyl, she remembered Irene suggesting she get the antimicrobial material she could easily clean, in case some dog or cat piddled on the furniture. The vinyl looked a bit sterile, but she had to admit it had saved her bacon on more than one occasion.

Olivia didn't register the unique disinfectant smell of her business, because it was something she immersed herself in every day. Some clients would wrinkle their nose when they stepped inside an exam room and caught a whiff of the combination of smells unique to many vet clinics.

Leaning on the curved reception desk, she knew she was probably forgetting something. Evie normally helped her close up, but Olivia had sent her home an hour ago, after assuring her she could handle things on her own.

Her assistant had tried to convince Olivia to keep the clinic closed for longer than three days, but puttering around in her empty house was far worse than coming into work and going through the motions each day. After only three weeks, she'd finally decided to close the clinic and get away from Moses Lake and all the memories that haunted her. Visiting her older sister, Maribel, for a week might provide the balm to her gaping wound.

Olivia decided not to wait until morning to make the trek to her sister's farm. She gathered her things, locked the front door to the clinic, and climbed into her truck. The bag she'd packed that morning occupied the passenger seat where Irene normally sat during their road trips. Evie had agreed to pick up Sasha and dog sit while she was gone, as well as look in on Olivia's cats and provide a bit of affection each day. Tom and Jerry were relatively self-sufficient, but cats were not as independent as everyone believed. Olivia was convinced they needed at least an hour of loving each day.

†

Olivia didn't have a specific plan as she eased onto I-90 west, heading toward Ellensburg. The trip to Klamath Falls was grueling. She figured she would drive until her eyes started to droop, then she'd find the first cheap hotel that didn't have an infestation of bed bugs. Motel 6 wasn't the greatest, but she thought the large chain would be fairly safe. She'd made it to Madras and decided on the Quality Inn, since it looked marginally better than her other choices. If she left at the ass crack of dawn, she might catch her niece, Briana, completing her morning chores. Spending a few minutes with Bri was sure to lift her spirits before enduring the uncomfortable looks from Maribel. Olivia was

sympathetic to the uneasiness of her sister. If she was in her sibling's shoes, she wouldn't know how to comfort her, either. Losing one's spouse at such an early age was not something she would wish on her greatest enemy.

†

She didn't need an alarm clock to awaken her, as she'd tossed and turned all night. After giving up on the pretense of sleep, she jumped in the shower and headed out well before the sun started to show its cheery face to the world. She rubbed her tired eyes and climbed back into her truck. She would definitely catch Bri at this rate. The three-hour drive was monotonous, and the silence wasn't at all helpful, as it forced her to revisit memories of a far-too-short life well lived with Irene.

Dust from the pocked dirt road kicked up behind her truck, as she traveled up the rough entrance to the farm. Olivia held her hand up in an attempt to shade the bright light from her eyes, as the faded red boards of the aging barn crossed her field of vision. Despite the sadness that draped over her, she smiled when she spied the golden hair of her niece reflected in the early morning sun. Bri was leading a chestnut mare into the pasture.

Olivia noted the gentle way Bri handled the high-strung horse, even though the large animal dwarfed her barely five-foot frame. *Maybe I should nickname her the horse whisperer.* Maribel had lamented the decision to buy the expensive breeding horse after being on the wrong end of a well-placed kick. Neither Maribel nor her husband, Greg, could get within five feet of the wretched beast. She'd asked Olivia for advice, but Bri sure seemed to know how to tame the wild mare.

The truck came to a complete stop, and Olivia saw Bri's crooked smile as she watched her close the pasture gate then run to greet her. Olivia grabbed the handle to her truck and the door creaked open, as she stepped down to meet her exuberant niece.

"Aunt Olivia, I'm so glad you're here." Bri wrapped her arms around Olivia, and that simple gesture was pure joy and love.

Olivia returned the hug and felt a tiny bit lighter. She reluctantly let her arms drop and slung her arm across her niece's shoulder. "Hiya squirt. I better go see your mom, she wasn't exactly expecting me."

Bri frowned as she turned her head and looked at Olivia. "Your eyes are sad again. Mom's been worried. She'll be glad you're here. She keeps mumbling about how we should have stayed longer to help you. Maybe I could come to live with you, then you wouldn't be so lonely anymore."

The innocent comment sparked an idea in Olivia's mind. She definitely could use the help in her clinic, and Bri would be able to spread her wings a little. The tiny seed began to take root, as Olivia focused on something other than her grief. Taking care of someone would give her a renewed purpose, something she'd lacked in the last couple of weeks.

"Maybe. You know you're my favorite niece."

Bri giggled. "I'm your only niece."

"True, but you're still my favorite." Olivia squeezed Bri's shoulder.

The two walked slowly to the side door of the large, white-washed farmhouse. Olivia removed her arm and reached for the screen door, letting it bang shut as they entered the spacious kitchen.

Maribel pivoted in front of the deep porcelain sink, wiping her hands on her pants and grinning. She moved quickly and pulled Olivia into a full body hug. "Hope you're staying for more than a day or two. We could use the free labor."

†

The morning breeze was a relief from the night's stifling heat. The old farmhouse didn't have central air, and sometimes the night temperatures didn't cool down enough to allow a reprieve, even when Olivia stripped down to nothing. She rolled over on her side, staring at the white wall and wondering how she might approach Maribel with her idea for Bri. When the clattering of the pots interrupted her thoughts, she threw on a pair of shorts and a t-shirt, and decided to toss out her idea while Bri was tending to the horses. She knew her niece would already be up finishing her chores before breakfast. Bri was far more diligent about work than most of the young people she had interviewed in the past, with the exception of Evie.

Shuffling into the large, open kitchen, Olivia spied her sister flipping pancakes on the griddle. She knew Maribel was making blueberry pancakes specially for her. The comfort food reminded them of their youth.

"Morning, Maribel," Olivia greeted.

Maribel offered a tentative smile. "How are you holding up, Olivia?"

Olivia shrugged. "Hey, can I talk to you about something?"

"Of course." Maribel turned the knob on the gas burner, removed the pancake from the griddle, and slapped it on top

15

of the stack next to the stove. "Come, sit, we can visit for a bit while Bri and Greg finish up their chores."

Olivia pulled out one of the weathered, wood chairs and sat. "I'm just going to blurt out my idea. Before you say no, can you listen to my whole spiel?"

Maribel narrowed her eyes, but nodded.

"I think Bri has a lot more potential than sticking around the farm and living her whole life here. I know you both love her, but she's a very talented young woman, and I'd like to take her back with me and give her a job in my clinic. I need the help and frankly, right now, I need a little ray of sunshine in my life. The loneliness and quiet at home is, well…"

A tear formed at the corner of Maribel's eye, as she laid her hand on top of Olivia's. "Oh, hon, you know when you add that last part into your argument, it's awful difficult to say no. She's my baby. I'm not quite sure how to let go. I suppose having an empty nest is something every mother goes through, but I thought that was one advantage to having a special needs child; she'd always be with me."

Olivia squeezed Maribel's hand. "You know, that probably isn't the best way to think about a child with Down syndrome. It's limiting," she gently chastised.

"Oh, you know I didn't mean it like that," Maribel defended.

"I know, but that's how those stereotypes get perpetuated. We need to work on how you think about Bri. She has so much more potential, if you'd let her venture out a little and be a bit less protective." Olivia smiled to blunt her criticism.

"You're right, and I suppose me letting her go to live with you is a start."

"So…we can talk to her about it?"

Maribel nodded. She stood and turned back to the stove. Olivia knew this was about as far as she could go with her sister's acceptance of Bri coming to live with her.

CHAPTER THREE

JUNE 2010

Deb rapped on the side door of Kathleen's house, then immediately barged in. A white stick protruded from her mouth, as she sucked on her lollipop. She stuck her nose in the air and sniffed. After she pulled the candy from her mouth, she asked, "How come I don't smell meat cooking?"

Kathleen was leaning on the counter with a scowl on her face. "Siera's not home yet, so I told Jeremy to hold off on grilling the burgers. Jeez, Deb, what are you, ten? A grown woman with a Tootsie Pop addiction."

"I'm still trying to find out how many licks it takes before I reach the creamy center. My data seems to change every time I stick in a new pop. Women are much easier. I only have to lick about eight to ten times before I reach their creamy center."

"La, la, la, la, I did not hear that. By the way where is your latest flavor of the month?" Kathleen asked.

18

"Old news. I dumped her a week ago." Deb snapped her fingers and waved her hand in the air. "Come on, Sis, keep up. So, back the info train up. Where is my favorite niece?"

Kathleen frowned. "That is the question of the hour. She's never late. I'm starting to worry. She's such a responsible child, and now I'm having visions of some pervert luring her into his web of deceit with a kitten or a puppy."

"She's nineteen and not a child anymore. Cut her some slack."

"I know, but I still worry about her. You'll do the same when you have kids of your own."

"Oh no, broached that subject before and scorched my nostrils from the rubber Carrie burned as she took off for greener pastures. I'm never getting married or having kids. Women are impossible to figure out, so I've stopped trying, and now I'm enjoying their creamy centers."

"Don't let one bad experience scare you off."

"Easy for you to say, you have the perfect spouse."

"Nobody is perfect."

"Well, tell that nearly perfect man of yours to start grilling, because I want meat." Deb hopped on the counter and swung her legs.

Kathleen chuckled. "Um…that sounds kinda weird coming from my lesbian sister."

"I know. It does, doesn't it, but you know what kind of meat I'm talking about."

†

Siera kicked a stone as she shuffled along the gravel path. With her head bent, she didn't see the other young

19

woman sitting on the bench, at first. The sun was shining bright, but her mood did not match the weather.

She'd had a horrible day at Walmart. When the group of teenagers walked into the store and snickered as Siera greeted them, she knew at least one of them, would say something mean. Teenagers were especially cruel. High school hadn't been easy for her, but she had flown under the radar for the most part and had finally graduated. It had been a long, lonely existence.

"I heard Walmart hires all the retards in town. It's stupid to have greeters, but I guess they figure hiring the handicapped makes them some kind of civic giant. I sure wouldn't want to greet people at Walmart all day long. How boring," a young woman said.

"Oh, that's Siera. I heard her mom made such a huge fuss at the school and threatened to sue if they didn't allow her precious daughter to attend the regular classes. She never said much in class. It's sad really. Her parents should have let her go to the special school where she could be with her kind."

Siera knew most people assumed she wouldn't understand when someone was saying something derogatory about her, but she always knew. Her mom had to fight with the school to keep her in the regular classroom. It didn't matter she'd proven she could do the work like everyone else. Each year the new teacher would take one look at her almond-shaped eyes and make the same assumption every other teacher before them had. When Siera would answer the teachers during roll call, she would notice the slight head nod indicating a verification of their assumptions. No matter how much speech therapy Siera had, there was still a slur to her words. Siera hated her thick tongue that she knew was the

culprit. Her mother had patiently explained how low muscle tone was a big contributor. That was a frustrating fact that added to her dumpy appearance.

Finally, in her last year of school, a guidance counselor who didn't have any preconceived notions about Siera's abilities had encouraged her to apply to Big Bend Community College. Siera loved Miss Moore for that. Besides her mom and aunt, Miss Moore was the first person who ever believed in her.

Siera heard the honking of the geese and looked up to see a frantically waving hand. She turned her head, thinking the young woman sitting on the bench was waving at someone behind her. She wasn't. Siera was alone on the gravel path along the lake.

As Siera took a few tentative steps toward the young woman, she noticed her crooked smile and couldn't help the grin that seized her mouth and made her lips turn up in joy. The young woman looked like her, with almond-shaped eyes and small ears like Siera's.

Siera hadn't been around others like her. Her mom had never acceded to the authorities when they'd wanted to relegate her to the special schools for children with Down syndrome.

Siera knew she had Down syndrome. Her mother had explained everything to her when she was a young girl but made sure Siera knew she shouldn't let having Down syndrome define who she was, or what she could accomplish in life. What her mom didn't realize was that mainstreaming, while helping to push Siera to reach her potential, had left her isolated and alone in a very scary world.

"Hi," the young girl called out.

"Hello," Siera tentatively responded.

"Do you want to feed the geese?"

Siera squinted her eyes and noticed the thick, golden-blonde hair pulled loosely in a ponytail. It was beautiful. She had an urge to touch the soft strands. Siera had always been a tactile child, wanting to touch everything soft and shiny. This young woman's hair glinted in the sunshine.

"You have beautiful hair," Siera blurted out.

The young woman blushed. "My name's Bri. What's yours?"

"Siera."

"You can help me feed the geese if you want. They won't bite," Bri offered.

Siera wasn't so sure about that. She'd seen the geese get aggressive before, but she had to admit they seemed subdued today.

"Okay," Siera said.

Siera sat next to Bri on the bench and closely scrutinized the young woman. She was about the same size, probably not more than five feet tall. Siera hated the extra few pounds around her stomach that made her look dumpy. She noticed the young woman wasn't as lumpy as she was and wondered if she did some kind of special exercise to combat the genetics associated with their syndrome.

Siera surprised herself when she asked her about it. "Do you exercise or something? I wish my stomach was flatter."

Bri squinted and smiled again. Her eyes traversed across Siera's body. "You look fine to me. I like to bike and feel the breeze in my hair. Aunt Olivia always yells at me to wear my helmet. As soon as I know she's not watching I take it off."

Siera couldn't help herself, she reached out to touch the golden hair. Bri didn't pull away from the fleeting touch.

"I think we're going to be best friends," Bri declared.

Siera nodded. She'd never been anyone's best friend. In fact, she'd never had any friends. Her heart raced at the thought of having just one. Somehow, she knew, in that instant, her life was changed and would never be the same again. It was a welcome adjustment.

She looked up at the sun in the sky. It was getting late, and she needed to get home before her mom started to fret. A late dinner wasn't a problem, because when her dad wasn't working his long shifts, he was always home tinkering away on something he argued needed fixing. Her mom was an obsessive worrier.

CHAPTER FOUR

Olivia stood in front of the picture and stroked the frame almost as if the wood was her lover. She sighed. Dinnertime was especially tough, because that's when she missed Irene's concoctions. Irene always tried to think of new and different ways to cook a vegetarian meal, even though she was a meat eater herself, and on occasion Olivia would eat chicken or fish.

"You always said life is short, but I never really believed it. Thank God for Bri, or I think I would have turned into a bitter old woman in a matter of months. How can I not embrace life with such a ray of sunshine surrounding me?"

With one last brush of her fingers on the picture, she retreated to the living room and picked up her e-reader. She expected her niece home any minute. A simple meal was on the counter, covered in tin foil to keep the food warm. Cooking had never been her forte, but she'd learned to make a dish or two after Bri moved in. The perpetually sunny young woman was her savior and had kept her from plunging

into the depths of depression after Irene died. Her help in the clinic was an added bonus and one she never took for granted. She hoped Bri was happy living with her, because she hated to think her beloved niece was a crutch to lean on. Olivia wouldn't keep her sequestered from branching out and making her own way in the world.

†

Bri walked with a spring in her step after saying goodbye to Siera. She reached her recumbent bicycle, locked to the bike rack, and squatted down, as she worked her fingers over the combination lock. Sometimes, her small stubby fingers made it difficult to turn the numbers, but Bri had a lot of patience. Her aunt always said that's what made her such a great assistant. Aunt Olivia had been her favorite aunt, not because she offered Bri a job, but because she encouraged her gift with animals.

"You've got the golden touch, Bri. It's your special gift to the world. Even if you don't want to work with me, I think you ought to bless the universe with your gift," Aunt Olivia had said, after she'd asked Bri to move to Washington and work at her veterinary clinic.

Three years ago, Aunt Olivia had come to visit. Bri could feel her aunt watching her with the horses and farm animals. She'd been upfront about needing an assistant, and talked privately with her mom. Aunt Olivia had explained to Bri how she'd eased her mom into their conversation of letting Bri spread her wings and branch out into new life experiences. Aunt Olivia had confided in Bri, chuckling while telling her she might have pushed it a bit and used some old-fashioned guilt. She didn't know what guilt her aunt had used, but she thought it might be something related

to how sad and lonely Aunt Olivia was after Aunt Irene went to heaven. Bri needed a job, or she was destined to remain in the shadows and under her family's well-meaning protection. It wasn't like they discouraged her in any way; they simply didn't expect much, and that had been slowly killing her zest for life.

She had felt bad for leaving the family. Her mom had cried as Bri took the final step and crawled into her aunt's red truck. Since then, Bri had blossomed under her responsibilities at the clinic. She was proud of herself when the staff at the clinic called on her special skills with a particularly difficult pet. She understood fear and was able to connect to the root emotion every time.

The short bike ride to her aunt's house on the lake was exhilarating. She ignored her aunt's admonishments that sifted through her brain and stuffed her helmet in her bike bag strapped to the back of the rack.

Darn, busted. As Bri rolled up to the garage, she saw her aunt's frown.

"Sorry, Aunt Olivia. I needed to feel the breeze in my hair. I met someone today. She touched my hair," Bri confessed.

Olivia's frown deepened.

"Come on in and sit down. Tell me all about it, and don't leave anything out."

"Thanks, Aunt Olivia. You're not too mad about the helmet, are you?" Bri asked.

Olivia smiled and shook her head. "I'm more concerned about this new person you've met. I know your mom warned you about talking to strangers. Being friendly is okay, but

sometimes people don't have the purest motivation. Do you understand what I'm talking about?"

"It's because I'm the way I am. People might want to take advantage of me. I'm smart with animals, but not people. I hate that I was born this way. You and mom don't have to be careful with new people."

"Oh honey. That's not what I meant. Anyone can be taken advantage of. You are perfect just the way you are. Never let anyone make you believe anything different. Now, tell me about this person."

Bri led the way into the garage and lifted her bike to set it on the hook her aunt had installed onto the wall. She opened the door into the mud room and sat down to remove her gym shoes. She looked up at her aunt and grinned. She was excited and couldn't wait to tell her aunt about her new friend. "She's like me, Aunt Olivia, but she's smart. She's going to Big Bend in the fall. I wish I was smart enough to go to college. I never met someone like me who was smart enough to go to college. We're going to be best friends," Bri declared.

"What do you mean she's like you?" Olivia tentatively asked.

"She's Down's too," Bri nonchalantly replied. Bri stood up and followed her aunt into the kitchen.

Olivia raised her eyebrow. "I think I need to meet this young woman who is your new best friend."

"Okay. I told her to meet me again tomorrow evening at the park. Can I ask her to come for dinner?" Bri sat at her usual place at the table, while her aunt walked over to the counter to retrieve the plates she'd prepared.

"Does she have a bike, or should I pick you up?" Olivia set the plate of salmon and grilled asparagus on the table in front of Bri.

Bri scrunched up her face and smacked her head. "See, I'm so stupid. I didn't ask. She was walking, so maybe she lives close to the park."

Olivia reached over and stroked Bri's head. "Don't ever call yourself stupid. You are a wonderful, talented young woman, and I am sure this new friend will be delighted to spend time with you." She sat down at the table with Bri. "How about if I rush through closing up the clinic and swing by the park tomorrow? We can toss your bike in the back of the truck and hers too if she has one?"

"Oh, thank you, Aunt Olivia. You're the best. I know you're going to love her like I do."

The frown returned to Olivia's face.

CHAPTER FIVE

Siera banged the screen door open. She knew she was late when she saw her mom sitting at the table tapping her fingers. She was probably wondering what happened to delay her return from work.

"Oh, honey, I'm glad you're here. I was about to call the National Guard," Kathleen joked.

"Aw, Mom, I was at the park. I met someone. I think I have a friend."

Kathleen paused, and her stiffened posture betrayed her feelings about Siera's declaration.

Siera had a knack for noticing emotions. People often underestimated her ability to observe certain nuances of human behavior. Even though her mom tried to act nonchalant, Siera noticed the nervous twitch as she asked about her new friend. Her aunt was sitting on the counter. She looked so much younger than her mom, even though only a few years her junior. Siera loved her aunt, she was

29

funny and a lot more comfortable to be around than her dad's brother, Uncle Frank.

"Oh. Why don't you tell me about it while your dad finishes his grilling masterpiece," Kathleen's voice quivered very lightly.

"It's all good, Mom. She was sweet. She has Down syndrome too. She's not like those other kids in the special schools you didn't want me going to. The geese weren't aggressive around her. It was amazing, and she has really pretty yellow hair. I touched it. It was so soft."

"What was she doing out at the park all by herself?" Kathleen asked. The clipped tone revealed her true feelings.

Deb glared at Kathleen but didn't say a word. Siera loved her aunt, because she treated her like she was normal. Not too many people did that.

Siera recognized her mom's fear. Even though she'd always encouraged Siera, sometimes her protective nature came out whenever Siera talked about her efforts at forming friendships in school. Siera had been hurt before, and she knew how much it wounded her mom to see her cry over another disappointment.

"She works at a veterinary clinic. Isn't that cool? She graduated from high school, too. She told me we would be best friends. I have a friend, Mom—a real friend."

Kathleen's shoulders relaxed a little.

Jeremy sauntered into the kitchen with a plate of bison burgers.

Toby, her younger brother, shuffled behind and made a face behind his father's back.

"Hi, pumpkin. How was your day today?" Jeremy asked, then looked over at Deb. "One or two extra plates?" he asked.

"One. Don't ask," Deb answered.

Jeremy raised his eyebrow, then shifted his eyes back to Siera.

"I have a friend now, Dad."

Jeremy frowned and Toby grinned.

Siera noticed how her mom caught her dad's eyes and the look seemed to reassure her dad.

"She met a young woman feeding geese at the park," Kathleen clarified.

"Why don't you invite this girl over for one of my famous burgers?" Her dad smiled.

"Dad thinks he's the best griller west of the Mississippi. He was trying to impart his expert knowledge on me today. 'No son of mine is going to make a lackluster burger, I'll teach you all my tricks,'" Toby mocked.

"Go ahead and ridicule me now, but when you get serious with a girl, she's going to expect you to demonstrate your grilling prowess. If you don't have game there, she'll throw you back in the pond. How do you think I got your mom to marry me? She was never the same after I invited her to a barbecue. I separated myself from the flock that day. Right, hon?"

"Sure, whatever you say." Kathleen grinned.

Siera knew her dad loved her, but it was hard to erase the memory of the argument she'd heard through the vent in her bedroom five years ago. On that night, she'd learned how her father had reacted to her birth.

Siera had heard angry loud voices in the small den below her bedroom and crawled from her bed to open the heating vent to listen. She knew she shouldn't. It was wrong

to invade her parent's privacy, but when she heard her name, it was hard to resist.

"You expect too much of her," her dad declared. "Why can't you let her go to that school where she'll be surrounded by kids like her?"

"And you expect too little. I haven't forgotten how you reacted when the doctor gave us the news. You passed judgment that day, and you've never seen her potential. All you can see is her condition. Well, she's as talented as every other kid, and I will not let them turn her into a pity project so some self-imposed executive can feel good about hiring the poor handicapped girl. Why do I have to fight you, too? It's bad enough I always have to do battle with the schools."

"Aw, Jesus Christ, Kat. Won't you ever let me live that down? I was a new father. I wasn't ready to hear the news. It simply took me a little more time to get used to the fact that our first baby wasn't perfect. It was a knee-jerk reaction."

Siera heard something crash. "Do you hear yourself? Not perfect. Even now, you consider your daughter less. I didn't think you could ever say anything more hurtful than 'we should have done that amniocentesis test and aborted when we had the chance.' But now here we are, fourteen years later, and your profuse apology means absolutely nothing. Your true feelings are coming through again," Kathleen shouted.

"Shit, Kat that's not what I meant. You know how much I adore Siera. She's lonely and hasn't been able to make one friend. It's not right you pushing her so much. Can't you see how awful the public school is for her? It's going to break her spirit someday, but you don't care about that, do you? You are so hell bent on making sure everyone treats her like

any other normal teenager, but she's not, and she'll never be. That is not something you have control over."

"She won't get the same opportunities in life at that school. Can't you see that? When she goes to college and proves them all wrong, then you'll see this is the right decision. I know you love her, but can you please temper that protective streak of yours and believe in her a little more?"

"Isn't her happiness and well-being important to you at all?" Jeremy countered.

"Of course it is. She's fine. I make sure she isn't the recipient of bullying. I'm on it. Trust me."

"Just because the kids don't bully her, doesn't mean she's happy. Haven't you noticed how she never talks about school? Every one of her teachers tells you that she's as quiet as a church mouse. Well that's grand for them, but what about her connection to other kids? It's nonexistent and you know it."

Siera crawled back in her bed. She didn't want to listen to their conversation anymore. She supposed they were both right, but the realization her father hadn't wanted her when she was born cut her to the bone. She knew deep down her dad loved her. His fear and protective nature were dictating his perspective.

In the end, her mom got her way—like she always did wherever Siera was concerned. She would attend Big Bend College in the fall, like her mom wanted, but at what cost to her health and well-being.

Suddenly, everything had changed. Today with Bri made all the difference in the world. She finally had a friend. It was something she'd prayed about every day since the age of five. God had finally answered her prayers.

"Can I, Dad? I think she would love your burgers as much as I do," Siera said.

"So, what's the girl's name?" Jeremy asked.

"Bri." Siera sighed. "She has the most beautiful yellow hair."

"She does? Hmmm. Dark and light like your mom and me. You got those beautiful wavy dark locks from your mom. Now I know you are destined to be best friends. Contrasts are good."

"She works at a veterinary clinic as an assistant. Isn't that cool? I wish I had a job working with animals. I love cats and dogs," Siera said with excitement in her voice.

"You know, those clinics see other animals besides cats and dogs. You would have to take care of snakes and other slimy reptiles," Toby teased.

"Ew. I don't like snakes," Siera answered.

"Don't you like your job at Walmart?" Kathleen asked.

Siera lost her smile and shrugged. "It's okay, I guess."

Kathleen narrowed her eyes. "Honey, did something happen today?"

"Just some stupid teenagers. I don't care. I'm going to study hard. I don't have to work at Walmart for the rest of my life. I don't want to talk about it. Can we eat now? I'm starved."

Siera didn't miss the concerned look Kathleen gave to Jeremy.

"Hey, Sis, tell me who they are and I'll pound them into the pavement," Toby stated.

"No one's pounding anyone into the pavement." Kathleen glared at her husband and son. "We don't regress to violence to solve issues in this household."

"Tell that to the vase," Toby grumbled.

34

Deb laughed.

"What was that?" Kathleen asked.

"Oh, nothing," Toby answered.

Jeremy chuckled. "I think he was referring to your abuse of inanimate objects whenever you're pissed at me."

"Do not encourage him. I know you're the one who told him to pound anyone who gave Siera grief," Kathleen chastised.

"Stellar advice." Deb raised her thumbs in the air.

"Who, me?" Jeremy batted his eyelashes.

Siera laughed. She loved her younger brother. He was as protective as her dad and aunt, but none of them could make the other kids like her. That was beyond their abilities.

CHAPTER SIX

Bri pedaled her recumbent bike down the road. She was anxious about getting to the park by five. Her aunt had noted her nervousness and finally allowed her to leave the clinic.

"Go on now, we can close up. Mrs. Thompson is bringing Rufus, but he's easy to handle. Don't forget to invite your new friend over for dinner tonight. I'll pick you both up in about an hour. Okay?"

"Thanks, Aunt Olivia. You're the best." Bri nearly sang her response.

Bri had her iPod stuffed into the pocket of the biking shirt, as she listened to her favorite female artists. She shared a similar taste in music to her aunt who had added the mix to her player. She was singing along to Brandi Carlisle, when she entered the park.

Carefully dismounting, she rolled her pride and joy over to the bike rack and locked it up. She'd saved her money to purchase the expensive bike and took very good care of it.

Her aunt made her put most of the money she earned into a high-interest-bearing account she wouldn't be able to touch for five years. Although Bri had complained at first, she bent to her aunt's will after she had carefully explained. Someday, Bri might want to purchase something that would foster more independence, and she would never be able to do that without a nice nest egg. Her aunt was smart that way. She always knew how to get through to Bri.

Bri had told her aunt about her dream of independence, when she first moved to Washington, and she suspected her aunt had filed that away to pull out at the right moment. It worked. Bri desperately wanted to feel normal, and living independently would be the first step.

Bri removed from her bike bag the ziplocked container of cabbage and cauliflower leaves. She skipped over to the bench and clicked her tongue.

Several of the regulars came waddling close, waiting for Bri to share the tasty treats.

Footsteps on the gravel scared the geese away. They were familiar with her, but not a new person sneaking up on them. Bri knew it was her new friend and jumped up to greet her.

"You came." Bri's smile threatened to take over her whole face. She set the bag to the side and impulsively pulled the young woman with dark, wavy hair into an enthusiastic hug. She was happy when Siera returned the hug with equal fervor.

"My aunt asked me to invite you to dinner tonight. Can you come? She wants to meet you," Bri declared.

Siera smiled. "I'd like to, but I have to ask my parents. They were hoping you would come to our house for a barbecue. My dad makes the best burgers. I think he wants to

show off for you. He grills other things too. They want to meet you."

"Do you have a cell phone? I don't. I never had anyone I wanted to talk to before now, and I spent all my money on this bike," Bri confessed.

"Yeah, I do. My mom wanted me to have one in case there was an emergency. The only people I ever call is my family. I don't have anyone else I want to talk to either." Siera blushed. "Except, now I do, and you don't have a phone."

"I can get one. If I ask Aunt Olivia, she'll let me spend some of my money on a phone, now that I have someone to call. So, can you call your parents and ask them?" Bri glanced at her watch. "Aunt Olivia said she would come pick us up in about thirty minutes."

"Okay." Siera slipped her backpack off her shoulder and rummaged around inside until she located her phone. She held it up and grinned. After pushing a few buttons, she placed the phone next to her ear. "Hi, Mom. Bri asked if I want to have dinner with her and her aunt, tonight. Can I go?… I don't know. I'll ask her."

Siera removed the phone from her ear. "Mom wants to know if she can call your aunt and talk with her. Do you know the number?"

Bri smiled. "Yeah, she made me memorize it, in case of an emergency or something. It's 509-974-6321."

"Can you tell my mom that?" Siera handed Bri her phone.

"Um, hi. This is Bri. My Aunt Olivia's number is 509-974-6321…. Okay." Bri handed the phone back to Siera. "Here, she wants to speak to you again."

"Hi Mom.... Okay. I'll wait for you to call back." Siera looked down at the ground.

"It's okay. My aunt is really protective too. I'll bet Aunt Olivia wants to talk to your mom as much as your mom wants to talk to her."

"I guess, but we're both adults. Sometimes my mom treats me like an adult. She pushes me to *reach my potential*. Other times, she's as bad as my dad. I try not to get mad about it." Siera picked up her backpack and awkwardly zipped it up while holding on to her phone. With her free hand, she placed one strap over her left shoulder.

"Come on, let's sit on the bench and feed the geese. I won't let them peck you. They're my friends. Now, they'll be your friends too."

Bri and Siera walked hand in hand to the bench. After Siera laid the pack on the ground next to the bench, they both sat down next to the treats for the geese.

Siera transferred her phone to her left hand and bravely took her new friend's hand. "I like it here. The geese aren't as scary now."

A few bold geese made their way over, squawking while they neared the bench. Bri tossed a bunch of cabbage and cauliflower leaves out to the birds, and they gobbled up the offerings in a split second. A white goose remained on the periphery, taking a tentative step forward, before one of the more dominant birds squawked at her.

"Beatrice, Hannah, that wasn't very nice. You need to let Silvia have some too," Bri chastised.

"They have names? How do you know who they are? How can you tell the difference between them? Except for that white one, they all look the same to me."

"But they're not. It's like us. We're the same, but we're different. I have yellow hair, and you have brown hair. I know our differences are more obvious. If you look close, Beatrice has slightly darker tail feathers and is a little bigger than Hannah."

Siera's smile grew as she looked closely at the geese. "Oh yes, I can see it now."

Ring, Ring.

Siera unclasped her hand and pressed the answer button. "Hi, Mom.... Oh, thank you.... Yes, I'll be sure to tell Miss Olivia I need to be home by ten o'clock, at the latest.... Yeah, I know I have to work tomorrow." Siera pushed the button to end the call and impulsively kissed Bri's cheek. "Mom said I can go."

Bri blushed. "I'm so happy she said yes. You're gonna love Aunt Olivia. She's like the best person in the world. She's the best vet in town, too. Do you have pets?"

Siera shook her head up and down. "Uh huh. Sampson and Delilah. We rescued them from the pound. They're brother and sister."

"Brother and sister what?" Bri asked.

"Kittens. Well, they were kittens when we first got them. I suppose they're cats now. Sampson is gray and white, and Delilah is kind of a gray tabby. They sleep with me. When we first got them, they would run all over my bed and wake me up in the middle of the night. Now they usually sleep through the night. At least when they play, it isn't as bad. I love them. They've been my only friends until I met you."

Bri grinned. "Aunt Olivia has cats and a dog. One time, she rescued a baby skunk. Of course, she had to do something so he wouldn't spray her. She found him a good home after that. Skunks are sweet if you raise them from

babies. I got to pet him and feed him from a dropper. She told me I was the reason he trusted people so much."

"When you come over for a barbecue, I'll let you pet Sampson and Delilah. They aren't as friendly with new people, but I'll bet they let you pet them. It sounds like animals like you."

"Oh, they do. Aunt Olivia says I have the magic touch." Bri beamed.

The geese started to waddle away after they'd finished all the treats Bri brought.

Siera shifted in her seat. "Can I ask you something?"

"Sure."

"Did you go to a special school with people like us or to the regular high school?"

"I went to the regular high school. They put me in a special class. I got extra tutoring and graduated a year later than the kids who were my age, but I graduated." Bri stuck out her chin.

"Did you have friends?" Siera asked.

"Only one. He moved my senior year. I think he wanted to be my boyfriend. I didn't like him like that. He was sweet. He wasn't Down's like us, but he had a hard time in school too. I ran a race in the Special Olympics when I was younger. That was fun. There were more kids like us. Sometimes, they were harder to understand than me. I didn't have a best friend like you though."

"Oh. I didn't have any friends. I was afraid. I'm scared to go to college in the fall. No matter what Mom says, I don't think I'll fit in very well. It will be like high school. Maybe worse," Siera admitted.

"I know. When someone new comes to the clinic, they kinda look at me strange. It takes them a while to warm up.

Aunt Olivia scowls at them if she thinks they're about to say anything mean. It only happened once. I had to beg Aunt Olivia to let him continue to bring his pit bull mix in to see her. I didn't say anything, but I was glad I talked her into it. He was training the dog to be mean. Rover, that was the dog's name. He was the first dog I was ever afraid of, until I understood he was scared of mean old Mr. Simpson. After that, Rover and I became friends."

"I wish I could get a job in a pet store or maybe at your aunt's clinic. I like cats. Dogs are nice too. Toby says you take care of snakes. Walmart is okay, but it's not an important job like yours," Siera stated.

Bri grinned. "Aunt Olivia is the best. We don't have any snakes that come in, but sometimes we get rabbits. Walmart is so big. I'll bet your job is important too."

"I just greet people. It's not important. Maybe after I graduate from community college I can get a better job. Was it hard to learn your job?" Siera asked.

"Nah. I mostly calm down the animals and get supplies for Aunt Olivia. I'm not very good with the computer. Evie takes care of all the front office stuff. She's nice to me—like a big sister."

Bri turned around and watched the clinic's big red truck pull into the parking lot. Sometimes her aunt would use the truck when she made home visits. She was anxious to have her new friend meet Aunt Olivia. She desperately wanted them to get along, because she knew Siera would become an important part of her life.

Bri noticed Siera twisting her body around as the truck approached.

Siera unzipped the front pocket of her backpack and slipped the phone inside. After zipping the pocket closed, she

stood and positioned the pack on her back. She began to shuffle her feet—shifting from her right to her left foot. Bri thought her new friend was nervous, so she slung her arm around her shoulder and pulled her close. It was an instinctive gesture meant to provide support.

"Hi girls. Are you ready to go?" Aunt Olivia stretched out her hand. "You must be Siera. I am so happy to meet you. Bri has been talking nonstop about her new friend, so you must be special. I'm Olivia."

Siera briefly clasped her hand, quickly averting her eyes and bowing her head. "Hello Miss Olivia. It is very nice to meet you," she whispered.

Olivia waved her hand in the air. "Please, no formalities. I don't think Miss Olivia suits me at all, so you must call me Olivia. All my friends call me Olivia, and I hope you and I will become friends, Siera."

Siera glanced up, and Bri could see a smile return to her face.

Bri removed her arm and turned in the direction of the bike rack. "I gotta unlock my bike."

"I can help," Siera offered.

"Okay."

Olivia followed them, waiting patiently as Bri worked the combination and pulled the chain from the spokes. She handed the lock to Siera and stood up, as she began walking the bike to the truck. Siera walked next to her with the lock dangling on her arm like a bracelet.

"How about we order a pizza tonight? Any special requests?" Olivia asked.

"Can we get Hawaiian, Aunt Olivia?"

"Sure Bri. Although if you don't mind, I'll ask them to make half of it vegetarian. Is that all right with you, Siera?"

"Uh huh. I like anything. I'm not particular. Thank you for inviting me," Siera answered.

Olivia pulled down the back gate of the truck and lifted the front wheel in. "Bri, can you lift the back for me please?"

"Sure, Aunt Olivia."

Siera stood awkwardly to the side, while Bri and Olivia rolled the bike into the back of the truck and slammed the gate shut.

"Sheesh, that's heavy. They're a lot heavier than a regular ten-speed, but Bri says they're more comfortable to ride. Do you have a bike, Siera?" Olivia asked.

Siera nodded. "It's not as fancy as Bri's. It only has one speed. Mom said it's called a cruiser. The seat is comfortable though. Maybe I can save my money and get something better. I never had anyone to go with before, except my brother, Toby. He doesn't like to take me with his friends, because I hold them back."

"I don't care how fast we go," Bri declared. "There's lots of great places to bike. We can go when we both have the whole day off. Okay?"

Siera smiled. "Okay."

"Come on you two. Stop dillydallying. I'm starving," Oliva teased.

†

Siera started to relax when she walked into the house. It wasn't anything fancy, but it had a kind of cozy warmth. She always liked houses with fireplaces, especially ones faced with stone or brick. Her eyes traveled to a picture prominently displayed on the mantel. Two women stood arm in arm in front of Mount Baker, which she recognized because her family used to go there to ski. One of the women

was Olivia. Siera wondered about the other smiling woman with the jet-black hair. The joy on their faces drew her in, and she took a step closer.

"That's Aunt Olivia and Aunt Irene before Aunt Irene got hit by a drunk driver and went to heaven," Bri explained.

Siera looked at Olivia, whose eyes began to glisten as she turned away and took a deep breath.

"Was she your best friend?" Siera asked.

Olivia turned back around and nodded. "Irene was my very best friend."

"My Aunt Deb had a best friend named Carrie. She didn't come around anymore, and Aunt Deb got real sad. Now she has a new best friend every time she comes to see us. She changes her best friends as often as I change my underwear. Mom doesn't approve. I bet you miss her like Aunt Deb misses Carrie," Siera stated.

"Every day." Olivia sighed. "I'd better go order the pizza before we all waste away to nothing." Olivia winked. "Make yourself at home, Siera. I'll be back in a jiffy."

Olivia walked down the hall, and Siera looked around the room. Two large cats were sprawled out on the couch, a gray tabby and an orange tabby. She walked over to pet the lounging felines.

"Aunt Olivia rescued Tom and Jerry from a big wood pile. Their momma was hit by a car, and this lady heard them meowing one day. She brings all her cats to see Aunt Olivia. She asked if we could find good homes for the kittens. She already has five cats of her own. It was plain ridiculous to add two more. Aunt Olivia fell in love with them and brought them home."

"They're soft." Siera continued to move her hand over their fur. The gray one rolled over and purred while she continued to pet his belly.

"He likes you. I can tell. Aunt Olivia says a cat's belly is very vulnerable. When they show you their belly, that means they trust you," Bri explained.

Siera heard a door open and the clip, clip, clip of nails on the hardwood floors. When she turned in the direction of the noise, a medium-sized dog with golden hair bounded in her direction, with a large, fluffy tail whipping furiously from left to right.

Siera held out her hand like her dad taught her to when meeting a strange dog. The dog licked her hand and she giggled.

"That's Sasha. She's Aunt Olivia's dog. She's mostly a golden retriever, but has a little bit of chow mixed in. That's what makes her stubborn sometimes and why she kinda looks like a puppy in the face—even though she's seven years old."

Sasha continued to wiggle and wag her tail, while Siera pushed her hand through her thick fur.

"Sasha, sit," Olivia commanded.

Bri grabbed Siera's hand. "Come on. I want to show you my room." She dragged Siera down a narrow hallway before turning into a small room on the right. Siera studied the built-in book shelves that occupied one whole wall. Strewn haphazardly amongst a vast collection of paperback books was an eclectic collection of rocks, shells, and driftwood. The other walls contained prints that conspicuously featured cats, dogs, birds, horses, and other wildlife.

"Wow. Have you read all those books?"

Bri nodded. "Most of them. Mom used to make me read at least an hour every night. She made me do all my homework first, then I would read for an hour. After that, she let me watch TV. I never got to watch much TV. It took me so long to do my homework. I didn't mind too much, because I started to like to read. I'm slow and have to look up words all the time, but it's worth it. Sometimes, I imagine I'm the heroine in the story. It's fun."

"I like to read, too. I don't think I've read as many books as you have. I like young adult romances." Siera blushed.

"Oh, me too," Bri chimed in.

"I wanted to read *Twilight*, but Mom thought it would give me nightmares. So she didn't let me read that. Have you read it?"

Bri walked over to her bookshelf and pulled out the first book in the series. "Here. You can borrow this. It wasn't that scary."

"Thanks."

Siera paused and lifted her eyes to Bri's. She wasn't sure if she should ask the next question. Her mom had warned her about asking questions that might be too personal. She decided it was okay, because Bri was her best friend. "Bri, have you ever kissed a boy—like in the books or on TV?"

Bri shook her head. "No. Most boys I know are sweaty and smelly. Kissing a girl would be okay. Aunt Olivia used to kiss Aunt Irene. She told me if you really loved someone, it was okay to kiss 'em. But I should be careful not to give my kisses away unless it is someone special. Have you ever kissed anyone?"

Siera looked down at her feet. "No. The boys teased me a lot in high school. They made kissing sounds, but I knew

they were just making fun of me. I've seen people kiss on TV and in the movies. I want to try it someday..."

"Girls, the pizza is here," Olivia called from the living room.

CHAPTER SEVEN

The old-fashioned grandfather clock chimed loudly, indicating the top of the hour, again. Kathleen frowned as she looked over at the clock that had been in her family for generations. She was amazed it still worked, but at this moment, it was another reminder that Siera wasn't home yet.

Jeremy clasped his wife's hand. "Hon, it's only ten. You're the one who is always encouraging Siera to make more of an effort to get to know other kids. High school was not easy on her. I think it's wonderful she's met a new friend who she has something in common with."

"Maybe I don't want her hanging out with other Down's kids and limiting her potential. Siera is going to college in the fall; she's special," Kathleen declared.

"Oh, for Christ's sake, Kat. Do you hear yourself? You're the one who's always blasting anyone for having preconceived notions about Siera. You haven't even met the girl, and already you're judging her in the same way that everyone judges Siera."

"Oh God, Jeremy, you're right. I can't believe I said that. Olivia seemed nice and very protective of Bri. I'm sure they were just delayed a little bit."

Jeremy chuckled. "You're acting like Siera is on her first date and you don't trust the young man. Bri is a friend and it's about time Siera had someone to hang out with. I'm glad she met this young woman, and I hope they continue to develop a friendship. It's good for Siera to be around other kids."

"You mean other kids with Down syndrome."

"It's not like she can catch it from them," Jeremy quipped.

"That's not funny. Crap. I'm doing it again, aren't I?" Kathleen sighed.

Jeremy nodded. "You told me Bri works in her aunt's vet clinic. I'll bet she has no problem keeping up with Siera."

"Her aunt did say Bri was advanced and relatively self-sufficient. She seemed to have a lot of pride about her niece's capabilities."

"Jeez, hon. What did you do? Interrogate her?" Jeremy asked.

"No, I did not interrogate her! We had a polite conversation, and she was very open about herself and Bri. I think she understood my need to be protective. She wasn't at all offended," Kathleen defended.

"So, what's her story? Is it just her and Bri? Maybe I should introduce her to Frank."

"Your creepy brother? No offense, hon, but the guy is a douchebag. I don't even like him spending time with Siera. I can't understand how two completely different people could have come from your mother's womb. Frank's never kept a

job for longer than six months, and the women he tends to spend time with are…." Kathleen shuddered.

"Frank's had a few bad breaks in life. He needs to find a nice woman to settle down with."

"Yeah, good luck with that. I don't think Olivia would be a good match at all. She's a successful vet, and I get the impression she's not one of those women who needs a man to complete her."

"Really? And you could tell this from one phone conversation?"

Kathleen shrugged. "I don't know. She had this confident air about her."

"You're probably right. Frank always tended to go for the girls who were somewhat more pliable, shall we say," Jeremy admitted.

"That's a delicate way of putting it."

The front door slammed, and Siera rushed into the family room. Kathleen noticed the wide smile on her flushed face.

"Hello, honey. Did you have a good time?" Jeremy asked.

"We had pizza, and Bri showed me her room. She has more books than me. She loaned me *Twilight* and told me it wasn't that scary to read. Olivia had a best friend too. She went to heaven. I told Bri she should come to a barbecue tomorrow. Can you make your famous burgers, Dad? Olivia said it was okay but wanted to call mom to make sure. They only live a few miles away. Bri said she could bike here. Her aunt said that wasn't a very good idea. She offered to drop Bri off after she closes the clinic. So can she come tomorrow?"

"Wow. That's a lot of information. How about if I call Olivia in the morning and we can work out the logistics? By the way, why are you calling her Olivia instead of Miss Olivia?" Kathleen asked.

Siera beamed. "She said I should call her what all her friends call her. Now I have two friends."

Kathleen patted the spot on the sofa to her right. "Why don't you sit down and tell us all about your night? We shouldn't stay up too late, because you and I have to work tomorrow, and your father needs his rest if he's going to create a culinary masterpiece for your friend after his early morning training."

Siera slipped off her backpack and dumped it on the floor next to the sofa. She grinned after she sat down. "Okay, but I have so much to tell you. I don't know if I can remember everything."

Kathleen was amazed at the transformation in Siera. She looked downright exuberant. Kathleen looked at her husband and saw him smiling. It was good to see her husband and daughter so happy. She wasn't sure she'd ever seen both of them smiling so much.

CHAPTER EIGHT

Siera waved goodbye to the bus driver. He was always nice to her. When she would daydream, he'd remind her that her stop was coming up. She'd had a good day at the store. Everyone had been polite and nice to her. Those days were rare. Most people weren't outwardly mean, except for some of the teenagers, but they would avoid looking at her or scrunch up their face. She could tell she made some people feel uncomfortable.

Her mom wouldn't be home for several hours, and Toby was probably still at his summer landscaping job. Toby was always showing off his muscles by taking off his shirt whenever a girl walked by. He would claim it was too hot, but Siera knew he wanted certain girls to notice him.

Her dad was at some training at the firehouse. He sometimes went to these events on his days off. She hoped he'd be home in plenty of time to make sure everything was ready. He nearly growled when anyone else tried to get close to his grill. He called it his domain. It made Siera laugh when

53

he would hug the big silver grill before firing it up. Her dad was silly sometimes.

Siera wasn't sure what she would do until it was time for Bri's visit. She wasn't positive her mom had been able to call Olivia to make the arrangements, but she was still counting on it. *Mom promised she would call Olivia's clinic first thing in the morning, when she got a chance.*

She decided to curl up on the couch and start reading the book Bri lent her.

Siera's mouth moved, as she slowly read the words of her new book. She didn't know if the cats were in the house, but Sampson finally came out from his hiding place and climbed up on the couch, spreading his paws over her legs. When she heard the garage door open, she popped up, ready to ask if Bri was coming over. Sampson meowed as if to say, *Hey, I was comfortable.*

"Did you call Olivia? Is Bri coming over? You didn't forget, did you?"

Kathleen set a grocery bag, a Dutch apple pie, and her handbag on the counter. "Yes, I called Olivia, and she's bringing Bri over after her clinic closes. I invited her to join us. I'm still not very comfortable with you calling her Olivia and not Miss Olivia, but I suppose you are turning into an adult." She pulled Siera into a warm hug. "My little girl is all grown up and ready for college. I'm going to have to start adjusting sometime, but it's hard. You can remind me when I start treating you like a child." Kathleen kissed the top of Siera's head.

"When's Dad coming home? He needs to start the grill. They'll be here soon. We won't have anything ready."

"Relax." Kathleen turned her head. "I think I hear your father now."

Jeremy was whistling as he entered the house and smiled as he tossed his keys on the counter. "Wow, my two best gals at the door eagerly greeting me. To what do I owe this honor?"

"I think your daughter is excited for her friend's visit. I invited Olivia as well. Where's the steak and chicken I asked you to pick up? I don't think everyone likes buffalo burgers." Kathleen leaned in and gave her husband a quick peck.

"Don't worry. Toby is getting it on his way home. He should be here any minute. I'll go fire up the grill, so it's the perfect temperature before I create my culinary masterpieces." Jeremy sauntered to the sliding glass door that led to the back patio.

Siera turned around when she heard the kitchen door slam. Toby barreled into the house carrying a large, brown grocery bag. His face was smeared in dirt and grime, and his t-shirt had large perspiration stains under his armpits.

"I come bearing gifts of meat. Argh, argh, argh. Nothing better than the man bringing home the meat." Toby tossed the bag onto the island in the kitchen.

"You're all dirty and gross. You better not have gotten it all over the food. Yuk," Siera exclaimed.

"It's in the bag."

"Go wash up. Siera's right, you're a sweaty ball of muck. Don't put on those ratty jeans, either. We're having guests, and I'd like you to pretend you're civilized."

"Aw, come on, Mom, don't you want to give me a big hug? I'll think you don't love me anymore. What about you, big Sis? Come on, give your brother some love." Toby stretched out his arms and lumbered over to Siera.

Siera screamed and ran to the sliding glass door. "Daaaad."

Jeremy pulled the door open and walked back inside. "Ah, that's what all the screaming is about—the prodigal son has arrived. Where's my meat?"

Toby pointed to the bag on the island.

"Go on, git. Quit teasing your sister." Kathleen smiled, plucked the dishtowel off the handle on the stove, and swatted Toby on his behind.

"Chicks dig that manly smell." Toby stuck his nose in his armpits and sniffed.

"Oh no, you did not refer to young women as chicks! And I guarantee your grubby body is not a turn on to anyone of the opposite sex. If your father gave you that crap advice, I would recommend never listening to another word he says."

"No, it was my buddies on the crew. They told me about the rich women who love getting it on with the hot sweaty laborers." Toby grinned.

Kathleen grabbed Toby's arm and swung him around. "You listen to me, you hormone crazed product of my loins. I did not spend fifteen hours in labor with you to produce a knuckle dragging Neanderthal. I'd better not ever hear you disrespecting women, young or old. I'll yank you from that crew and make you work in a flower shop if I ever hear that shit come out of your mouth again."

"Aw, Mom, I was kidding. I'm heading to the shower right now, and you'll be amazed at my transformation. Besides, I might have a date with Amy tonight. I think she saw my bulging muscles. She told her friend, who told Kevin, she thought I was cute. Kevin said they were all heading to see the new *Twilight* movie, and I'm supposed to look like Jacob. Go team Jacob. It's a chick flick...oh sorry, Mom, I mean the girls love those movies. I finally caught Amy's eye. Can I take the car, please?"

"You be home by midnight. Remember you have to work tomorrow. You treat Amy like a lady; she's a nice girl."

"I will, Mom." Toby charged up the stairs whistling.

Siera looked down at her baggy jeans and favorite t-shirt. She felt dumpy and unattractive. She didn't want Bri thinking she didn't have any nice outfits to wear. She hadn't considered taking a shower after work, and now she felt as grubby as her younger brother. "Mom, do you think I have time to take a shower too? I want to change into my blue shirt."

Kathleen turned her wrist and glanced at her watch. "I think so. Your father and I will entertain Olivia and Bri while you get ready, but I'm sure your friend doesn't care what you're wearing. It's not like this is a date or anything."

Siera stomped her foot. "I don't want to look sloppy."

"Okay, honey, I'm sorry. Go right ahead. You look lovely in your blue shirt," Kathleen soothed.

Siera ran up the stairs and decided she would try to put on a little makeup. She'd never had a date before. She could pretend her friend, Bri, was a date. Bri said her Aunt Olivia kissed girls so in Siera's mind that meant two girls could date.

Siera thought she would enjoy kissing Bri a lot more than any of the boys who teased her. She bet her lips were really soft.

†

Bri held the bunch of flowers from Aunt Olivia's garden in her hands, while her aunt carried the bottle of wine and pressed the doorbell. Bri was nervous to meet Siera's family. She wanted them to like her, because she was desperate to

continue spending time with Siera. They got along better than she could remember clicking with anyone else. It was more than the fact they both had Down syndrome. Siera was sweet and so pretty. Bri liked how her long, dark hair whipped around in the wind.

When a beautiful woman answered the door, Bri knew it was Siera's mom. She had the same wavy hair, and her smile made Bri relax.

"Oh, I'm so glad you could join us. We need some additional female energy. The testosterone is driving me nuts. Now we can tip the balance in our favor. Since Olivia insists on Siera addressing her by her first name, you'll have to do the same, Bri. I'm Kathleen, not Miss Kathleen, okay?" She stuck out her hand, and Bri tentatively clasped it.

Kathleen opened the door and gestured for them to enter the house. "Come on in. Olivia, it's so nice to meet you in person. I've heard great things about your clinic. I think I'll change vets. Our rambunctious kitties might take a shining to you. They hiss and growl every time I take them in for a checkup. I heard you have quite the touch with animals, Bri."

As if on cue, a gray and white cat wove in and out of Bri's legs, as she bent down to scratch his ears.

"Wow, that's Sampson. He doesn't usually come out when strangers arrive. I wonder where Delilah is hiding."

A small gray tabby darted out from under the couch and screeched to a halt in front of Olivia, who slowly bent down and stuck out her hand for the cat to smell. "This one is smart. I think she detects that faint, vet-office odor. She isn't about to wind around my legs, until she knows I don't have a big needle or a thermometer to stick in her behind."

Kathleen chuckled. "Well, can you blame them? I'm glad we get the thermometer in the mouth when we're sick.

Siera is primping but should be down any minute. Her younger brother is also primping. I swear he spends more time on his hair than Siera." Kathleen leaned in and whispered, "He has a big date tonight."

Bri looked up, as Siera came walking down the stairs. She was wearing a royal blue shirt and flowing black pants. Her bright-blue eyes sparkled, and Bri thought she looked like a beautiful angel. Her crooked smile landed on Bri, whose heart skipped a beat.

"Hi," Siera whispered.

"Hi. You look so pretty. We came right from the office." Bri smoothed down her t-shirt. "I look ugly next to you."

Olivia stroked Bri's hair. "No you don't, hon. You're wearing your dress T today, and that color makes your hair shine."

"It does. You have the shiniest hair I ever saw," Siera exclaimed.

"She does, doesn't she?" Olivia agreed.

"We all look fabulous. The boys will have to wear their sunglasses all night long to shield them from the glare of our brilliance." Kathleen led the group out to the back patio. "Jeremy, can you pause from your meat Picasso to say hello to our guests?"

Jeremy closed the lid to the large, shiny, stainless steel grill and set his tongs on the tray covering the side burner. He wiped his hands over his *King of the Grill* apron and waved at his guests with a boyish grin. "I'm Jeremy, Siera's dad. You ladies are in for quite the treat. The steaks and chicken are almost done. Please tell me neither of you like your meat well done, because it would be a crying shame to cook all the flavor out of those magnificent meat specimens."

Kathleen smacked him on the arm. "Hon, not everyone likes their dinner still mooing."

Bri giggled. "I like it rare, Mr. Jeremy."

Jeremy touched his heart. "Oh, if only I wasn't already married. Clearly, you appreciate the only way to prepare a steak. Just Jeremy, please." He winked. "Olivia, how do you like your steak, or would you prefer some chicken?"

"At the risk of offending you, I don't eat red meat, so I'd appreciate you grilling up an alternative. Chicken works for me," Olivia answered.

"Whew. I almost had Toby pick up some Portobello mushrooms, because I wasn't sure if you ate chicken. Siera mentioned something about a vegetarian pizza. We're a family of carnivores, so that was different for her." Jeremy stuck out his tongue. "See, hon, I am not a meat snob."

"I think the operative word is almost. I, on the other hand, did pick up vegetables and the Portobello mushrooms, just in case. I've been wanting to try them anyway. I think all the meat we eat isn't very healthy for our arteries."

"Oh, that's a bunch of hooey. My dad is still going strong, and he's never paid a bit of attention to limiting his red meat intake. Not that being a vegetarian is wrong or anything," Jeremy added.

Olivia laughed. "It's just that certain animals are too close to the ones I fix up in my clinic. I see those big cow eyes, and I can't bring myself to eat beef. I feel the same way about pigs. They're so darn cute when they're born."

"What about baby chicks? They're adorable, and you don't have a problem with chicken," Jeremy teased.

"Well, I don't eat the baby chicks, and when they grow up, they're not cute and cuddly. I suppose pigs aren't very

cute when they get to be a thousand pounds, but I still think of that children's movie, *Babe.* I can't do it."

Bri was listening intently to the conversation. She'd never thought about the fact that she was eating cows and pigs. She wasn't sure she wanted to eat chickens now, because they reminded her of the geese she loved.

"Could I maybe try those mushrooms?" Bri tentatively asked.

"Me too, Dad," Siera echoed.

"I think I'd like to try that too." Kathleen grinned. "Good thing I marinated them. They shouldn't take too long to grill up. I'll go get them." She brushed against her husband and kissed him on the cheek before going back into the house.

"You people are killing me. Okay, I'd better move the meat to the warmer section before they taste like leather. More for Toby and me."

Bri turned her head, when she heard the banging of the sliding glass door.

"What do we get more of, Dad?" Toby asked.

"Meat. The ladies here are having mushrooms."

"Epic. I'm starved. I worked up an appetite today. I think I can definitely eat two steaks. Ick, mushrooms, really? Hey, I'm Toby, Siera's good looking younger brother. Siera has been talking nonstop about her two new friends, Bri and Olivia." Toby walked over to Siera, slung his arm around her shoulder, and revealed a lopsided grin.

Bri liked the easy way Siera's family interacted with one another. She felt the warmth and love that hovered all around them. She knew her mom and dad loved her, but this seemed different. Even Toby seemed to treat his sister like she was a normal girl. Sometimes she forgot she was different around

Aunt Olivia, but even her aunt could be overprotective—
reminding her she wasn't exactly like everyone else.

Toby removed his arm and grabbed one of the plates on
the patio table. "Can I grab the steaks off the grill and chow
down now? I kinda got plans tonight and need to leave pretty
soon. Mom said I could take the car." He lifted the lid to the
grill. "Dad, you're letting the steaks cook too much."

"Oh, shit. Oops, sorry, ladies. If you'll excuse me, I need
to salvage our meal." Jeremy grabbed the tongs and expertly
moved several pieces of chicken and steak to the top shelf on
the grill. He placed two large steaks on Toby's plate.

Toby took his plate to the table and began slicing up the
meat and shoveling it into his mouth.

Kathleen returned to the patio, carrying a cookie sheet of
large, brown mushrooms. She raised her eyebrow. "Why are
you serving Toby before our guests?"

"Hot date, I think. He told me you said he could use the
car, so I assumed you already knew." Jeremy grabbed the
mushrooms with his tongs and placed them on the grill.

"Sorry, Mom, but I'm gonna be late if I don't hurry,"
Toby mumbled around a mouthful of food.

"Chew, please, and remember to be home by midnight. I
mean it Toby, not one minute after. I don't care if you've
managed to convince Amy to take a romantic walk in the
moonlight. You treat that young girl with respect and get her
home at a reasonable hour." Kathleen crossed her arms.

"Ooh, Amy. She's the cute little blond, right?" Jeremy
held up his thumb.

Toby nodded.

"Need some pointers from your old man? That first kiss
is the one that reels 'em in, ya know. The famous Kaufman
smoocharoonie."

"You did not just say smoocharoonie, did you? As I recall, Mr. Smooth, you waited until our fifth date, and when you went in for the kiss, you missed my mouth completely," Kathleen noted.

Olivia held her hand over her mouth snickering quietly, as Bri and Siera giggled.

Toby finished his steaks and was still chewing when he got up and smacked his father on the back. "Nope, don't need any pointers from you, Mr. Smooth."

Bri couldn't remember the last time she'd felt as comfortable around other people. She took a seat at the table next to Siera and ate the mushroom Kathleen had nestled inside a hamburger bun. It was different, but she decided she liked the taste and not having to think about eating a cow with those big brown eyes.

Siera was munching on her own mushroom burger and kept looking in Bri's direction, smiling between bites. She dumped a large pile of potato chips on her plate, along with a generous portion of potato salad.

Bri kept eyeing the potato salad and deviled eggs. She wanted to fill her plate with seconds, but didn't want Siera to think she was piggy. When Siera dipped the large spoon into the bowl of potato salad and served her a big scoop, Bri couldn't stop the smile from blossoming on her face. "I love potato salad."

"Me too. Dad always brags about his steaks. I like filling up on mom's potato salad." Siera leaned in close and brushed her lips against Bri's ear. "Don't tell Dad. It'll hurt his feelings." The whisper in her ear caused goosebumps on Bri's skin, but she liked how it made her shiver.

The pie that Siera's mom served after dinner was the best pie she'd ever tasted, and she felt so full she was

squirming on the big wooden bench Jeremy had moved in front of the fire pit. She sat right next to Siera. Their knees were touching. It was nice to sit close to her best friend. "I think I ate too much."

"I did too. I love pie. Are you gonna feed the geese again tomorrow?" Siera asked.

Bri nodded. "Do you wanna go see that *Twilight* movie with me after we feed the geese?"

Bri hoped Siera asked about the geese because she wanted to meet her at the park again, and she thought seeing a movie would be fun. Kind of like a date. She'd never been on a date before. Aunt Olivia told her sometimes boys asked girls on dates and sometimes girls asked other girls. She'd said there wasn't anything wrong with two girls going on a date.

"I'll ask my mom and dad. How will we get there?"

"I'll ask if Aunt Olivia can take us. She won't admit it, but I saw her. She read one of my *Twilight* books. I think she liked it. It was different from some of the other books she reads. They have just girls on the covers. I know she likes mushy books where people fall in love."

Siera sighed. "I want to fall in love."

"Me too." Bri clasped Siera's hand. It was nice holding her hand. She wanted to do that all night long, but pretty soon her aunt was telling her it was time to go.

CHAPTER NINE

Kathleen pulled back her dark, wavy hair and splashed warm water over her face.

Jeremy was brushing his teeth next to her. He yawned and stretched his tall frame. "Olivia seems nice, but I guess setting her up with Frank is out of the question. We should try to set her up with your sister instead."

Kathleen grabbed the hand towel and began blotting her face. "What? Olivia's not a lesbian."

"Jeez, hon, how can you have a gay sister and not recognize other gay women? I think you still have issues with her. I never could understand why you always insisted Deb's lovers were her roommates or good friends of the family, when she brought them over. I could see the hurt on her face when you did that."

"The kids were younger and it would have been too confusing for them. Besides, how did you know all of them were her lovers? There's been so many since Carrie, and she also brought home a fair number before she met Carrie."

Jeremy shook his head. "I can spot 'em a mile away. It makes sense now. Remember when Siera told us Olivia had a best friend who went to heaven?"

"Yeah, but that doesn't mean she's gay and her best friend was her lover."

"It's all in the way lesbians interact with other men and women. I can always tell. Your sister does it too. It's the eye contact and intensity. There's this woman-to-woman energy that's different from when they talk to men. You're just pissed I'm more observant than you. I'm a sensitive guy." Jeremy lightly smacked Kathleen's behind. "I pick up on emotions you often miss, like with Siera."

"What do you mean?"

"You never did see how miserable she was at school. She was all alone. I'm glad she met Bri. I worry about how she'll feel when she goes to Big Bend. I'm still not sure that's the right thing for her."

"We've talked about this before. I'm not about to expect less from her because everyone else tells me I should. Look how far she's come. She was accepted to Big Bend and earned the right to attend that school. Don't take that dream away from her."

"Whose dream, yours or hers?"

Kathleen sighed. "I have to fight the school and everyone else. Do I have to fight you as well?"

"I want you to pay attention to the subtle things now and again. For example, you might want to pay a little more attention to how Siera feels about Bri."

Kathleen raised her eyebrow. "What's that supposed to mean?"

"Well, homosexuality is hereditary. Siera could be a lesbian, and so could Bri."

"Now, you're being ridiculous. Besides, you don't seem to have much intuition when it comes to your creepy brother. There is something definitely off about him, yet you fail to recognize that."

Jeremy frowned. "No, I know he's a bit odd, but he's my little brother. I'm supposed to look out for him, like Toby looks out for Siera."

"I am grateful for that. Toby's a good kid under all that adolescent bluster. Amy is cute, isn't she? I wouldn't mind if he started dating her. I also wouldn't mind if my free-spirited sister settled down with a nice woman. Maybe we should try to get them together, if your so-called gaydar is accurate. I'm still not convinced."

"How much do you want to bet?"

"You're on, Mr. Sensitive. Winner gets a one-hour massage every night for a week."

"Deal." Jeremy stuck out his hand, and Kathleen vigorously shook it.

"So, how are we gonna find out?"

"Call her up tomorrow and ask." Jeremy walked into the bedroom and pulled back the covers on his side of the bed.

"I'm not doing that. She'll think I'm nosy or have a mild form of Asperger's. People don't blurt out something like that to someone they barely know." Kathleen shook her head. "You ask her."

"All right, I will."

"No, don't do that. She'll think we're nuts. I'll figure out a way to find out. And do not get Siera to ask, either. I know how that little pea brain of yours works. You think if the question comes from sweet little Siera, she'll answer without thinking it's odd." Kathleen climbed in beside Jeremy.

Jeremy pulled Kathleen into an embrace and kissed her lips. "Pea brain, huh? At least I have a ginormous…"

Kathleen slapped her hand over Jeremy's mouth. "Do not finish that sentence."

Jeremy grinned. "Well I do, you know."

"Braggart. Please do not teach your son to be uncouth. I'd rather you role model that sensitivity you seem to think you have an abundance of."

"Mr. Sensitive. Yup, that's me."

Jeremy looked at his beautiful wife who was half Italian and half Cuban. The combination was lethal at times. She was a strong woman, someone who got her way often, as she barreled through life. Her strength was both a blessing and a curse. Sometimes he loved her tenacity, and other times he wondered if she'd ever allow a different perspective to seep into her stubborn head.

When they'd first started dating, he considered himself lucky. He'd only asked her out on a dare. His friends wanted to watch as she turned him down. When she agreed, he said to her, "Really, you'll go out with me?" He smiled to himself, as he remembered her chuckling and tossing back her beautiful hair. It was love at first sight, and on their fourth date, he knew this was the woman he wanted to marry.

They were both in the medical field. People in health care don't think like normal people. They were sitting out on her front porch, gently sliding back and forth, and she was absently stroking his arm. It was so sensuous and arousing. Then she said, "You've got great veins. I could slip a 14-gauge needle in there."

Most guys would have run for the hills, but he understood the compliment—he was a paramedic. They'd laughed about it later.

Yeah, Jeremey adored his wife, but when it came to Siera, she was blind to the obvious. He couldn't think of a single way to penetrate that tough exterior.

†

Kathleen woke up early the next morning and stared off into space, as she replayed the conversation she'd had with Jeremy the night before. She'd never considered the possibility Siera would feel attraction to anyone, male or female. If she were honest with herself, she supposed she saw Siera like most people saw Down's adults—childlike, asexual beings with a degree of innocence, regardless of their age. She was hypocritical to ignore the possibility Siera would develop any kind of sexual feelings. Add the possibility Siera might be a lesbian, and it was too much for her to handle.

She'd agreed to let Siera go to see *Twilight* with Bri, and now she was regretting her decision. She wondered how she was going to squash this new friendship, lest it evolve into something she was definitely not ready for. Maybe she should call Olivia and invite her over for a serious chat. Certainly, she'd understand the need to watch over the two friends and make sure things didn't get out of hand.

Kathleen brought her coffee mug to her lips and took a large sip. When she heard Jeremy come into the kitchen, she looked up and watched him pour his own cup.

"You're up early."

Jeremy brushed his hand over Kathleen's shoulder. "I thought I would fix that old glider on the porch. I think the girls would like spending time in the evenings talking and watching the stars and moon. Summer nights are made for star gazing."

Kathleen frowned. "Are you sure it's a good idea to encourage their friendship in light of your observation last night? If Siera really does have confusing feelings toward Bri, we should try to corral them before it's too late. I know she can't get pregnant if they take their relationship too far, but other disastrous things could happen."

Jeremy's voice rose in irritation, "Like what?"

"You know."

"No, Kathleen, I don't. Please, don't tell me you have a problem with your daughter being a lesbian. I thought you'd worked through all that with your sister, so what's the issue?"

"I can't talk to you about this. You're always fighting with me on what's best for Siera. She's had to fight her whole life for acceptance. Surely you don't want to add to her burdens."

"No Kathleen, she hasn't had to fight for acceptance. She would have easily gotten that. You were the one who fought for it, not her, and whether you like it or not, you didn't really win."

"She's going to college, isn't she?"

Jeremy sighed. "Yes, and I'm very proud of her, but I'm not sure that's what she really wants. She told me she wanted to work with animals like Bri. She'd be a whole lot happier doing that this summer, and maybe for the rest of her life, rather than spend the summer at Walmart and trudge off to community college in the fall without the foggiest idea of what to do."

"I love her and only want the best for her. Her life has been hard enough. Don't you think?"

"On that, I agree."

"I'm going to talk to Olivia."

"Good idea, you should ask if she has a spot for her in her clinic."

"No, not about that. I want to discuss…oh, you know…my concerns about Bri and Siera. Do you want to join us? I can probably get away for lunch, and we can go to her clinic today."

Jeremy shook his head. "Nope, you leave me out of this. You're on your own. I sure hope you don't offend the woman with your regressive stance. Maybe you should weave into the conversation you have a gay sister who you accept and adore. Perhaps she'll ignore the ignorance that will surely follow." Jeremy stalked out of the room and slammed the door.

"Damn! I am not an ignorant bigot!" Kathleen shouted to the empty kitchen.

Kathleen decided to call Olivia from her office. Most days, her position as the emergency department director meant craziness from the time she entered the hospital until well past the dinner hour. Maybe it wouldn't be too busy in the emergency room today, and she could get away for lunch.

She wasn't sure if there was someone else to help with Olivia's clinic besides Bri. *Surely there's another doctor or tech that helps out. Bri seems like a high-functioning kid, but that would be a lot of responsibility to place on her.*

She propped her head in her hand and wondered if maybe she was blowing things out of proportion. It was preposterous to imagine Siera and Bri would be anything besides sweet friends. *Why did Jeremy try to suggest it was something more than that?* Kathleen convinced herself a conversation with Olivia would clear everything up.

†

Olivia was having a rough morning. First, the aptly named Mrs. Piddles peed on the stainless steel examining table. The cat had a tendency to squat and urinate wherever the mood hit her. The next appointment was Mr. Simpson, who brought in Rover for his annual exam. Rover was a vicious pit bull-rottweiler mix Mr. Simpson had trained for hyper aggression. Bri was the only person who had ever managed to calm the nasty dog, but she was busy with Mrs. Carlson's nervous mini lop. Before Olivia was able to calm Rover down, he'd chomped down on her arm. Mr. Simpson smirked and looked close to handing Rover a treat for maintaining his ferocious reputation. An apology was not forthcoming.

She chastised herself for not recognizing Rover's aggression before it was too late. He'd telegraphed his intentions with a loud growl, but by the time she reacted, he'd already lunged. Olivia was seconds away from kicking Mr. Simpson's despicable ass out, along with his fierce companion, when Bri rushed into the room and soothed the savage beast. Sometimes, Olivia regretted her decision to continue caring for Rover and dealing with his vile owner. She was thankful Bri had heard the commotion. Rover was not a quiet attack dog.

"I can help, Aunt Olivia. Rover didn't mean to hurt you." Bri smoothed his fur, and he licked her hand. He even rolled over, showing Bri his belly.

Mr. Simpson screwed up his face but didn't say a word, as Olivia managed to complete the exam and administer Rover's annual shots. "Next time you bring Rover in, you need to muzzle him if Bri isn't present."

"Mmf." Mr. Simpson yanked Rover, pulling violently on his collar.

Rover yelped and tucked his tail underneath his backside, as he dutifully followed his owner.

Olivia's arm began to throb. When she looked down, she noticed the blood flowing down her wrist. She turned to the sink to wash away the germs and disinfect the bite mark.

"I'm sorry, Aunt Olivia. I saw Rover on the schedule this morning. I should have come quicker. Why is Mr. Simpson so mean to him? You know he bites out of fear. Is your arm okay?" Bri grabbed a large piece of gauze and some antibiotic ointment. Olivia turned back around, and allowed Bri to apply the ointment and wrap the wound in the white gauze.

"I don't know, hon. Sometimes people aren't very nice and it's hard to figure out their reasons." Olivia sighed. "If I didn't have you around, I would refuse to see Rover. I suspect the loving attention you give him is the only kindness that poor dog will ever experience. If I had proof Mr. Simpson was abusing him, I would call the authorities, but he skates right on the edge."

Olivia's cell phone buzzed in her white coat. She pulled the phone out and glanced at the number. Whenever she didn't recognize the person calling, she would hit the red button to ignore the call. If it was anything important, they could leave a voice message. Then she could decide whether to call back or not.

When the ding indicated a message, she pushed the button to listen and tilted her head as Kathleen's voice played through the tiny speaker.

"Is it bad news, Aunt Olivia? You have a funny expression on your face."

"No, no, it's your friend's mom, Kathleen. She wants to meet for lunch today."

"I can't have two best friends. Maybe Kathleen can be your new best friend. You can't kiss her like Aunt Irene, 'cause she's married. Married people can't kiss anyone but who they're married to. Right?"

Olivia smiled. "That's right. You can have friends you don't kiss."

"Siera's not married. I could kiss her, right?"

Olivia chuckled. "You could. Do you want to kiss Siera?"

Bri shrugged. "She's pretty and nice. She said she likes my hair. I wish I had dark hair like hers. It's so thick. I like holding her hand. It's soft. Sometimes I wonder if her lips are soft too."

The wood door to the exam room slid open, and Evie poked her head in. "Your noon appointment just cancelled, do you want me to call the next person on the waiting list to get them in?"

"Wow, perfect timing. No, I think I'll call Kathleen back and tell her I can meet her for lunch."

Evie wiggled her eyebrows. "About time you started dating again."

"Oh no, Kathleen is Siera's mother, straight and married."

"Oh, too bad. Is that the Siera Bri has talked about, nonstop, for the last two days?"

Bri grinned. "Yes, my new best friend."

"Well, have a good time anyway. You deserve to get a proper lunch away from here now and again, especially after dealing with Rover." Evie glanced in the direction of Olivia's bandaged arm. "He bit you, didn't he? I'll bet that a-hole Simpson didn't even try to stop it."

Olivia nodded. "Next time, can you please remind Mr. Simpson to muzzle him? No muzzle, no appointment." She turned to Bri. "I'm sorry, but if he's a threat again, I'll have no choice but to refuse to care for him. You understand that, right? What if he'd bit Evie?"

Bri frowned. "I understand. If I would have been in the room, he never would have bit you."

Olivia patted Bri's arm. "You're a good soul. Okay, make sure there aren't any other appointments when Rover is scheduled. That should help."

"Will do, Olivia. Now about that dating thing...." Evie began.

CHAPTER TEN

Olivia eased her massive red truck into the last parking space in front of the bistro. It had been a long time since she'd had a leisurely lunch sitting at one of the outdoor tables. Irene had sometimes asked Evie to leave the schedule blank during the noon hour, to entice Olivia away from the clinic when the weather was nice.

She took a deep breath before exiting the truck. Kathleen was leaning back in her chair, with her head tipped back and her face to the sun. Olivia couldn't tell if her eyes were open or not; dark sunglasses hid the evidence.

When she slammed the truck door shut, Kathleen's head snapped up.

"Sorry, I didn't mean to startle you."

Kathleen smiled. "I was just enjoying the sun and catching a few rays. The ED was blissfully quiet today, definitely a rare occasion. All the planets seemed to have lined up. I'm glad you had a last-minute cancellation and could join me."

"I must admit to being intrigued by your call. Not that I'm an expert or anything, but it sounded like this isn't really a social chat. Did you want to discuss something important?" The chair scraped over the cement sidewalk, as Olivia pulled it out to sit.

"I don't know how to broach the topic without it somehow coming across as judgmental."

Olivia quirked her eyebrow. "Why don't you simply spit it out? We can navigate the murky waters of etiquette later."

"Do you ever worry about Bri forming an unnatural attachment to her friends?"

Olivia narrowed her gaze. "Unnatural?"

"It's just that I get worried the girls will form such an affection for each other and it will distract Siera from school. You know how hard it is for them to stay focused. Siera is going to college in the fall, and she'll need to concentrate if she is going to succeed. Bri is her very first friend, and I'm afraid she is quite enamored with her. Has Bri had other close friends before?"

Olivia leaned back in the chair and crossed her arms. "No, Bri is very isolated here. That's why I'm glad she met Siera. Personally, I don't think having a good friend is a distraction at all. I think it's an advantage. Good friends enhance the quality of our lives and bring out the special gifts that exist in us all. I've seen a positive change in Bri in the last couple of days, and I believe Siera has played a large role in that. Bri seems more confident."

"My husband has this silly notion that maybe the two of them have an attraction to one another beyond friendship."

Olivia leaned forward. "Are you afraid they'll experiment and become intimate with one another?"

"Aren't you?"

77

"Why would I be? Down's adults have the same feelings and urges that people without the syndrome have. Why shouldn't they be able to express those feelings in a loving way?" Olivia glared at Kathleen. "Unless what you really have a problem with is homosexuality. You do know I'm a lesbian?"

"No, of course I don't have an issue with gay people, my sister is…Deb?"

Olivia turned in the direction of Kathleen's concerned gaze to witness an attractive woman whose wavy dark hair was pulled back into a ponytail. The woman sat heavily at a table and angrily banged down a bottle of beer. She held her head in her hands and was quietly crying.

"Excuse me, please." Kathleen pushed back her chair, stood, and moved over to the woman.

Olivia wasn't sure how to avoid listening to the two women talk. She felt awkward sitting there, but she needed to finish the conversation with Kathleen. Siera was the best thing that had happened to Bri, and she was damn sure not going to let some well-meaning, but overprotective, mother ruin their friendship.

"Deb, what's going on?" Kathleen asked. "Why are you here and drinking a beer in the middle of the day?"

"The trauma that came in yesterday. We lost him. I had to get away. Don't worry, Martha sent me home 'cause I couldn't get my shit together."

Olivia stole a look at the woman sitting across from Kathleen. Sadness vibrated all around the woman, and Olivia wanted to wrap her in a hug to make it all go away. Olivia didn't often feel that way toward people, but she could always tell when an animal was in pain. Olivia wondered if the attractive woman was one of Kathleen's nurses.

"The little boy?" Kathleen asked.

The woman nodded. "Hey, I'm sorry. I interrupted your lunch, and you never get away. Who's your friend? Does she work at the hospital? I don't think I've ever seen her before. I would have noticed."

Olivia turned away, but it was too late. Those piercing brown eyes settled on her, and she knew the woman had caught her eavesdropping on their conversation.

"Oh, I should introduce you. It's Bri's aunt, you know, Siera's new friend."

"Oh yeah, the vet, right? Can I join you, or would that be awkward? I guess it already is awkward, huh? Maybe you two can manage to make sure I don't drink myself into oblivion."

Olivia stood and walked over to the other table. She wasn't sure what motivated her, but she'd always been a direct person. "I might as well come clean, as I couldn't help overhear the conversation. I suppose this is kind of awkward, but you look like you could use more than one sympathetic ear today. How about if we join you?"

The woman brushed her cheek and the small amount of mascara left a smudge of black. Olivia picked up a napkin from the table and held it out for the crying stranger. When she didn't take the offering, Olivia gently wiped under each eye where the evidence of crying remained. "A little running mascara."

"Hi, I'm Deb, Kathleen's younger sister—oh God, I just realized I'm one of those."

Olivia tilted her head. "One of those what?" *So this is Siera's famous aunt with the rotating best friends.*

"Ugly criers. You know, not the Hollywood type of crier who lets a single tear escape down her cheek looking

79

beautiful and vulnerable, but the hiccupping, slobbering, mascara-running, snot factory, ugly weeper."

"I wouldn't exactly categorize you as an ugly crier, just a little extra black makeup in a place you probably don't want it. I'm Olivia. I hate losing one of my patients. I know it's not the same, but I cry every time as well. I don't recommend a liquid lunch. How about I go in and order the meals, while you two chat for a few minutes. Just let me know what you want."

Kathleen took a few steps back to their original table and retrieved the bag hanging on the chair. She dug inside and pulled out three twenties and held them out as an offering. "Here, I invited you to lunch, so I insist on paying. I'll take a smoked turkey on focaccia."

Olivia waved away the money. "Don't worry, I got this. Deb, what would you like?"

"I'll take the veggie wrap. Normally, I would argue about a beautiful woman paying, but I don't have the energy. Of course, I never pass up a chance to let Kathleen pick up the check. You should take her money."

"Really, I got this. I don't have to mess with health insurance for most people who want Fluffy or Spot well taken care of, and pet owners are never stingy about paying to ensure their fur babies get the best treatment. I think I can afford this lunch." Olivia chuckled and pivoted to enter the bistro.

As she was opening the door, she heard Deb whisper, "She's cute and financially stable, why didn't you tell me the aunt was a lesbian?"

Olivia smiled, despite the fact she was not about to start dating anytime soon. She had excellent hearing after years of deciphering what ailed her patients through listening to the

subtle clues. It wasn't easy when your patient couldn't use words to tell you what was wrong. The different barks, meows, growls, and other sounds were their mode of communication, along with other nonverbal cues. She was good, but Bri was better.

†

Deb took a big swig of her beer and eyed her older sister. She felt better already. Kathleen knew what it was like when the babies died—she could relate after years in the ED. He was only three, and he'd died all alone—well maybe not entirely alone. Deb had taken him in her arms after they'd pulled the vent and disengaged all the wires and life support equipment. A group of nurses, technicians, housekeepers, diet aides, and even the hospitalist had surrounded him. They all hummed *Amazing Grace*, while he transitioned to what she hoped was a better place. His frail, battered body broke her heart.

Deb watched through the glass, as Olivia joined the queue. "I like her. She's got good vibes, and I'm glad Siera has a friend. She needs to have kids her age in her life. You're a good mom, but Siera hasn't had it easy in that school. She's been so alone and lonely."

"Did Jeremy call you to double team me or something?" Kathleen's jaw tensed.

"What? No. I've been a little busy. When would he have called, before that poor little boy made it to the unit, or after he died in my arms?" Deb asked bitterly.

"Oh God, Sis, I'm sorry I'm being shitty. Look, I know we emergency department nurses can be a crusty bunch, but I'll bet my last dollar they're just as shaken up. He came into our ED yesterday. Would you mind terribly if I took my

81

lunch to go? I want to make arrangements for the Employee Assistance Program to come in. I suspect there will be quite a few people that will need to process this, and I'd prefer they do it with a trained counselor versus at the bottom of a bottle. I'll expect you to attend one of those sessions. Um…I may have left the impression with Olivia I'm some kind of homophobe. Will you set her straight please?"

"You are a homophobe, and I would never want to set her straight. I prefer the lesbian version." Deb winked, and before Kathleen answered, she held her hand up. "Yes, I will tell her you've come a long way and aren't that narrow-minded, pig-headed sister I grew up with. Oh wait, yes you are still narrow-minded and pig headed—but not about me being a lesbian, anymore."

"I am not…oh, never mind. I'll go inside and make my apologies. Can I give you some advice?"

"Ooh, this ought to be good. Love advice from my sister."

"Olivia doesn't seem like your usual flavor of the month. Don't treat her like one. I think she may have had a longtime lover who passed away not very long ago."

"I thought you wanted me to find a good woman to settle down with." Deb grinned.

"Just be careful, okay? I don't want to have to pick up the pieces again, like with Carrie. She wasn't ready and you pushed."

"We were together five years. Do you know what that means in the lesbian world? We bring a moving van to our second date. I think I had every right to expect she'd want to become registered domestic partners. Don't worry, I'll not make that mistake again. I hope they never legalize marriage; makes it easier to avoid the conversation altogether. Now, if

I can only dodge those U-hauls, my life will be perfection in a bottle."

Olivia's petite form pushed open the doors and she smiled. Deb had to admit this woman was stunning and sophisticated in a down-to-earth way that created quite the dichotomy. She should be friendly toward the woman and not chase after her, for Siera's sake, she rationalized.

"Lunch should be out any minute. I asked them to put a rush on it, since I left Bri and Evie back at the clinic. With Evie taking her lunch, Bri will be the only one to watch the office. She gets flustered if she has to do anything more than answer the phone."

"Doesn't like computers, huh? Me neither. I hate the new EMR, that's our new computer system that is supposed to make it easier to document, but now takes us twice as long."

Olivia shook her head. "No, she doesn't like the computer. She thinks she'll break it or something. I keep reassuring her she won't."

Kathleen stood. "Look, I'm sorry I have to cut our lunch short, but I have to get back to the hospital. Um...after the uh...well I need to arrange for the debriefing sessions. My ED nurses were in the thick of it yesterday, and they'll be a mess. I'll just grab my lunch to go."

"Go ahead. I'll keep your sister company for a little while. Maybe I'll drag her back to the clinic, so she limits her alcohol intake to one beer. Nothing is more soothing than a litter of kittens. My first appointment this afternoon is with a client who breeds Himalayans. Those kittens are about as adorable as they come. I'm trying very hard not to add the one that looked like he stuck his face in a bowl of milk to my own menagerie."

"Ooh, I love fluffy pussycats." Deb shifted her eyes up to meet Olivia's, and the one corner of her mouth turned up in a seductive grin. She barely registered her sister rushing into the bistro to collect her lunch. The sadness had evaporated, replaced with a hint of mischief. She did feel better. The sting of the tragic loss of a young boy's life was a little less painful, now that she had the distraction of a beautiful woman. The sun would shine for several more hours, and she had the afternoon off. Things were looking up.

†

Was this gorgeous woman flirting with her? Deb's shift in mood took Olivia by surprise. As Kathleen rushed off, Olivia sat at the table and set her strawberry lemonade down. "You don't mind coming back to the clinic and cutting lunch a little short?"

"No, not at all. As long as I don't have to go back to the hospital and be reminded..." Deb's eyes watered.

"Do you want to talk about it?"

"No, I don't. Kathleen will make me attend one of the sessions, so I'll have plenty of time to perfect my ugly crying. I'd rather not start that up again."

"Can I ask you a question?"

"I believe you just did."

Olivia licked her lips and took a sip of lemonade. She was nervous, but she wanted to understand why Kathleen would have a problem with homosexuality. She was almost positive Deb was gay, and Kathleen didn't seem fazed by it. She didn't detect any of the tension that usually clung in the air when a person wasn't comfortable with their relative's sexual preference.

"Go ahead, ask. I'm sorry; I was joking. You look so uneasy. Do I make you nervous?"

"You're a lesbian, right? I mean, I don't want to make assumptions."

Deb nodded. "Yep, 100 percent, full-blooded, gold-star lesbian."

"So why does your sister seem to...oh, how can I tactfully put this?"

"It's okay. No, Kathleen isn't really a homophobe. Although she could win an Oscar for playing the role of one. She said something stupid, didn't she?"

"Not exactly. I think she's worried Siera is a lesbian. The way she started to talk about it, I got the distinct impression she was less than thrilled."

"Hmmm, interesting. My sister is quite logical in her assessment of situations. She has a hard time believing, for the most part, people in Washington don't give two shits who is sleeping with whom. I'll bet whatever drove her to invite you to lunch is rooted in her belief Siera doesn't need any more challenges tossed her way. She sees having to deal with people's ignorance as a challenge. What she doesn't understand is her own ignorance is driving the bus now, and it's going to take Siera to hell and back."

"Siera and Bri have already developed a very special bond. I won't let her take Bri on that bus. I don't want to see Bri caught up in your sister's struggles to accept certain realities."

"What realities?"

"Persons with Down syndrome can and do express their feelings in an intimate manner. I've done a considerable amount of research and met a few couples through some of

the groups I've connected with. I never cease to be amazed by the number of people who try to push the couples apart."

"Groups?"

"Yes, Bri is like a daughter to me. So, I connected with a support group that's mostly parents. They let me hang with them." Olivia grinned.

"Wow, that is so cool. Kathleen never got involved in the support groups, but to be fair she has stubbornly advocated for Siera. Too bad she can't see how she is doing the very thing she rails on others for. She's not seeing Siera as a beautiful young adult. Instead, she still views her as a child that needs protection. It's fairly common to treat adults with Down's like children or adorable pets, even if they're forty years old. I've tried to enlighten her, and so has Jeremy."

"She can't see it. She won't let go of her disappointment and anger about Jeremy's initial reaction to Siera. Jeremy was so young when Siera was born, and he suggested they should have had the amniocentesis test and aborted."

"I see. That must have been hard."

"It was, but he came around. Sometimes, it takes a little time to process things. She had a hard time with me being a lesbian at first, but when she realized not being who I was would only cause more pain, she got it. She'll come around about Siera, too. Give her time. I'll help steer that bus in the opposite direction. So, is Bri a lesbian too?"

Olivia shrugged. "I don't know for sure, but I think it's entirely possible. Perhaps Siera and Bri are trying to figure that out. I won't change my message to Bri because your sister isn't further along in her journey to full acceptance, even if you manage to steer the bus to a new location. I've consistently told Bri there is nothing wrong with expressing affection, as long as the other person shares your feelings and

is comfortable with touch. I can't see either one of them pushing the other beyond their comfort zone. I think, if it happens, it will be a slow process of sweet exploration."

"Speaking of sweet exploration, you're single, right?"

"Single, yes. Available, no."

"Aren't they the same thing?" Deb asked.

"No. I've been driving my own bus to hell, and I'm not taking on any passengers. I haven't gotten over my partner's passing, and honestly, I'm not sure I want to. I can offer friendship, though."

"Doesn't it get lonely?"

"Terribly. Even when I surround myself with great people, potential long-term partners, or family, I still feel alone. I haven't found the secret to filling the void yet."

Deb's soulful eyes met Olivia's. "I guess you're right. I never thought of it like that." Changing the subject, she added, "Um, I need to pick up something from my condo before visiting with the kittens."

Olivia looked at the pain and hurt in Deb's eyes. Somehow, she knew it didn't have anything to do with the little boy's tragic death. This time, when she felt the urge to wrap her arms around the woman, the waitress showed up barely in time to stop the insane gesture.

"Um, I'll meet you at the clinic, okay? Do you know how to get there?"

"Yeah, I think so, it's the one on Third, right?"

CHAPTER ELEVEN

Bri sat at the front desk, swinging her legs in Evie's chair. She was glad to see her aunt's smiling face. Instead of trying to make the appointments in the computer, she'd carefully written the names and phone numbers down on the message pad. Olivia had offered to show her how to make appointments on numerous occasions, but Bri didn't want to make the machine beep and turn into a blue screen—like it did that one time she'd messed with her mom's computer.

She jumped up and greeted her aunt. "Hi, Aunt Olivia. Two people called for appointments. I wrote it all down. You're smiling. Did you have fun? Is Kathleen your best friend now?"

"Kathleen had to go back to work early, but I met her sister, Deb, and we had lunch."

"Is she as pretty as Siera and Kathleen? Are you going to be her next best friend? She's not married. You could kiss her." Bri frowned. "But then Kathleen won't have a best friend."

Olivia chuckled. "I'm pretty sure Jeremy is Kathleen's best friend, and I'm not looking to replace Aunt Irene. But it is good to have people to lean on and do things with. You can have more than one person to go to the movies or go on picnics with. I'm sure you'll be able to add Deb to your growing list of friends."

Bri wrapped her arms around her aunt and squeezed. "I'm so glad I came to live with you. I love working with the animals and making a lot of new friends."

"I'm glad you came too. You've been indispensable to me."

Bri scrunched up her face. Sometimes her aunt used big words, and she didn't exactly know what they meant. She figured it was a compliment by the way her aunt was looking at her.

"It means you are very important to the success of the clinic."

Bri beamed. "Aunt Olivia, can I use some of my money for the movie tonight? I want to pay for Siera too and get some popcorn and candy. I've been saving almost everything. I want to use some of the money I earn."

"Sure, honey. I'll give you some cash."

Bri folded her arms over her chest. "I don't want your money. I want it from my job."

"It will be part of your paycheck. I'll give it to you in cash. Okay?"

She unfolded her arms. "Okay. It'll be like a real date then."

"Yes, it will." Olivia slung her arm around Bri's shoulder. "By the way, I invited Deb to come by and see the kittens. Are they here yet?"

"No. They're supposed to be here soon. How come she didn't come back with you? Were you embarrassed by your messy truck?"

"No, silly. She had to drop by her condo to pick something up." Olivia's brow furrowed. "I'm not sure why though; she didn't say. Oh, and before I forget, your mom called earlier. She mentioned she hasn't talked to you in a while. Can you please call her tomorrow?"

Bri nodded. She knew her mom worried about her, and she felt bad she hadn't called sooner to tell her mom about her new friend.

†

Deb rushed back to her condo to pick up the pet carrier. She knew she should have gone to the humane society and picked out a new kitten after Artemis died, but Himalayans were her favorite breed. They tended to be very affectionate, and she missed having a little ball of fur to snuggle up with at night. Besides, she'd have to keep coming back to see the lovely vet if she bought the kitten. She'd have to make sure her beloved pet got all his shots.

The tinkle of the bells on the door announced Deb's arrival, and she immediately heard the chorus of tiny meows. She knew the woman sitting at the desk wasn't Bri. A young woman with thick, blonde hair and a big smile poked her head out from one of the exam rooms off to the side, and Deb couldn't help but return the warm greeting.

"The kittens are in here. Aunt Olivia says you should come on back. They're so cute. I've been petting their fur. It's really soft. Hey, how come you have a carrier? Did you bring your cat to meet my aunt?"

"You must be Bri. I'm Deb, Siera's aunt. Can you keep a secret, Bri?"

Bri nodded her head enthusiastically.

"I brought the carrier, because I want the kitten your aunt described to me. The one that looks like the spokeskitten for those *got milk* commercials." Deb pointed to her mouth. "You know, the one with a large white marking on his nose and mouth."

"Oh, you mean, Socks. He's my favorite. He has white paws too. Aunt Olivia says he gets that from his Birman daddy. They're a Himalayan/Birman mixed breed. It gives them those special markings. Come on in."

Four adorable balls of fluff were squirming around, stepping over one another in a large carrier, while an older woman watched over them. Olivia plucked one out and began checking him or her over. Deb wasn't sure how you could tell the sex when kittens were only six or eight weeks old. Their junk wasn't very big. She never got the sex right when they were young.

"Hey. I'm glad you came. I was about to give this little guy his deworming medication." The kitten squirmed in her hand. His mewl was pitiful. "Bri, can you pull out some more medicine please?"

Bri prepared the eyedropper and handed the loaded medicine to her aunt. "It's all ready to go, Aunt Olivia."

"Thanks, Bri." Olivia expertly turned the kitten until she was able to push the dropper into his unsuspecting mouth and squeeze while gently massaging his throat. "One down and three to go."

"Is the one named Socks still available?" Deb asked.

The older woman smiled and glanced in Olivia's direction, lifting her eyebrow.

"No, I cannot add another kitten to my household, no matter how cute he is," Olivia announced.

"Yes, he is," the woman answered.

"I'd love to take him." Deb squatted in front of the carrier and peered in. She saw Socks yawning, and it was love at first sight. She reached in to stroke his soft fur. "Can I pick him up?"

"Sure." The woman nodded.

Socks curled into Deb's neck and began purring.

"I think he's found his new mama." Olivia handed the kitten she'd wormed to Bri, who put him back in the carrier and handed Olivia the next kitten.

"How much?" Deb asked.

"Are you a friend of Olivia's?" the woman asked.

Deb glanced at the lovely doctor.

"She is," Olivia answered.

"Then he's free. I was going to give him to Olivia. She's been my vet for a long time and saved quite a few of my babies over the years. I know you'll take good care of him, and now Olivia can visit him whenever she wants." The woman winked.

"I will take great care of him, and Olivia is welcome to visit him anytime." Deb grinned.

"You should come to the movie with us tonight. We're going to see the new *Twilight* movie. You can be Aunt Olivia's date. Siera is mine," Bri announced.

"I accept."

Olivia coughed and looked away, but hadn't corrected the date comment. Not only was Deb getting a new kitten and had finagled a movie date, but now she had a reason to invite the gorgeous doctor over. Yes, things were looking up.

†

Siera skipped along, swinging the loaf of bread she'd bought at Walmart after finishing her shift. She wanted to contribute in some small way to feeding the geese and wasn't exactly sure what they ate. Her boss told her chunks of bread would work. She tried to remember what Bri brought to feed them. She knew it wasn't bread, but she'd forgotten to ask her the night before.

Bri was swinging her feet on the bench and tossing something yellow to the geese who were brave enough to come close. Siera saw her bobbing her head and wondered if she was listening to music. When Siera got close, Bri turned her head and pulled out her headphones. Her wide grin let Siera know she was pleased she'd finally made it to the park.

"I brought bread for the geese," Siera said proudly. When Bri's smile disappeared, Siera wondered what she had done wrong. She couldn't help it when her eyes began to water.

"I'm stupid. I should have asked what to bring." Siera flopped down on the bench, dejected.

Bri tossed another handful to the eager birds before putting her arm across Siera's shoulder and pulling her close. "It's okay. I can teach you about what they eat. I didn't always know either. Aunt Olivia had to tell me. Bread is not the best thing for them. Sometimes we throw too much out. It stays on the ground and gets moldy. When they eat the moldy bread, stuff gets in their lungs and can hurt them. Bread isn't very nutritious. We're supposed to feed them cracked corn, birdseed, or other grains. You can also bring stuff you put in a salad. Aunt Olivia says they like leafy greens, especially cauliflower leaves."

"Oh." Siera looked down.

Bri kissed her cheek. "It was sweet of you to think of them. Aunt Olivia always says, 'it's the thought that counts.' It was a real nice thought. We can save it to make peanut butter and jelly sandwiches. I like those. Maybe we can have a picnic lunch. Do you work tomorrow?"

Siera shook her head. She touched the place where Bri had kissed her cheek and felt something fluttering around in her tummy, but not in a bad way like when she got the stomach flu.

Bri grinned. "Neither do I. Do you want to have a picnic here by the lake tomorrow? We can bring some more food for the geese."

Siera wanted to say yes, but she'd already told her mom she'd spend the day with her. She liked to have special mom days sometimes. Dad got to have those with her a lot when he wasn't working his long shift or having a man day with Toby.

"I wish I could. I promised I would do something with Mom. Just the two of us. Could we do it on Sunday?"

"You don't work on Sunday?" Bri removed her arm and began scooping up more bits of corn from the plastic bag. She tossed a handful to a lone bird, who slowly approached the group. Siera noticed how Bri always seemed to make sure everyone got a share of the food. She thought that was kind.

"Nope. I have the whole weekend off. I have to work next weekend."

It was too bad Bri had removed her arm. Siera wanted to sit with Bri's arm around her shoulder all night long, but then they would miss the movie. She was looking forward to that.

"I wish we had the same schedule." Bri sighed.

94

"Me too. I wish I didn't work at Walmart. I hate it. I'd rather work with animals. I'm probably not as good as you. I'm not as smart about what they should eat. I work really hard and I'm strong. I could carry things or move heavy boxes."

"I'm gonna ask Aunt Olivia if we need another person to help at the clinic. I'll bet she would hire you if we do. Can we have our picnic on Sunday then?"

Siera beamed. "I'll make the sandwiches. Do you like strawberry jam?"

"It's my favorite," Bri answered.

"We got some from the farmer's market. It's so good. I put it on everything—even my pancakes. I like it better than maple syrup."

"I don't like maple syrup. Aunt Olivia buys blueberry syrup. 'Cause she makes blueberry pancakes. She says the syrupy goodness makes the berries burst with flavor."

"I might like that."

"You should come over for Sunday breakfast."

"Okay. I'll ask my mom if I can."

They sat on the bench engulfed in tranquility, tossing bird seed and cracked corn to the geese and a few ducks that had wandered over for the free food. Bri tossed the last of the bird seed out across the lush, green grass. As Siera leaned back into Bri's embrace, Olivia's truck pulled into the parking lot.

Siera turned her head and saw Olivia walking over to them. She thought her Aunt Deb was sitting in the passenger seat. She squinted to get a better look, but the sun created a glare.

"Hey girls. Are you ready to grab a Subway sandwich before we head to the movie? We won't have a lot of time

before the show starts. I hope you don't mind that I picked up a hitchhiker who wants to join us." As Olivia walked up the path, the geese scattered.

"That's dangerous. My mom said you should never pick up strangers," Siera parroted what her mom always told her.

Olivia chuckled. "She's not a stranger. Sorry, Siera. I was teasing. Your Aunt Deb decided to join us. I met her today at lunch, when your mom and I were talking. She's been hanging out at the clinic and helped me close up tonight, after Bri took off for her nightly ritual. Bri's been leaving a little earlier than usual these days. I can't imagine why." Olivia winked.

Siera blushed. She sensed Olivia was teasing her and Bri. She liked how Olivia treated them as if they were like everyone else.

Bri turned her head, placed her hand above her eyes, and looked in the direction of Olivia's truck. "Is Socks in the truck? We can't leave him while we're at the movie. Can we, Aunt Olivia? That wouldn't be good for him."

"Don't worry, I followed Deb back to her condo, so she could drop off her car and Socks. We stayed for a few minutes to make sure he got used to his new digs. He seemed quite content when we left. I believe he staked a claim on her bed right away."

Bri shook cracked corn and seed crumbs from her lap onto the ground and stood up. "I gotta get my bike."

Siera jumped up and linked her free hand with Bri's. "I'll help you."

"I hope you girls don't mind crawling into the back. I know the seats aren't very big, but there's four of us. Even if we had room in the bed of the truck, it's not safe to travel back there."

"It's okay, Aunt Olivia. We're both a lot shorter than you and Deb. We don't mind. It'll be like a double date."

"Really?" Siera's eyes opened wide. "I never went on a date before."

"I got my own money and everything. It's my treat." Bri smiled.

CHAPTER TWELVE

Kathleen glanced at the clock on the wall for the tenth time. It was only nine thirty, but she couldn't help her nervousness. She was expecting Siera home any minute. Jeremy had picked up a last-minute shift, so it was up to her to interpret how Siera's evening went and whether her budding friendship with Bri was cause for concern.

When she heard a truck door slam, she jumped up and peeked out the window. Bri and Siera were walking up the sidewalk, hand in hand, with huge smiles on their faces. How could she squelch the pure joy she saw emanating from Siera? Besides, how dangerously could the relationship evolve? They were two innocent girls, who probably didn't have the foggiest idea about attraction or physical intimacy. She shook her head at her earlier thoughts and concerns.

She hovered by the front door and couldn't help eavesdropping on their conversation. She continued to observe them through the opening in the blinds.

"Thank you for asking me to the movie. This was the best date ever," Siera said.

"I'll see you on Sunday. Do you think we could ride our bikes to the park? Can you make it that far?"

"I think so. I'll have my dad look at my bike. He likes to make sure everything is in tip top shape. That's what he always tells me."

Bri hugged Siera and kissed her cheek. "Goodnight. I hope you have very sweet dreams."

The porch light illuminated Siera's blush. "Goodnight, Bri."

Kathleen stepped back, when she heard the door handle turn. She rushed to the couch. She didn't want it to appear obvious she had been impatiently waiting for Siera to return.

Siera bounded into the room. "Hi, Mom. The movie was so good. I felt sorry for Jacob, because Bella chose Edward. He was so hurt. I'm glad Bri doesn't have another best friend. I would be really sad if she chose her over me."

"Did I hear something about Sunday?" Kathleen asked.

"Oh yeah. I forgot to ask. Can I go on a picnic with Bri on Sunday? She asked about tomorrow. I told her I couldn't, because that's our special day. I'm making the peanut butter sandwiches with the bread I got." Siera held up the loaf of bread clutched in her hands.

"Why do you have bread?"

"I was going to help Bri feed the geese. She told me bread wasn't very good for them. I'm going to use it for our picnic lunch. Dates are fun." Siera sat on the couch next to her mother.

Kathleen frowned. "Dates?"

"Yeah, me and Bri are dating like Aunt Deb and Olivia. Aunt Deb went to the movies with us tonight. We had a

double date. She said Olivia isn't one of her new friends."
Siera knitted her eyebrows. "I didn't understand. It kinda
looked like it to me, and I said so. That made Olivia choke
on her Coke."

"Do you know what a date means, Siera?"

"Yeah, it's when you like someone a lot and want to do
things with them. I like Bri. I'm happy when I go to the park
to feed the geese with her. Or when I go to her house and
have pizza. Or she comes here for dinner. When two people
who like each other go to the movies together, it's a date. Bri
said it was a date. She paid for my movie and popcorn. That
was nice of her, wasn't it, Mom?"

Kathleen absently nodded. "Sometimes, when people
date for a long time, they decide they want to live together
and get married. Dating leads to a different kind of
friendship. Friends who like each other don't necessarily go
on dates, but they still get to spend time with one another.
Bri can still be your best friend, and you can spend time with
her, without it being a date. Do you understand?"

Siera knitted her brow. "But I want to date Bri. Maybe
someday I can live with her. Can two girls get married? I'd
want to marry Bri."

"Two girls can't get married, but they can live together
and love each other the same as your father and I. They can
register as domestic partners. That's the same as marriage,
but it isn't called marriage," Kathleen explained.

"How come the domestic thing isn't called marriage?
That doesn't make sense to me. I wish I was smarter, so I
could understand that."

"Oh honey, sometimes the laws don't make sense. I
don't understand it either. Believe me, you're a lot smarter
than most of the politicians."

"Maybe after I finish college and get a better job, I can ask Bri if she wants to do that domestic thing."

"I'm glad you're focusing on college, because you shouldn't let your friendship with Bri distract you from school. You know how important that is."

"I know, Mom." Siera yawned. "Can I go to bed now? I'm kinda tired."

"Of course. We can talk more tomorrow. I have a lot of fun activities planned for us."

Kathleen leaned back on the couch. She wasn't sure how she felt about their conversation. Siera's simplistic view made more sense than any argument against gay marriage. She had to really dig deep and explore why she'd expressed concerns about where Siera's relationship with Bri was heading.

Didn't she want her daughter to live a normal life as independently as possible? Wasn't that what she fought so hard for from the very beginning? Maybe she was a closet homophobe. How ironic. On the other hand, Siera had enough prejudices to deal with. Adding one more complication wasn't something she wanted for her beautiful baby girl.

She sighed. How was she supposed to both protect her daughter *and* encourage her independence? It was a conundrum she didn't have all the answers to, yet. If she admitted to Jeremy she might have been wrong, he'd never let her live that down. How would she approach Olivia, now that she'd done such an awful job of broaching the subject?

†

After dropping Bri off, Olivia pulled in front of Deb's condo and put the truck in park, leaving the engine running.

She turned in her seat. This was the awkward part of the evening. She did find Deb attractive, and that was hard to hide, but she was determined not to let her baser instincts overtake her brain. The bottom line was that she was not prepared to begin a relationship with anyone, even a casual one that wouldn't lead to anything but a bit of fun or a pleasant distraction.

Deb undid her seatbelt, swiveled in her seat, and faced Olivia. "So...listen...I'm sorry Siera caught you off guard. She's a perceptive little shit. You know how Bri has a special talent with animals? Well, Siera has a way of...oh, I don't quite know how to describe it. I guess she makes the complicated, simple. Look, I'm not going to deny I'm attracted to you. I would like to date you. It could be casual or not. Your choice."

"My offer of friendship still stands."

"Friends with benefits. I can live with that. You've got yourself a deal." Deb leaned in and brushed her lips against Olivia's.

Startled, Olivia pulled back and almost smacked her head on the window. "Um...that was not a negotiation. It was a statement of fact. Sex isn't on the table. It adds an unnecessary complication, one I'm not willing to throw into the mix. Besides, from the sounds of it, you are not lacking in female company that could provide the scratch to that particular itch."

"Okay, I'll admit I don't have the best track record right now. I've been licking my wounds lately, or more accurately letting someone else lick them." Deb grinned. "I haven't met a lot of women worthy of anything more than a bit of fun. I sort of get it, though. After Carrie left, I retreated for a little bit. Phase two of my recovery was casual dating. I thought

she was the love of my life. Turns out she wasn't, but I still wasn't ready to replace her. Your situation has to be so much more difficult. I caved and got lonely. It happens, but like you said, I haven't found the magic pill to fill the void."

"I'm sorry, Deb. I'm not capable, right now, of being the antidote for your pain. I do hope you find it though." Olivia patted Deb's hand.

"Well, if I can't con you into being my lover, how about my trusted vet? Will you come in for a few minutes to make sure Socks is adjusting well to his new home? I'd be ever so grateful." Deb batted her eyelashes.

"Just for a few minutes and then I have to go. He is a cutie."

Deb crossed her index finger over her heart. "I promise—cross my heart—I won't keep you too long, unless you want."

†

Deb wasn't about to give up on exploring a possible relationship with Olivia but was smart enough to know timing was everything. Olivia was the first woman, since Carrie, of any substance worth waiting for. It was time to let go of her apprehension about entering into anything serious with anyone. Olivia was proof there were women who could make long-term commitments. It seemed like that long-term promise had extended well beyond her lover's passing. Deb recognized the obstacle, but also admired the loyalty. She'd felt that depth of love and loyalty for Carrie, but it hadn't been returned.

Carrie had loved her, but maybe she hadn't been in love with her. They were good together, yet something was

obviously missing, or she wouldn't have been scared away by the prospect of making a lifetime commitment.

Deb waved Olivia into her cozy condo. The home was perfect for Deb on her own. After Carrie and she split, she'd decided to get something that would be easy to take care of. The condo on the lake was perfect.

Socks greeted the two women at the door. Deb scooped the ball of fur into her arms and was delighted when he started purring. He was exactly what she needed. She'd missed having a cat to snuggle up with at night—especially now that, for the most part, she slept alone. Normally, she would go back to her date's place, rather than sully the sanctity of her private retreat from the world. On days like this, when a small child had died in her arms, Deb needed to spend time alone to work through her emotions.

The day came flooding back, and she couldn't help the tears that leaked from her eyes. She tried to turn away and rein in her emotions, but Olivia must have noticed.

"Hey, what's wrong? I'm sorry, I tend to be blunt when I explain where I'm at with my inability to enter into any kind of relationship." Olivia lifted Deb's chin with her finger and swiped away a tear. Her eyes revealed a genuine apology.

Deb shook her head, while Socks crawled further up her body and nestled in her neck. "No, I'm sorry. This has nothing to do with your honest declaration. I respect and accept that, for now. I had a rough day, and for some reason, I flashed back to why I took off early from the hospital."

"I remember. The little boy, right? You never did talk it through with your sister at lunch today. I'm a very good listener if you want to borrow my ear instead."

"You don't want to hear about that. It's very depressing and not a happy story at all."

"Actually, I do. I can tell you from experience it helps to talk things through rather than to bottle up your emotions. Sometimes, talking with someone who is somewhat removed is the answer. How about I take that cup of coffee I know you were about to offer? While you're making it, I can keep Socks company. Is it okay if we have a seat on your couch?"

Deb handed Socks to Olivia. "Okay, if you're sure. What would you like in your coffee?"

"Black is fine."

Deb filled the kettle and put ground coffee into the French press, while stealing glances at Olivia. It was endearing how she kissed Sock's nose and murmured to him. Deb wished those lips would find their way to her, but she'd prefer them on her own lips versus the nose. She leaned against the counter and continued to watch, as Olivia turned Socks over and tickled his belly. When he started to bite, she removed her hand and said, "No bites."

"What do you expect, when you start teasing the poor thing?" Deb called out.

"I'm not teasing him. I'm teaching him hands are for petting, not playing with. You need to start his education on this at a very young age. Too many people wave their hand in front of their new kittens and then get mad when the kitten acts like their hand is a new play toy. To a kitten, wiggling fingers are something to attack."

"Hmm, I guess you're right. I never thought it of like that. Even when they're little, those tiny teeth and claws are sharp."

"Yes, they are." Olivia smiled.

Deb was enamored with her new friend, who practically lit up the room with her brilliant smile. Olivia was a very beautiful woman. Her long blonde hair fell softly to the top

of her shoulders. The ends curled up slightly, with enough body that Deb longed to run her fingers through the slight wave. Deb had a hard time describing Olivia's eyes. They were the lightest blue she'd ever seen on someone and reminded her of a shimmering river, silver with a splash of blue. Against Olivia's golden tan, they stood out like two beams of light.

The kettle began to whistle, and she finished making the coffee while Olivia continued to teach Socks her hands were not play toys. Deb carried the two cups of coffee to the table in front of Olivia and took a seat next to her.

"Thanks for coming inside. Honestly, I guess I wanted a few more minutes of company; which is really strange. I normally prefer retreating to my condo alone to work through my complicated emotions," Deb confessed.

"So, I know you lost a little boy. That is always hard, but I sense there was more to the story and the reason it's affected you so much today."

"Wow, beautiful and intuitive. Too bad you're off the market. Yeah, it was particularly hard on me. Most of the time, when we lose the little ones, they're surrounded by loving family members—that wasn't the case this morning."

"So, what happened?" Olivia asked.

"He was in the car with his mother and father, who are fairly well known in the community. They aren't the best parents and have serious drug and alcohol issues. The dad was driving under the influence, and the result was a head on collision with a Hummer. His mom didn't make it, and then they arrested his dad for vehicular homicide. The bastard practically walked away from the wreck, while his wife and son died, and the couple in the Hummer also didn't make it." Deb took a deep breath, and her tears started to flow freely.

She paused, unable to form a new sentence, as her emotions choked the words away.

Olivia took her hand and held it.

"The doctor told us the results of the tests indicated no brain activity and they were about ready to remove the breathing tube. I thought it was a tragedy this little boy wouldn't have anyone by his side as he passed. I was his primary nurse, and when I heard his grandmother was in the waiting room, I thought 'thank God, he has someone.' I went out to explain to her about her grandson's condition." Deb angrily swiped away a tear.

"That's a good thing, right? That he had someone there for him."

"I thought so, but boy, was I wrong. When I started explaining to her that her grandson was critical and there wasn't any brain activity, she held her hand up. She told me she was there to get the keys to the car her no-good son stole, and she'd heard they were locked up in the hospital safe." Deb took a sip of coffee. "I went to get the keys for her and then naively thought maybe I was using too much hospital vernacular. Maybe I needed to break it down for her, so she would understand her grandson was going to die. When I gave her the keys, she started to leave. I followed her to the elevator and stuck my foot in the door. I started to explain again, and do you know what she said to me?"

Olivia shook her head and squeezed Deb's hand.

"She told me, 'what's done is done.' Nothing she did would change that. She continued to say she wished the damn car wreck would have taken her son as well, because then she wouldn't have to deal with his shit anymore. Then she kicked my foot, and the elevator doors closed."

"I'm so sorry," Olivia exclaimed.

"I couldn't let him die alone. I went back to the room and gathered him in my arms, rocking and singing to him, while he went to what I hope is a better place. We all sung to him as he passed. He didn't die alone."

Olivia held Deb, who sobbed freely with her head resting on Olivia's shoulders.

"Sometimes these experiences turn into the defining moments in our lives. Not that you weren't a fabulous nurse before, but this will help shape how you view everything in the future. You did something great today. Don't ever forget that."

Deb felt Olivia's arms tighten around her and create a protective cocoon, as she expelled all her sadness of the day.

CHAPTER THIRTEEN

Bri woke up with a smile on her face, thinking about her date with Siera. She'd wanted to kiss Siera's lips but had decided that might be too forward. She'd settled on kissing her cheek. Aunt Olivia had told her a kiss on the cheek could be a nice gesture. Lately, kissing was all Bri could think about, and she wondered if that was okay. Aunt Olivia didn't seem to think it was wrong if Bri wanted to kiss Siera, but for some reason, Bri wasn't sure. Sometimes, she overheard people talk about Aunt Olivia, and they said a lot of mean things. She didn't understand, because her aunt was one of the nicest adults she'd ever known.

Bri pushed her fingers through her thick hair, trying to untangle it. Her mom would say it was in a disarray and tell her to shower and brush it out. Siera said it was pretty. Bri wanted to make sure her hair always looked nice, even on the days she wasn't going to see Siera, because then she was in the habit of taking care of it.

Skipping into the kitchen, she saw her aunt leaning against the counter with a faraway look in her eyes.

"Morning, Aunt Olivia."

"Morning, Bri. I feel like a bike ride today. What do you say? Will you let your old, out of shape aunt tag along with you when you ride to the park?"

"That would be fun. You should call Deb and invite her too. We could ride to where she lives. Then I could pet Socks."

Olivia sipped her coffee and peered over the cup. "Um, I'm not sure we should disturb her on her day off. This is her free weekend, and she had kind of a rough day yesterday, before she came to visit us at the clinic."

Bri scrunched up her face. "I thought when people were sad, you should visit them to cheer them up. Like when I got sick and had to stay in the hospital. I liked having visitors. Even if it was only my family. I bet Siera would have come to see me. Isn't that what friends are for?"

Olivia smiled. "I suppose you're right. Deb may act all tough, but I think a day out bike riding in the sunshine may be the right medicine. Although, I don't know if she has a bike. I guess we'll find out. Let's have some breakfast first, then I'll see about tracking down her number. I suppose I can call Kathleen to get it."

"You should call early. 'Cause Siera is having a girl's day with her mom. Can I use some of my money to get a cell phone, Aunt Olivia? Siera has one. I want to be able to call her. Maybe I can learn how to text her too."

Olivia patted Bri's back. "That's a good idea. Besides, I'd like a way to get ahold of you when you're out and about on your bike. I'll put you on my cell phone plan and make it

a family plan, okay? Then you won't have any excuse not to call your mom and dad more often."

"Thanks, Aunt Olivia. You're the best. I promise to be better about calling mom."

"Don't forget your dad. He loves you too."

"I know."

†

Siera pulled her arms from under the covers and stretched them over her head. The blinds kept the light from shining through the windows, but Sampson had decided it was time to wake up. He jumped on top of her and began to knead her chest and lick her. She giggled and scratched his chin where he liked it.

When Delilah meowed, Siera peeked over the side of the bed and saw two green eyes staring back at her.

She patted the bed and called out to her, "Come on up, Delilah. I can pet you both at the same time."

Delilah jumped on the bed and snuggled on the opposite side of where Sampson had claimed his spot. With both cats soaking up attention from their favorite human, Siera thought about her first date. It brought a smile to her face.

She frowned when she remembered talking with her mom afterward. Her mom hadn't said anything bad, but Siera still had the feeling something wasn't quite right. The impression wasn't as strong as the outright disapproval she sometimes picked up on, but something odd was there. Siera wanted her mom and dad to like Bri, because she was planning on spending a lot of time with her. Maybe someday, they could live together, even if they couldn't get married.

Things were very confusing to Siera. Shouldn't love and friendship make everything better? She supposed it might be

111

like in the movies. Before two people could live happily ever after, they had to remove a big obstacle. She grinned at the thought that maybe someday there would be a movie about her and Bri.

Siera heard rustling in the kitchen and assumed it was her mom getting breakfast ready. She knew Toby had left early for his landscaping job, and her dad was still at work doing his long shift. It was going to only be Siera and her mom for their special day. Although she liked those days with her mom, a part of her was going to miss seeing Bri. Siera was anxious for their picnic date on Sunday but didn't want to hurt her mom's feelings by telling her that.

"Siera, breakfast is almost ready," her mom called from the kitchen.

She kissed both Sampson and Delilah on the nose and scrambled out of bed.

When she reached the kitchen, her mom was placing waffles on the table—Siera's favorite. The whipped cream was out, next to a big bowl of fresh strawberries mixed with a little bit of sugar. She was eager to dig into the special breakfast.

"Waffles, my favorite. Thanks, Mom." Siera pulled one of the kitchen chairs back and sat down.

"I thought we'd head to Cave B and do a spa treatment. How does that sound?" Her mom sat across from her and placed two waffles on her plate.

"That sounds like fun." Siera covered her waffles with a large scoop of strawberries. She reached for the spoon sticking out of the handmade whipped cream and placed a dollop on top of the berries. She giggled as she thought about the word dollop. Her mom liked to use that word to describe how much cream to put in coffee. The first time she'd heard

her mom use the word, she'd asked why her mom wanted to put her doll in the coffee.

"I know that it's our special day, but Aunt Deb had a hard day yesterday. Do you think maybe we could invite her to join us?"

"Mm hmm, sure Mom," Siera answered around a mouthful of food.

"Siera, don't talk with your mouth full."

"Sorry, Mom."

Siera glanced at her mom's cell phone when it started buzzing on the counter.

"Maybe that's Aunt Deb calling to give an update on her date with Olivia." Kathleen chuckled.

She picked up her phone from the counter. "Hello.... Um, sure, I can give you Deb's number.... Oh, that sounds like a nice gesture. I was going to ask her to join us, but I'll bet she would prefer spending the time with you and Bri. She's an avid cyclist and sometimes uses her bike to clear her head, so that's perfect. Thank you for thinking to include her in your plans. That's very nice of you. She did have a very bad time of it yesterday, and I'm glad you invited her last night. Her number is 763-5412. Listen, about yesterday, I'd like a chance to talk more with you and apologize.... Okay, I'll call next week, and maybe we can have a do-over of lunch."

Kathleen ended her call and returned to the table. "I guess it's just you and me again."

Siera tilted her head. "Was that Olivia?"

"Um hm. She called to get Aunt Deb's number."

"How come you have to apologize to Olivia?"

"Oh, just some adult stuff."

"Mom, I'm an adult now too," Siera huffed.

113

"Yes, you are, but sometimes things are private between people. Can we leave it at that?"

"You mean like secrets between best friends? Like they tell you something but ask you not to say anything to anyone else." Siera put another big bite of waffle in her mouth.

Kathleen frowned. "Do you and Bri have secrets?"

Siera paused, as she finished chewing her food. "No, she hasn't told me anything she said I couldn't tell you or Olivia about."

Kathleen nodded her head. "Okay, that's good."

"She might, though. I would keep it private. That's what best friends do."

"Well, it depends. If she tells you something you shouldn't keep private, because it might hurt her, then you should tell someone."

Siera furrowed her brow. "Like what?"

"Well, if someone was picking on you or her, you shouldn't keep that a secret. Besides you know you can always tell me anything, right?"

"Uh huh. I think the secrets best friends tell each other are more about how they feel about things. If Bri tells me stuff like that—it's okay to promise you won't say anything, right?"

"I suppose so," Kathleen admitted.

†

Olivia rubbed the bridge of her nose, as she stared at the picture on the fireplace mantel. "Oh Irene, I can't help myself. There is something about Deb that is a little hard to resist. She's very different from you in many ways, and yet, there's this vulnerability she lets slip through, every once in a while. I'm like a moth to a flame and can't help wanting to

make it all better for her. I suppose she has the same zest for life you always had, and that's also hard to repel." *Maybe I'm one of those people who likes to rescue others from pain.*

She picked up the framed picture and remembered when they'd first met. Irene had come into the clinic where Olivia was an intern, holding her beloved kitty, Zippy, in her arms as tears ran down her face. She was the very definition of an ugly crier, but Olivia still saw Irene's incredible beauty. Olivia was a sucker for a crying woman. When Irene's bleary, green eyes captured Olivia's, it was love at first sight. She'd confessed that to Irene on their second date, but Irene never questioned Olivia's sincerity. Olivia fell a little bit more in love when Irene accepted those feelings and told her they were fated to become one. Ironic, that was one of the few times Olivia had ever seen Irene cry.

Bri came bounding into the living room, with her helmet in her hands. "Did you call Deb? Is she going to come riding with us? Can we leave now?"

"Whoa, wait. One question at a time. Yes, I called Deb, and she sounded happy about the invitation to ride. I guess she's quite the avid cyclist."

"What does avid mean?"

"It means she has a passion for it, like you have a passion for feeding the geese. It's one of her favorite things to do. It grounds her like feeding the geese grounds you. Remember when I said grounding is like giving you a sense of calm or peace?"

"Are you going to be able to keep up with us?"

115

Olivia laughed. "I'll do my best. Do you think you can pretend to struggle a little and slow down so I won't look so bad?"

"Okay, Aunt Olivia, I'll go slow. You can keep up, and I won't tell Deb the reason." Bri grinned.

"Thanks, I'll owe you."

"Deb makes you smile. I haven't seen you smile much since Aunt Irene went to heaven. I think you should let Deb become your best friend."

"Oh, hon, things are a bit more complicated. Nobody can replace your Aunt Irene."

"Why not?" Siera asked.

Why not? That was a very good question, and Olivia wasn't sure she had the answer. She redirected the conversation, because she didn't know how to respond. "Hey, how about we ride to that ice cream place today and get some handmade cones?"

"After lunch, right? We have to eat real food before we can have a treat."

Olivia chuckled. "Yes, we'll get some lunch at the deli. It's on the route. I sure am glad this town has great bike paths. I would worry about you riding all over the place if this wasn't such a bike-friendly town. It's about time I started riding again."

Olivia was finally ready to admit to herself she'd unconsciously avoided her bike. She had so many memories of lazy summer days with Irene. They would pedal around the lake and enjoy Irene's special chicken salad she'd lovingly tucked into a mini-cooler.

Bri bounced up and down on the balls of her feet. "This is going to be so much fun. If Siera was here it would be

116

perfect. She might be as out of shape as you. Today, I can practice going slow so I don't hurt her feelings."

"Good plan. Don't tell her she's out of shape. That wouldn't be something to be honest about. Sometimes it's better not to say anything at all even if it's the truth. Remember, if you can't say something nice, don't say anything at all. As William Blake said, 'A truth that's told with bad intent beats all the lies you can invent'."

"I know Aunt Olivia. I would never hurt her feelings."

"I know you wouldn't, hon. You don't have a single mean bone in your body."

"Bones can be mean?"

"It's just an expression. It means you're very sweet and kind, and that's what everyone loves about you."

"Do you think Siera loves that about me?"

"Absolutely, who wouldn't love a great kid like you?"

Bri stomped her foot. "I am not a kid."

"You'll always be a kid to me, because I'm so much older than you. It's not a bad thing. Even when you turn fifty and I'm seventy, you'll still be a kid to me." Olivia smiled.

"Okay. As long as you help me be more independent and don't treat me like a child, you can call me a kid. Sometimes, can you also think of me as an adult?"

"I do think of you as an adult. A very mature and responsible adult, or I wouldn't leave you in charge at the clinic like I did yesterday."

Bri beamed. "I'm going to learn to use the computer. Then you can leave me for longer periods and the work won't stack up for Evie."

"That's a great goal. Now let's head out. It's going to take us longer than normal to go to Deb's house, and I want

117

to save some energy for our ride once she joins us, or else I'll embarrass myself."

†

Deb was squatting next to her racing bike, attaching the nozzle to pump her tires with air, when Olivia and Bri rolled into the parking lot. She squinted into the sunshine and noticed the sleek recumbent trike that Bri was riding. Deb thought that might be a bit more comfortable for a long ride than her skinny racing seat. She liked speed and had resisted purchasing a heavier, more stable bike as her body started to let her know she wasn't a teenager anymore. She imagined the loud complaints from her back, wrists, and shoulders, together with the painful chaffing of her nether regions, might make a disjointed symphony if put to music. Even Olivia rode a more appropriate cycle, as she sat atop the mountain-road combo bike with the cushy-looking seat.

Olivia turned her right foot before clicking out of her clip-on pedal, and came to a stop a few feet away from where Deb was now pushing the handle up and down on her pump. "Your bike looks fast." She slipped her sunglasses down her nose and peered over the frames.

"Maybe fast, but I'll wish I was riding Bri's bike after twenty miles."

"Twenty miles, how far do you think we're going today?" Olivia choked out the words.

"Is a twenty-five-mile ride too far for you?" Deb grinned.

Olivia pushed her sunglasses back up her nose. "Um no, but remember we've already ridden eight miles. I think it's only fair you escort us back to my place and have to pedal the final eight of your ride all by yourself. If I'm in pain

tomorrow, I want to know someone else is sharing the misery."

"Oh, I see how you are." Deb stood and brushed her dirty hands on her shorts. "Maybe we should plan a short ride if this is your first time out this summer."

"Do not insinuate this old lady cannot keep up. I'm very competitive, you know." Olivia smiled.

Deb looked at Olivia's taut legs and well-defined deltoid muscles. The sleeveless bike shirt revealed arms that had the perfect combination of femininity and strength. "I don't think you'll have much trouble today. You look like you're in great shape."

"Oh, there's no doubt I'll be sore. I haven't ridden in a long time, and those muscles may have forgotten how much I do enjoy riding a bike. I've been considering purchasing a trike like Bri's. It does appear more comfortable than either one of our bikes."

"Maybe we should check out the bike shop in Wenatchee. I've always wanted to try out their trikes," Deb said.

"You can take a short ride on mine if you want," Bri offered with a huge smile on her face.

"That's okay, I don't want you to have to move the seat or readjust everything. I'm a lot taller than you," Deb replied.

"I don't mind. Aunt Olivia can help."

"Maybe we should take a drive there tomorrow, while the girls are on their picnic lunch. I really do want to check out the recumbent bikes. I almost dragged Irene there before…"

Deb saw the look of sadness pass over Olivia's face, despite the sunglasses that hid most of her emotion. She jumped in to lead the conversation down a different path, at

least until they were alone and she could return the favor by offering her listening ear. "It's a date. I'll come pick you up at nine. We can grab some brunch and head to the bike shop after our bellies are full. The drive will give us plenty of time to digest and get ready to take a test spin on several different brands."

"Perfect, I know a great place for brunch. So, for today, we thought we should ride to the deli first and grab a bite to eat. How does that sound?" Olivia asked.

"Wonderful. Lead the way."

†

Kathleen looked over at her daughter, who giggled as the nail specialist filed and buffed her toenails. She'd grown so much, and Kathleen was proud of the young woman she'd become. Maybe Walmart wasn't the best employer, but the job had taught her responsibility and discipline. Jeremy might be right about seeing if Olivia needed additional help at the clinic. At least Siera might enjoy her work more than at the discount superstore. Still, for all her growth and hard work to get into the community college, Siera was very naïve and childlike. Kathleen wondered if that was because she'd encouraged her academically without treating her like an evolving adult. It was a hard habit to break. Treat her like a child, and she'll act like one. View her as an adult, and she'll blossom into an amazing young woman.

"There's nothing like treating yourself to a pedicure. Have you decided yet what color you want?"

"I like the rose color. I think I want that. I can wear my pink shorts tomorrow."

"That might not be very comfortable on your bike. I bought you those bike shorts because that's what most

people wear when they're riding a bike. Black goes with everything."

"Can I wear my pink t-shirt—the one I got for the cancer walk?"

"Sure, honey, but you know you can't ride barefoot or in your sandals, so you'll have to show Bri your toes when you stop and have your picnic lunch."

"Okay, Mom."

"I'll have your father make sure your bike is in good condition when he comes home from his shift tonight."

"I was going to ask him to do that too. I think Dad likes tinkering."

Kathleen chuckled. "Yes, he does. Listen, I want you to be sure to carry your phone with you, in case something happens, like if you get a flat tire."

"Bri doesn't have a phone. I wish she did. Then I could call her up anytime I want."

Kathleen frowned. "Why doesn't she have a phone? Doesn't her aunt worry about her when she's riding her bike alone?"

Siera shrugged. "I don't know. She said she was going to ask if she could buy one with the money she has saved up. She's saving all her money. Then she can get her own place someday. Isn't that cool?"

"Yes, that's a good goal."

Kathleen played back the conversation in her head and chastised herself for doing it again. Did all mothers treat their adult children the same way, or was she also falling into those age-old biases toward children with Down syndrome? Perhaps that was something she could discuss with Olivia to help them find a new common ground without her offending the woman again. It was hard being a mother and knowing

what was the best thing for your children. She was far from perfect, but she didn't want to turn into a helicopter mom, constantly hovering over her child. Lately it seemed like she was veering down a bad road and needed to get herself back on track.

CHAPTER FOURTEEN

Olivia groaned and rolled on her pillow-top mattress when she heard the chime on her smartphone. Picking up the offending device, she glanced at the text, squinting to read the small words.

How RU doing this AM?

She smiled, despite the ache in her legs. When she'd gotten out of bed in the middle of the night, she'd realized what a terrible decision it was to ride the extra ten miles.

It reminded her of the time she'd accepted that shot of whiskey. As the liquid burned all the way down her throat, she'd declared to her friends, "Oh that tasted like a bad decision." And it was. She'd ended up stripping down to her underwear and singing *Kum Ba Yah* at the top of her lungs at her friend's pool party.

The extra miles hadn't seemed much farther, until they turned into her driveway and dismounted. Deb had offered to give her a leg massage, but Olivia had politely declined. The mild flirtation in her offer was enough to sober Olivia. She'd

participated in the day's banter a tad too much. She needed to nip that in the bud. *What the hell was I thinking?* If she gave this woman an inch, she was sure to take a mile.

Olivia grimaced as she swung her legs onto the floor and sat on the edge of the bed thumbing her response.

I blame you for my condition. Don't laugh when I hobble along today.

Hair of the dog. We'll work out the kinks when we test drive the recumbents.

Ugh...

On my way. CU in 10

Olivia moved the phone away, making sure she read the text correctly, then pressed the power button twice to read the time. When it registered in her foggy brain it was 8:45, she called out, "Bri, why didn't you wake me up?"

Silence was the response. *Oh, holy hell, she must have left early for her outing. Serves me right for not setting my alarm.*

Each tiny step to the bathroom sent a shot of pain up her legs, as she attempted to swivel and shuffle to her destination. She imagined most people would find her odd walk hilarious—like a decrepit penguin.

Olivia was determined to work out the stiffness and pretend she wasn't as out of shape as she appeared. Walking like a ninety-year-old woman was sure to give her secret away. *Maybe she'll think old penguins are cute. Oh, stop that, why do you care what she thinks?*

When she finally made it to the toilet and slowly let her bottom hit the seat, she cringed and wondered whether the paramedics would need to burst into her house to remove her from the cold porcelain. At least Deb wasn't working today,

but being the butt of the ED nurses' jokes was not Olivia's idea of a good time. She chuckled at the inadvertent pun.

"Ahhhhh." It felt good to empty her bladder after the sparing trip in the middle of the night. Normally she got up several times a night, but after learning the consequences of her poor judgment, she'd avoided a second or third jaunt with her sore muscles.

Olivia knew there was no way she could move fast enough to take a nice hot shower and certainly not a heavenly bubble bath, so she pulled herself up using the edge of the vanity. Bracing herself against the sink, she rummaged around in the drawer, selected a hair tie, and gathered her thick mop into a messy bun. As she stood in front of the mirror with her feet wide apart to provide the necessary balance, she managed to brush her teeth.

She hoped Deb would take pity on her and give her some time to sooth her sore muscles in a hot shower, as she attempted to make herself a bit more presentable. When she heard the doorbell, she hobbled to answer it.

Deb was smiling when she handed her a purple gift bag with yellow tissue paper poking out of the top. It felt heavy.

"Please tell me you're a little sore. My ego needs a bit of stroking, and it would help for you to admit that. I don't care if you lie to me, in fact, please lie to me, because you look entirely too chipper and well put together this morning."

Deb chuckled. "The bag contains some healing bath salts. Kathleen called me this morning. Bri let the cat out of the bag you might not be up early. Go on, I see you haven't showered yet. Take a bath, relax, and I'll go out and get us some nice, rich coffee. We can still make brunch and have plenty of time to thoroughly check out the bikes."

"Aren't you sore at all? Not even a tiny bit?"

"My legs are okay, but I wouldn't even let you, as hot as you are, go anywhere near my crotch. God, I swear if you want to make it easy on someone to stay celibate, send them on a thirty-five-mile bike ride," Deb confessed.

"Oh, thank God. Well, I mean sorry about your, um...sensitive parts, but at least you aren't iron woman. I guess I can be thankful for the nice wide seat on my bike. Too bad I'm horribly out of shape. Thanks for the bath salts. Are you sure you don't mind the delay?"

"Not at all. I woke up early and took my own bath. It really does help. I'll be back in half an hour. Will that give you enough time?"

"It might take me that long to walk back to my bathroom." Olivia laughed.

"Oh, okay, how about..."

"I'm kidding. See you in thirty minutes. I owe you big time."

Deb waved and started walking back toward her car. "My pleasure."

Olivia kept the door open and watched Deb walk away. The slight sway seemed to mesmerize her, and she had to shake her head to remind herself she was not on the market. Friends, just friends.

†

Siera noticed her mom seemed less stressed than in the last few days. When she told them to have a good time, she smiled her real smile and not the fake one she sometimes put on when she was being polite. Siera had gotten up early and made her own breakfast, before rolling her bike out of the garage. Her dad checked over everything and pronounced the whole kit and caboodle was in good working order. He'd

pumped up her tires, oiled the chain, and told her to have a good time.

Since Siera only had a small basket in front, Bri offered to put the picnic lunch in the large bag she attached to the rack on her trike.

They were moving along the trail at a leisurely pace. Siera was glad Bri didn't mind going slow. She knew she had a long way to go to be able to keep up with Bri, and she wanted to ride a lot more to build up her stamina. Her dad said the more she rode, the easier it would get. He always talked about doing exercise at the firehouse to keep his stamina up so he wouldn't let others down. Siera didn't ever want to let Bri down.

Bri talked about the long ride her aunt, Deb, and she had taken yesterday. She said she was glad they wouldn't go as far today, because even though she took her bike everywhere, it was a lot more miles than she normally journeyed.

Halfway to the park Bri offered to let Siera try her special bike.

"You're the same size as me. I wouldn't have to adjust anything if you wanted to try it out."

"Really? I would love to," Siera answered.

When they entered the park where Bri usually spent her early evenings after work, Siera dismounted and flipped down the kickstand with her foot. She was eager to try the trike, because it looked a lot more comfortable and easier to ride than her own cruiser.

Bri showed her how to straddle the bike, grab the tube in the middle, and fall back into the seat. It was awkward, and Siera sat too quickly, rattling the trike.

"I'm so sorry. I didn't break it, did I?"

"Nah. It's really sturdy. Just put your feet on the pedals now. The bars on your right and left move so you can steer."

Siera pushed on the pedals in front of her and moved a few feet forward. She experimented with the handles on her right and left, moving them a little to turn.

"The brakes are on the handles you steer with," Bri shouted out, as Siera began to travel farther away.

Siera started to pick up speed and lost her tentative touch, as she careened around the parking lot.

"Wheeeeee. This is so much fun," she said, as she whipped around the black top and passed Bri. After she'd completed three large circuits in the lot, she squeezed hard on the brakes and flew forward as the bike came to an abrupt stop. Although her behind lifted out of the seat, she managed not to fall too far forward and injure herself on the tube sticking up in the middle.

"I guess I shouldn't pull on the brakes too hard." Siera giggled.

"Did you like it?" Bri asked.

"Oh yes. It was a lot more fun than my old bike. I want to save up my money and buy one for myself." Siera scrunched up her face. "Was it very expensive?"

"Yeah, it was. It was important to have a way to get to the clinic on my own. My hours are different from Aunt Olivia's. I didn't want to take the bus. I don't like busses." Bri frowned.

"Why? The bus drivers are really nice here."

"They weren't nice where I grew up. They never smiled. They would yell at me to hurry up. I like being independent. When I bought the bike, a whole new world opened to me. I don't have to depend on anyone anymore. I can go wherever

I want. Whenever I want. Except, I don't ride late at night."
Bri smiled.

"Doesn't it get too cold in the winter?"

Bri shook her head. "I have winter clothes. As soon as I
start riding, I warm up a lot. When it's really cold, Aunt
Olivia gives me a ride and closes the clinic early. That's only
for a couple of weeks in the winter. She knows I'd rather get
there on my own."

"I know what you mean. I had to convince my mom that
taking the bus was safe. Dad says she's overprotective. I
want to be more independent, too. I guess it's hard on my
mom seeing me grow up. She says I'll always be her little
girl no matter how old I get."

"That's what Aunt Olivia says too. She told me even
when I'm fifty years old, I'll still be a kid to her. I don't
think she meant that in a bad way. I know she loves me. She
gives me a lot more responsibility than my mom ever did. Do
you think if you lived with your Aunt Deb she would let you
go out on your own more?"

"Probably. Aunt Deb is a lot of fun. She treats me
different than Mom does, but I don't want to hurt my mom's
feelings. Maybe someday we can live together on our own?"

"I'd like that. It can be kinda tricky getting off the trike.
Do you need some help?" Bri asked.

Siera nodded.

"Give me one of your hands. Use the other one to grab
the bar in the middle and push up."

"Okay." Siera offered her right hand, and Bri grabbed it,
pulling at the same time Siera held onto the tube in the
middle. "Thank you for letting me try out your trike."

"You're welcome. Are you hungry yet?"

"Uh huh. I hope you like the sandwiches I made. I brought some apples and brownies. Do you like brownies?"

"I love them. They're one of my favorite desserts. Aunt Olivia and I make them all the time."

"Me too. Mom and I made them last night, after our day at the spa. I got a pedicure. Do you wanna see?"

"Uh huh." Bri unzipped her bag and removed what Siera had packed for them. She carried everything to one of the empty picnic tables in the park.

Siera walked over to join her, sat on one of the benches, and removed her shoes and socks. She lifted her feet off the ground and pointed to her toes. "I picked out this pink color. It's my favorite."

"That's really pretty. It goes with your t-shirt," Bri said.

Siera swiveled around to face the picnic basket Bri had set on the table, while Bri maneuvered herself onto the bench and sat next to her. Siera began pulling all of the food out of the basket and setting it in front of them. The two girls eagerly dug into their sandwiches, as the sun beat down on them.

"It's hot out today. I put the water in the freezer so it would still be cold when we stopped for lunch." Siera had pulled the extra water from the basket earlier and now handed one to Bri.

"Wow, that was really smart of you. The water bottle on my bike is kinda warm now." Bri unscrewed the cap and took a large swig of the water. "It's still cold," she exclaimed.

"I'm having the best time. Is this our second date?" Siera asked.

Bri blushed. "I think so."

"Do you think it's okay to kiss on the second date?"

Bri shrugged. "I don't know. I guess. Do you want to kiss?"

Siera blushed and nodded.

"Okay. I think we should kiss at the end of the date. Isn't that what you're supposed to do?" Bri asked.

"I don't know. I guess I should have asked my mom. Maybe there's some kind of dating book we can get. I feel kinda funny asking my mom about it."

"I can ask Aunt Olivia. She told me I could ask her anything. I'll bet you could ask your Aunt Deb."

"Okay. I'll call her tonight and ask. Maybe we should wait to kiss until we both ask our aunts."

"That's a great idea." Bri grinned and took a big bite of her sandwich.

†

By the time Olivia and Deb arrived at Go-Bent Bikes in Wenatchee, it had reached ninety-five degrees and the sun blistered down on the blacktop in the parking lot. A variety of trikes and two-wheeled recumbent bikes lined the outside, and Deb jumped out of the car excited to try one. She watched, as Olivia grimaced and grabbed the edge of the roof to pull herself up, enabling her to slowly emerge from the car.

"Ow, ow, ow. That hour and a half drive did not do my body any favors. I didn't think my legs could stiffen any worse than when I woke this morning, but I would be wrong about that."

"The bath didn't help much did it?" Deb asked.

"Oh no, it did. Without the bath, I wouldn't have agreed to come at all. Just give me a few minutes to walk a bit and stretch my legs."

Olivia hobbled after Deb, as she walked over to the bikes that were on display outside.

Deb ran her hand along a recumbent tandem bike and smiled. "Hey what do you say to giving this tandem a shot?"

"Oh, I don't know about that. What if my stiffness causes us both to crash? I've never ridden a recumbent before. I'll bet they take getting used to. The trikes seem more my speed, because there isn't any risk of toppling over. I like the idea I'll be able to ride one of those well into my eighties."

"Spoilsport. Maybe they have a tandem trike." Deb looked up as a burly man opened the front door and smiled broadly at them.

"Are you ladies interested in a tandem? That one right there is a sweet ride. I'm Jerry, the owner of this fine establishment."

"Hiya Jerry, I'm Deb, and my chickenshit friend here is Olivia. You wouldn't happen to have a tandem trike we could try out, would you?"

"As a matter of fact, I do. It was a special order, but the customer decided to go with something else. I almost convinced my wife we should buy it ourselves, but she nixed my suggestion. It's an absolute blast to ride," Jerry said.

"Sold, well not sold as in we're going to buy it. But can we take it for a test ride along the path?" Deb asked.

"You bet. I'll get my assistant to help take it down and pump the tires. We'll have to get you two fitted, and then you can take it for a spin."

Jerry walked back into the store, and Deb grinned at Olivia. "This should be fun."

"Just remember, you have a semi-cripple to contend with. If I don't contribute as much to our forward propulsion, you'll understand, right?"

"Of course, but I think it'll only take a few minutes for you to warm up, and then we'll be cruising along with the breeze in our hair, enjoying this fine summer day."

"It's kinda hot today. Are you sure we should be going for a long bike ride in this heat?"

"You're one of those glass half empty types, aren't you?" Deb grinned.

"I am not. I'm a realist. Do you think he has some cold water or Gatorade we can buy? You're a nurse, you know how dangerous dehydration can be."

"I don't know, let's check." Deb opened the door and burst inside the bike shop. When she looked around and saw the glass refrigerator filled with plain water, vitamin water, and Gatorade, she smiled and turned back to inform Olivia.

Olivia was pushing open the door and taking small steps as she limped inside.

Deb pointed to the case full of beverages. "Ta da. Your wish is my command. What would you like?"

"You drove. This is my treat. Better pick out several. I have a feeling it's only going to increase in temperature today. I'll take some vitamin waters. I'm not too picky about flavors, so whatever you want. It'll probably take me half an hour to get to the case and grab them, so I'll let you do the honors while I stumble to the counter to pay."

The tandem hanging from the ceiling was a massive machine. Jerry and a young woman were struggling to bring it down. Deb estimated the trike was a least ten feet long. It was similar to Bri's, but a double with a coupler in the middle to connect the two trikes together. It was ingenious

engineering, and she couldn't wait to try it out. She was almost afraid to ask Jerry how much it cost. She'd been pricing trikes, and they could run as much as six thousand dollars for a single. She suspected this one would be nearly the cost of an inexpensive car. Yet, if buying the tandem would guarantee more time with Olivia, she'd whip out several credit cards in the blink of an eye. Kathleen always railed on Deb's impulsive nature, but life was too short. In Deb's opinion, you needed to grab life by the horns and hang on, lest you miss out on something wonderful.

When the bike owner had finally wrangled the bike from its loft, Deb tossed out her question, "So, Jerry, how much does that tandem run?"

"Eleven thousand and some change," he answered.

Deb whistled. "Yikes! I could buy a Korean car for that."

"Greenspeed is the Cadillac of recumbent trikes. They're made in Australia, and you won't find a better bike in the market. It's an investment for avid cyclists who want to enjoy the sport well into their golden years. After you take a spin on this, I'll put you on another trike. You'll definitely feel the difference."

"Another tandem?" Deb asked.

"No, that's the only tandem trike we have, but I can let you ride the recumbent two-wheeled tandem that's on display outside."

"That looks fun, too." Deb was grinning from ear to ear.

"So, which one of you lovely ladies will be in the back? That's where all the power and control comes from. The rear seat is not only the power-rider position, but that's the person who will steer the bike."

"Well, I don't know if I like Deb having the control—she has that evil glint in her eye—but she definitely has more power than I do, especially since my very bad decision to ride thirty-five miles on a crossbike I haven't been on in years," Olivia interjected.

"Ouch, got a little lactic acid buildup, huh?" Jerry asked

"That, my friend, is an understatement." Olivia smiled. "Just push me into the seat. I'll pray I land in the middle somewhere and can wiggle my butt into position."

Jerry's deep belly laugh filled the cramped store. "Come on, I'll help you climb aboard, and we can adjust things while you're sitting. Mary, can you grab some helmets for them?"

"You do realize once I'm sitting in that bike it will take an act of congress to remove me," Olivia joked. "And, I'll have helmet hair when you transport me to the nearest hospital for a psych evaluation on my ability to make good decisions," she added.

Deb grabbed her hand and pulled her next to the bike. "Come on, I promise I'll be good when I give you that rub down tonight. I have a very special ointment I guarantee will provide some relief."

"I'll roll the bike outside, and you can take off from the parking lot. There's an entrance to the bike path right around the corner," Jerry said.

Once they were outside, Mary provided a helmet for each woman to secure to her own head. Jerry and Deb each took one of Olivia's elbows and eased her into the reclining seat. She groaned as she settled in.

Deb pulled a twenty out of her pocket and handed it to Mary, who was standing to the side watching the comedy of errors with a smile on her face. "Would you mind terribly

grabbing several bottles of vitamin water for us? I noticed there are multiple bottle holders on the trike, and I want to make sure we stay well hydrated."

"Hey, you distracted me from my mission. I thought I was paying for the beverages," Olivia argued.

Jerry waved his hand in the air. "On the house, girls, I'm hoping to make a sale today."

Deb chuckled, "Okay. If this bike or some of the others we're about to try out are as comfortable and fun as I hear they are, you probably will sell me a bike today."

"Excellent, I knew I pegged you as a bike enthusiast, my favorite kind of person. Grab four for the girls," Jerry directed.

Mary went back into the store, and Jerry began adjusting the front of the bike so Olivia's feet landed on the pedals in the perfect position to be efficient. Deb climbed on back, and moved the handle bars to her right and left, grinning as she called out, "Zoom, zoom. Gosh, I feel like a kid on a Big Wheel. I can't wait to get this baby on the road. It feels like a little racing car."

Olivia turned her head, calling over her shoulder, "Hey now, hey now, can you please tamp down your excitement a tad? I don't want you to be the first one to manage to find a way to topple this bike over. Trikes are supposed to be more stable, not less."

"You'll be fine. It's nearly impossible to crash on a trike," Jerry explained.

Mary pushed the glass door with her hip, carrying the four cold drinks in her hands. She bent to place them in the four bottle holders arranged in various places on the trike.

Jerry finished moving the tube frame, using the quick release. "Can you put your feet on the pedals and pedal backward for me please?"

Olivia started moving the pedals back slowly and groaned a little as she followed his instructions. "I'm still working out my sore muscles. Give me a few minutes."

"Okay, that's good," Jerry said.

Deb put her feet on the back pedals and made several rotations backward. "I think I'm already set. It looks like whoever rode this bike before was probably close to my size."

"Yes, my wife finally acquiesced to a ride after I begged her for a few months. She's about your height."

"Is she a powerful cyclist?" Deb asked.

"Nope. A control freak." Jerry chuckled.

Mary slapped him on the arm. "I'm telling her you said that."

"Go right ahead. She'll readily admit to it. In fact, I think she's proud of it."

"Okay, partner, ready to roll?" Deb asked.

"Sure, why the hell not? I do need to work the kinks out," Olivia answered.

"Ooh, I like the sound of that. Kinky is good..." Deb pushed on her pedals, and they rolled out of the parking lot on their way to the short road that led to the bike path.

†

Olivia was enjoying the small breeze as they cruised along at a good clip. With each rotation, her sore muscles loosened a little bit more. She had to admit, the bike was a blast. The recumbent felt so responsive to Deb's every minor

137

adjustment in a new direction. She imagined the single trike would probably turn on a dime and offer more joy.

"I really, really, want one of these, but it would be an over the top purchase. Especially as a single person, unless I can count on a regular riding partner, hint, hint," Deb called out.

"Oh no you don't. I am not letting you spend your hard-earned money on a tandem, regardless of how much fun I'm having on this machine," Olivia responded.

"Killjoy."

Olivia chuckled. "Are you always this impulsive?"

"Yep, it's one of my better traits, don't you think? It keeps all the women guessing."

"Actually, I think you are wonderfully transparent. You say exactly what you're thinking, no games or subterfuge. I like that about you," Olivia admitted.

Olivia couldn't see Deb's face, but she heard the smile.

"Thank you. I think that's about the nicest thing someone has said to me in a long time. Of course, I haven't been all that nice lately. Now, I'm going to play mean old nurse and tell you to take a drink. It may feel a lot cooler as we cruise along at a healthy clip, but dehydration can sneak up on you."

Since Olivia didn't need to steer, she had two free hands to reach down and grab her drink. She pulled the vitamin water from the bottle cage, undid the cap, and took a large swig. "Mmm this is pretty good. Kiwi-strawberry. We should pull over to the side, so you can take a drink. I don't think I want you trying any hands-free steering."

"Oh, ye of little faith. I have a very talented mouth and can open the bottle with my teeth, while I hold it in one hand and steer with the other. Winking at you now. I have to

describe my non-verbals because you can't see my face."
Deb chuckled.

"You are quite the little flirt. Do you really want to purchase a bike today?" Olivia asked.

"I am, and yes, I do want one of these trikes. I wish they weren't so spendy, but I really am an avid cyclist. I don't mind spending a lot on a quality bike. I'm single without kids and make a fairly decent income, so I deserve to pamper myself with a purchase that is an investment in my health."

"Nice rationalization. I might have to consider buying one for myself. I really am enjoying the ride."

"Let's buy this together. It'll be an investment in our future. We can look back twenty years from now and say our first purchase together wasn't a house, but a bike. We could be trendsetters."

"I do appreciate your unwavering commitment to outlandish flirtation, but no, best case scenario…we both get trikes and become frequent riding partners. That's my last and final offer," Olivia said.

"Deal, but we should check out the other bikes and the single trikes so we can decide which one we want to purchase. I sure am glad you're not a control freak and let me drive your truck so we can transport our new babies back to Moses Lake. I read online they have folding trikes. I think I want one of those so I can easily transport it in my car."

"I can't believe I'm about to buy a several-thousand-dollar bike. You are a bad influence on me."

"Woo hoo, I was hoping for that because, girlfriend, life is way too short."

Deb's laughter floated in the air, and Olivia thought it was about the most delightful sound she'd heard in quite some time. She didn't want to analyze how much fun Deb

was to hang out with, because that might lead to other contemplations she wasn't yet prepared to tackle. For now, she'd enjoy the time with her surprising new friend. Deb was right—life was too short. Irene had taught her that sobering lesson.

CHAPTER FIFTEEN

Bri had suggested they ride back to her aunt's house and pick out a DVD from the collection her aunt kept in the TV stand. She was curious about the movie, *Fire*. On the front of the DVD were two beautiful women with dark hair like Siera's. She'd heard her aunt tell someone it was one of her all-time favorite lesbian films. Bri wondered if maybe she was a lesbian like her aunt, because she wanted to kiss Siera and go on dates with her. Bri knew Aunt Olivia used to do those things with Aunt Irene until she went to heaven.

She remembered when Aunt Olivia was up late one night, watching the movie, and tears were streaming down her face. Her aunt told her it wasn't because the movie was sad, it was because she used to watch it with Aunt Irene. They had both loved watching "such a beautiful movie about two women in love."

The movie was almost over, and Bri was hoping everything would work out for the two characters. There were a few scenes in the movie that were very difficult for

141

her to watch. They made her uncomfortable. She knew about sex, but when the man was doing those icky things, she didn't like watching that. She liked watching the two women kiss and wanted to experiment with Siera, but she would wait until she could ask her aunt about dating and kissing. She wanted to do things the correct way.

She heard Olivia and Deb laughing as they rushed into the house. Bri was glad Deb was able to make her aunt happy, because she always seemed to have a little bit of sadness that overtook her eyes and lingered in her smile.

"Hi girls. We have a big surprise. Oh, it looks like you two are watching a movie. I'm sorry, we can wait and show you after you finish," Deb said.

Bri glanced at Siera who grinned. "Okay. I think it's almost the end."

Deb walked into the room and craned her neck, looking at the TV screen. "Ooh, *Fire*, that's one of my all-time favorite movies."

Olivia tilted her head. "It is?"

"Mmm hmm. Can we sit and watch the end, please?" Deb begged.

"Of course," Olivia answered.

The four women sat in comfortable silence, until the credits started rolling.

"Aunt Olivia, is there a right time when you kiss your date?" Bri asked.

Olivia coughed. "Um...do you mean a right time during a date?"

"No. I mean how many dates do I need to have with Siera before I can kiss her?"

"Well, there isn't a set number, Bri. When the time is right for both of you, you'll know. It's a nice way to show the other person you care about them," Olivia answered.

"That's what I thought. Is there a right way to kiss a person?" Bri asked.

"No, not really, but some people like a certain style of kissing better than others. It's okay to experiment a little and find out what your partner likes best. It's kind of hard to explain," Olivia said.

Deb was snickering in her chair.

"Deb, feel free to jump in any time," Olivia added.

"Oh, no, you're doing a bang-up job. Unless you want to do a demonstration for the girls, you know, purely to help them understand the different styles of kissing." Deb laughed.

"Oh, would you, Aunt Deb?" Siera asked. "We've been so curious. I don't think Mom is comfortable talking about stuff like this. She gets this scrunched up look on her face—kind of like she's constipated—when I ask her about kissing or sex."

"You ask Kathleen about sex?" Deb asked.

"I did once. You know they teach us about it in health class." Siera shrugged.

Deb chuckled. "God, what I wouldn't give to have been a fly on the wall for that conversation."

"Girls, it's getting late, and both of you have to work tomorrow. Why don't I run Siera home now? Deb and I will load her bike, while the two of you say goodnight to each other. Okay?" Olivia stood up, and grabbed Deb's hand and pulled her toward the front door.

"Okay, Aunt Olivia," Bri responded, as Olivia and Deb left the room.

Bri turned to Siera with their hands already intertwined. "Is it okay if I kiss you goodnight?"

Siera nodded. "I'd like that."

Bri brushed her lips against Siera's. "Your lips are so soft. Just like I thought they'd be."

Siera brought her free hand to Bri's hair and tentatively patted the thick strands. "Your hair is soft. It feels nice." The tactile sensation of moving her fingers over Bri's thick, silky hair was every bit as glorious as she thought it would be.

"I like when you pet my hair." Bri giggled. "It feels like you're petting me like a cat."

"It's softer than Sampson and Delilah. I didn't think anything would be softer than the kitten's fur," Siera said. "I want to go to the library and check out a book on kissing. Do you think there will be a book to show us different styles?"

Bri shrugged. "I don't know. It seems like we can watch more movies and get a better idea. That would be easier than reading a book about kissing. The two women in the movie kept their lips together longer. Maybe we could try that sometime?"

"Okay," Siera answered.

Olivia and Deb opened the door and came back into the living room. "Siera, are you ready to go now? Your bike is all loaded up in the truck along with your aunt's new trike."

"You got a new bike, Aunt Deb?" Siera asked.

"I did. We both did, actually. That was the surprise we were going to share with you girls before we got engrossed in the movie."

"Oooh, can I see them?" Bri asked.

Siera and Bri jumped up from the couch and crossed the room.

"Sure, come on outside. I unloaded mine so there was room for Siera's. After you check out our purchases, I'll run Siera home. Deb, you can follow me, unless you want to try to fold up the bike and see if it will fit in your car?"

"Do you mind if I try to fold it up now? I'd better see if it'll fit sooner rather than later. I sure hope my spatial observation skills are accurate and it fits," Deb said.

"I think it should work, they pack up pretty nicely," Olivia answered.

Siera stuck out her lip. "Now I'm the only one with a crappy bike."

Deb slung her arm around Siera's shoulder. "I'll take you to the bike shop we went to. If your mom says it's okay, maybe she and I can go in together and buy you a bike as an early combination birthday and Christmas present."

"Oh, Aunt Deb, would you? Would you really do that?"

"Of course, kiddo," Deb answered.

"Can Olivia and Bri come with? I want them to help me pick one out. Bri is smart about trikes. She'll know which one I should get."

"Yes, she is. If she wasn't already busy today, I would have asked her to help me pick out mine. But the shop owner was very nice and gave us an excellent deal since we both bought one. I'll bet he would give you a great deal on a new bike," Olivia said.

Siera was grinning from ear to ear, and Bri was happy she would be getting a new bike. She'd noticed how difficult it was for Siera to keep up with her, though she'd done her absolute best to slow down and ride at a more leisurely pace.

†

Olivia had propped herself up in her bed to read a little bit before falling asleep, when her smartphone buzzed on the side table. She picked up the phone and smiled when she read the text.

Hey, Miss Sex Therapist.
Any more questions from your niece tonight :)

Ha, ha, ha. You could have stepped in to help...

Oh no, you were doing a bang-up job. Why would I want to interject and ruin your perfect answers?

You're evil

I had fun today. When are we going to take our new bikes out for their maiden journey?

Do you work next weekend?

I do...frowning.

I suppose I could do a short ride mid-week.

How does Wednesday sound?

Good. Can we leave from the clinic?

Sure, I'll meet you there at 5:30? 6:00?

I'll close early. How about 5:00?

Perfect. Sweet dreams. Can I pick your brain about kissing techniques on Wednesday? I might learn something...

Stop flirting and go to sleep

Goodnight beautiful

Goodnight

Olivia was smiling, as she placed the phone back on the nightstand. A little innocent flirtation wouldn't hurt, would it?

She set her tablet next to her phone and slid down into her soft bed. *Damn that woman is almost irresistible.* That was her last thought, as she drifted off into a deep sleep and dreamed about riding around the lake with Deb.

They'd stopped for a picnic lunch, and Deb brushed her fingertips along Olivia's arm. Surprised when Deb took charge and seized her lips in a passionate kiss, Olivia was shaking with need. As Deb backed off and nibbled Olivia's bottom lip, Olivia automatically responded by wrapping her arms around Deb and pulling her down. Deb began to move on top of Olivia, and the sensual movements caused an instant pool of moisture, as her craving for Deb's touch exploded.

Deb's hand snaked beneath Olivia's bike jersey and rubbed against her erect nipples. The touch drove Olivia into a state of frenzy, as she bucked beneath her and reached out to stroke Deb's behind.

When Deb's hand traveled down Olivia's stomach and brushed down to her inner thigh, barely grazing her mound, Olivia's eyes popped open.

Her ragged breath invaded the quiet of the room.

She was wide awake now, as she pressed her tablet to view the time. 1:00 am. *This is so bad. I can't be having erotic dreams about Deb. I just can't.*

It took Olivia more than forty-five minutes to settle back into a restful sleep.

CHAPTER SIXTEEN

Kathleen was twirling the pen in her hand, as she sat in her cramped office in the emergency department. Monday was usually a slow day, as people settled from their weekend activities. She thought about calling Olivia to do some suitable groveling. She'd come to the conclusion she'd been horribly inappropriate the last time she attempted to reach out. It was time to make amends and possibly explore the option of Siera working at her clinic. She rationalized she wasn't reaching out and offering an apology simply to gain something in return.

She picked up the office phone and dialed the number she had written on a Post-it note after Googling Olivia's clinic.

"Hello. Can I speak to Olivia please? This is Kathleen Kaufman.... No, I can wait.... Hi, Olivia. First, let me apologize for being such an ignorant, horrible excuse for a human being. I want to make it up to you. It's obvious Bri's friendship with Siera is very important to her, and honestly,

I've seen a great deal of positive growth in Siera since the two became friends. I'm afraid I was acting like a helicopter mom and needed to do some serious soul searching to recognize the error of my ways. Would you have some time today to try this again and grab some lunch? I would like to talk to you about something else related to Siera.... Okay, wonderful, I'll meet you there."

Kathleen was thankful Olivia seemed receptive to putting their previous interaction behind them. Deb had mentioned Olivia several times over the past few days and seemed enamored with her. Kathleen had to admit there was something very appealing about her calm, down-to-earth aura. She clearly loved her niece and had treated Siera with nothing but respect. Every indication pointed to Olivia's understanding of kids with Down syndrome, and she seemed to treat both Siera and Bri as though they were like any other *normal* young women. *Normal, such a loaded word.* There wasn't a hint of the prejudice most people had when they interacted with Siera. Their subtle differences were like a neon light to Kathleen. She thought she might learn a thing or two from Olivia about how not to treat her own daughter.

She supposed she should admit to Jeremy he'd been right all along about a lot of things, but if she did that he would do his peacock imitation, and that irritated her. She loved him, but he could be such a guy sometimes. They rarely fought. If she were honest with herself, she'd admit the times they argued and ventured into dangerous territory were mostly to do with her reluctance to let go of old hurts— namely his initial reaction to Siera's birth. It was time for her to deal with that head on and stop letting those ugly tentacles wrap themselves around her psyche. He'd often asked when she was finally going to forgive him for that transgression. It

was a good question—one she didn't have the answer to. She'd have to admit her own wrong doing, and sometimes it took a while for her to process what part she played in the various conflicts in her life. Taking the initiative to apologize and admit to her own prejudgments about Bri and Siera's relationship was a good first step, in her estimation.

†

It was another scorcher, as Olivia sat at one of the outdoor tables waiting for Kathleen to arrive. A droplet of sweat slowly traveled down her neck and between her breasts. She mopped her brow with the napkin she'd grabbed after ordering the strawberry lemonade. The cool, refreshing drink passed her lips and soothed her throat. She leaned back in the chair and closed her eyes, allowing the sun's rays to beat down on her. She briefly considered moving to a table under the shade, but when her eyes flickered open, Olivia noted the option did not exist. If she wanted to remain outside, which was her preference, she'd have to endure the heat. Sitting in a stuffy bistro, with only the ceiling fans as protection against the stifling heat, was not a welcome alternative.

Kathleen's call had definitely piqued her interest, and she'd registered the conciliatory tone. Olivia was not one to hold grudges, and Deb had mentioned sometimes her sister needed to process things and come to a different conclusion after thinking everything over. She sensed that beneath the woman's overbearing and overprotective outer covering, there was a good person. Besides, she would make nice with the woman if it meant Bri would continue to blossom with Siera in her life.

"Hey. I guess we're in for some hot days. I suppose we could have met at the hospital, at least it's air-conditioned. The food sucks, so I was willing to brave the heat. You look like you're melting. Too bad they don't have any shaded alternatives." Kathleen sat down in the chair across from Olivia.

"You might want to get yourself something cool to drink while we wait for our food. I hope you don't mind, I already ordered my sandwich." Olivia brought her eyes to rest on Kathleen, who hid her eyes behind dark sunglasses. "I'd offer to go and get you some lemonade, but I'm still hobbling after this past weekend's marathon bike rides."

Kathleen removed her jacket and draped it over the chair. "No worries, I need to order something anyway. Did Deb bring over the ointment for your muscles?"

"She did and offered to give me a leg massage. I politely declined." Olivia chuckled.

"She likes you. Just so you know, you aren't like one of her normal flings. Be careful with her, she's more fragile than she reveals to anyone."

Olivia narrowed her eyes. If Kathleen was trying to make amends for her earlier gauche behavior, it wasn't going so well. "I've been nothing but completely honest with her about what I can and cannot offer."

Kathleen waved her hand in the air. "Please, don't misunderstand. You aren't doing anything wrong at all. Deb can't help herself. She's her own worst enemy sometimes. I love my sister, and I know her well enough to decipher her feelings for you are different. She can't help the way she feels any more than you can. Look, I didn't want to offend you, and here I've gone and done it again. Peace." Kathleen extended her hand.

Olivia smiled despite her uncomfortable feelings around Kathleen. "Sorry, peace it is." Olivia offered her hand.

Kathleen shook and released Olivia's hand, offering a genuine smile. "I'll be right back after I get some of that delicious-looking lemonade."

Olivia pondered whether her friendship with Deb was a good thing. She didn't want to lead the poor woman on, and yet, she enjoyed her company. If she was perfectly honest with herself, she enjoyed the flirtatious banter. It was good for her ego. No other woman had paid her that kind of attention since Irene. It felt wonderful for someone to admire her and unabashedly state their attraction. She would have a serious conversation with Deb about this, because the last thing she wanted to do was hurt her feelings.

Kathleen came back to the table carrying her cold drink and interrupting Olivia's thoughts. Olivia watched as the condensation dripped down the sides of her glass, and this reminded her of the sweat that continued to drip down her neck. She felt like asking for a glass of ice so she could hold it against her skin.

"I should have asked you to get them to bring me a refill," Olivia said.

Kathleen smirked and sat down in the seat opposite of her. "I did. They should bring it out shortly. I told them to supply us with two pitchers, one with ice, and the other with lemonade. Kind of like when the distraught person sits on a bar stool and says leave the bottle, I basically said, keep the cool beverages coming."

"Thanks. So, I know you didn't ask me to lunch to tell me you had some kind of epiphany. What's on your mind?"

"Well actually, I did…have an epiphany that is. I realized I am treating my daughter and your niece exactly in

the same fashion I criticize others for. When I looked at my behavior, I realized my overprotectiveness is holding Siera back from growing into an independent, successful young woman. If I continue my misguided behavior and treat her like a child, she'll remain a child. I also have a favor to ask of you, and you can feel free to say no."

"Wow. Good for you to recognize and admit that. It can't have been easy. Go ahead, ask your favor, and I'll give it a fair consideration."

"I know Siera hates her Walmart job. I was wondering if there was any way you had a place for her at your clinic?" Kathleen asked.

Olivia paused while she considered Kathleen's request. She watched as Kathleen shifted uncomfortably in her seat during the silence. "I've wanted to do something for a while now, and this might be the perfect solution. Bri is very talented with the animals, but I don't think she wants to try to go to vet school or become a vet technician. I get a lot of requests for recommendations on grooming services or pet sitting. I'd like to develop a partnership where Bri feels like she has her own business to run and takes the lead on this side business. I know either Bri or Siera could learn the fundamentals of scheduling appointments, setting up a price structure, and running a small business. What do you think?"

Kathleen's smile stretched across her face. "Oh my God, that's brilliant. I'd be willing to be a silent partner and provide some start-up funding if that is needed."

"Actually, I don't think it would take much funding at all. There's space in the clinic I could rent to the girls for a reasonable price. I want this to be their venture, with little assistance from us. Bri has been saving her money, and I

think she would feel better about this if she believed it was her business."

"Although Siera struggled a little bit with school, she worked hard and persevered. She learned how to use the Microsoft Office programs after a lot of hard work and Big Bend Community College accepted her to begin this fall. She'd probably think her schooling has a specific purpose if she focuses on business classes that would help with the new venture," Kathleen responded in an excited voice.

"I've got a few clients I know would use their services once they are open for business. I could pay Siera minimum wage to start, until their business gets off the ground."

"Oh Olivia, I cannot express how happy this makes me. You are a godsend."

"So, how do you propose we float this idea to the girls?" Olivia asked.

Kathleen grinned. "No time like the present. Would you like to come over for dinner tonight? If I know Siera, she'll probably head to the park after her shift to meet up with Bri. I think they have a sort of standing date at the park."

"Noticed that, did you?"

"Uh huh. I'll admit, at first, I wasn't too pleased, but I've since had a change of heart. Can you swing by and pick up the girls?"

"Sure. Are you inviting Deb over?"

Kathleen raised her eyebrow. "Why? Do you want me to?"

"I thought she might want to hear the exciting news first hand. She loves her niece very much."

"I know she does. Yeah, sure. Deb always adds a bit of liveliness to every party. I'm sure you've noticed that infectious energy of hers. She doesn't get off until seven

though, so she'll be a bit late. Wednesday is her next day free if you think we should wait."

"I know. We're supposed to go riding Wednesday night. Hopefully, I will have recovered by then."

Kathleen smiled. "Oh, riding, huh?"

Olivia blushed. "We can wait to talk to the girls after Deb arrives. Will that work?"

The bistro worker stepped up to the table and set down a pitcher of ice and another one with lemonade. "Your orders should be up shortly. I don't blame you for sitting outside, even though it's hot. At least it's not stuffy."

"Amen to that," Olivia answered.

After the worker left, Kathleen responded, "I'll get Jeremy to pick up some garden burgers. Will that work for you?"

"Sure. I love garden burgers. Thank you for remembering."

"Every once in a while, I let my better traits shine through to make up for when I stumble so badly and offend people with my brash and direct approach to life. I sincerely apologize for our earlier lunch, and I'm glad you're not the type to hold grudges. I'm not as forgiving, but I'm working on it," Kathleen admitted.

"Hey, we're all works in progress. There is no such thing as perfection. Besides, perfection lacks depth or texture."

Kathleen raised her glass of lemonade in the air, and Olivia joined her as they clinked their glasses together. "Hear, hear, ain't that the truth."

†

Kathleen tossed her keys on the granite counter and carefully set the two plastic bags full of fresh tomatoes, lettuce, and potato salad on the island in the kitchen. She peeked outside, following the sound of a whistled tune, in search of her husband. He was meticulously running the scraper on his beloved grill. She stood at the glass window watching him.

He was still a very handsome man and hadn't lost his muscled physique. She watched his bulging arms work up and down the grate inside the grill. She was a lucky woman.

He'd never once stepped outside the bounds of marriage, and she knew he'd had plenty of opportunities. The nurses in the emergency department threw themselves at him all the time. It didn't matter she was their boss. When they thought she wasn't looking, their flirtations were absurdly ridiculous. She would shake her head as she watched him dodge every subtle invitation.

She opened the glass doors and called out to him, "Hey honey, did you get a chance to pick up the garden burgers?"

He shivered. "Yuk, yes I did. If you ask me it's a waste of my grilling talents." He shook his head. "Vegetarians, hmmf, I don't understand them, and now Siera thinks she should be one too."

"Now honey, Olivia works with animals. I think it's understandable she might have some discomfort over eating flesh."

"I guess if that's her only flaw, I can live with it." He chuckled. "I'm glad she brought Bri here to Moses Lake. The transformation in Siera is nothing short of a miracle."

"Wait until I tell you why I invited Olivia over. Miracle will be an understatement. It's a dream come true for Siera. You were right about everything."

"Wait, what did you just say? Will you repeat that please? I believe it was something about me being right about everything. Arh, arh, arh." Jeremy beat his chest.

Kathleen chuckled. "Sometimes you show a certain measure of intuition and intelligence," she admitted. "Although I'm not quite there yet with Bri and Siera potentially being a couple, everything else was spot on. Olivia is a lovely woman and thankfully doesn't hold a grudge like me. She accepted my apology and had an idea for Siera and Bri that is nothing short of brilliant. I know you think it's my dream for Siera to go to college and succeed in life, but she also wants to be independent. I had a sort of epiphany that in many ways I am treating her like a child. It's hard for me to recognize she's growing into a wonderful young woman."

"So, what's this brilliant plan the two of you cooked up?"

"You'll have to wait and see like everyone else," Kathleen answered. "By the way, did you know Deb and Olivia have been spending time together?"

"Hmmm, no I didn't. You know your sister could do a lot worse," Jeremy noted.

"Oh, I know, but unfortunately Olivia made it very clear she isn't looking for anything beyond friendship. I get the sense she isn't ready to move on from the death of her previous lover."

"Makes sense, if something ever happened to you, I don't think I could ever move on either."

"Oh my God, you are so getting some tonight. Sometimes you say the sweetest things." Kathleen stepped outside, walked over to Jeremy, and gave him a quick kiss.

Jeremy turned up the corners of his mouth and pumped his fist in the air. "Works every time."

Kathleen punched him in the shoulder and walked back into the house at the same time Siera burst in with Bri and Olivia following closely behind.

"Hi, Mom," Siera greeted her.

"Hi, honey. Your father is out getting the grill ready. It won't be anything fancy tonight, just some burgers and potato salad. Jeremy picked up some garden burgers if you girls want that instead."

"Thanks, Mom."

"I really appreciate you picking those up special for me." Olivia nudged Bri.

"Yes, thank you Miss Kathleen," Bri added.

"Just Kathleen, remember? We're friends."

Toby sauntered into the kitchen covered in dirt. "Hey everyone. We having some kind of party again?" He took a few steps inside and left dirt and grass tracks on the floor.

"Hey, take your shoes off, and get your ass in the shower before you cover my floor in dirt and grime."

"Ooh, Mom said a bad word. You owe the swear jar."

Kathleen pointed. "Fine, go."

Toby kicked off his gym shoes and started walking toward the stairs. "Tell Dad I want two really big ones with meat, not those crappy vegetarian versions."

Siera stuck her tongue out. "I like vegetarian food."

"Me too," Bri added.

Toby chuckled, as he took the stairs two at a time. Kathleen shuddered thinking how much dirt he was probably tracking into the house.

"Come on in, I have some tea and lemonade already made up in the fridge. On hot days like the ones we've been having, I automatically keep the pitchers full," Kathleen said.

"Is there anything I can help with?" Olivia asked.

"Nope, I'll slice the tomatoes, wash the lettuce, and set everything on the counter for people to make their own burgers the way they want." Kathleen opened the refrigerator and pulled out the pitchers filled to the brim with cold drinks. "Siera, would you mind pulling some glasses from the cabinets?"

Siera pulled open the doors and pushed up on her tiptoes in an attempt to reach the glasses. "I wish I wasn't so short."

"Here, let me get those for you." Olivia reached into the cabinets and pulled down seven glasses.

"That's too many," Bri noted.

"I invited Deb. Seven is the right number, but that was very observant of you, Bri." Kathleen turned back to the refrigerator and pulled out the ground bison and frozen garden burgers. She handed them to Siera. "Here, take these out to your father for him to do his magic."

"Iced tea or lemonade?" Olivia asked.

"I'll take some tea. Siera usually wants lemonade, and so do Toby and Jeremy. I can make up some more lemonade if we run out," Kathleen answered.

"No worries, I love iced tea. Bri is tea okay for you?"

Bri nodded. "Uh huh."

Olivia filled all the glasses with the preferred beverages.

Siera came back into the house with the empty plate. "Dad said the burgers will be ready soon. He wanted to know if we would be eating outside or inside."

"I think it's over one hundred out there now, so let's eat inside tonight and avoid the stifling heat," Kathleen answered.

"If you let me rummage around in your cabinets, I can set the table," Olivia offered.

"We're not fancy. We don't set tables. We just set out plates, utensils, and napkins. You can do that while I'm slicing the tomatoes and getting the rest of the condiments ready," Kathleen answered. "Siera, would you mind washing off that plate, please, and then taking it back out to your father with another for the garden burgers?"

Olivia pulled out eight plates and set them on the counter.

After washing up, Siera picked up the top plate and exited through the sliding glass door.

"I sure hope that mudball son of mine gets down here soon. It sounds like we're almost ready to eat," Kathleen said offhandedly, as she continued to slice tomatoes on the cutting board she had retrieved from one of the drawers on the kitchen island.

Toby strolled into the room flicking back his wet hair. "Here I am. Let the party begin."

Kathleen noticed Bri looking a little lost in the kitchen and decided to give her a job to make her feel useful. "Bri, hon, will you pull out the hamburger buns from the pantry, please?" She pointed to the doors to the right of the refrigerator.

Bri smiled and opened the doors, surveying the inside, and retrieved two packages of buns from on the middle shelf.

Everyone seemed to pitch in. When Jeremy walked in with the burgers, their well-oiled machine had all the

condiments and dining utensils set up on the counter for everyone to make up their burgers.

Jeremy set the food on the counter. "Dinner is served. Dig in while it's hot."

†

Olivia sat back in her chair and wiped her mouth, setting the napkin on top of the plate. "That was delicious. Thanks."

She was bursting at the seams to lay out the plan to Siera and Bri, but wanted to wait until Deb arrived. The more time she spent with this family, the more she liked them—even Kathleen, who had, at first, appeared narrow-minded and pushy. Olivia could see the love between Jeremy and Kathleen and the protectiveness Toby displayed toward his older sister. They were a lovely family. She only hoped that as Siera and Bri's relationship developed, they would still be accepting of the direction she was sure it was going to take. She knew Deb was okay with it, but she wasn't sure where the rest of the family would land on the subject.

Finally, she heard two quick knocks on the door leading to the garage, and Deb burst in.

"I don't suppose you have any burgers left for me? I'm starving," Deb declared.

"One of each is on the counter. You might want to reheat it though," Kathleen answered.

"I think I'll nuke the garden burger. It probably tastes better reheated." Deb locked her dark brown eyes to Olivia's and smiled. "Hey stranger."

Olivia gave a little wave. "Hurry up and join us, we have some news and wanted to share it with everyone at the same time."

"Mmm, a little intrigue. I like it." Deb quickly tossed one of the garden burgers into the microwave and fixed up her plate. After taking an open seat with her dinner, she asked, "So what's the big announcement?"

Olivia ventured a side glance at Kathleen, who nodded. "While in college, I had a small grooming business that helped pay for vet school. I've been wanting to expand my clinic business for some time now, to venture into other services such as dog and cat grooming, pet sitting, dog walking, things like that. But I haven't had the personnel to do it. Siera and Bri, if you are willing, I could teach you how to groom cats and dogs. Siera, you know that room we use for storage right now? It can easily be converted. We'd need to get someone to plumb it for us. I'd like to hire you, Siera, to help clean up the room to get it ready. For now, I propose being a silent partner, but I could contribute some of the capital needed for professional grooming equipment."

Siera smiled and glanced at her mother. "I would love to work for you, Olivia. I would work really hard."

"Siera, I'm not only asking you to work for me. I'm asking you to create a business. I'll need your expertise, especially after you complete some of your college courses, to grow this business and make it successful. I'm counting on you and Bri to be the ones to run it, completely."

"I've been saving my money, Aunt Olivia. Do I have enough for the equipment?" Bri asked.

Olivia smiled. She was so proud of her niece. "Almost, Bri. That's why I'm offering to be a silent partner and contribute some capital funding as well as the room in the back that we'll convert. In exchange, I'll take five percent of your net profits."

Siera's knees were bouncing up and down. "I have some money saved. I want to contribute. That will make it a true partnership, right?"

"Yes, it will," Kathleen answered.

"Should we ask a lawyer to draw up some official papers?" Siera asked.

All eyes turned in the direction of Siera. Olivia smiled. She presumed Siera had shocked everyone with her astute approach to the plan. This was additional evidence Siera had so much more to offer than people gave her credit for. "I think that is a very good idea. We'll all want to agree on the finer details and can get some assistance applying for a business license."

"One of the nurses I work with is married to an attorney who, I think, specializes in business law. I could ask her how much he would charge to help you set this up," Deb offered.

"Perfect. I did a little research last night, and there is an excellent manual on dog and cat grooming. I hope you two don't mind; I went ahead and ordered it. I think it would be a good idea for you both to study it in detail, while we're preparing the room and waiting for the equipment."

Siera and Bri's excited head nods were a delight to see.

"I'm going to give my notice to Walmart tomorrow. I can start in two weeks." Siera popped up from her seat next to Bri and ran over to Olivia, wrapping her short arms around Olivia's neck and squeezing her in a hug. "Thank you for this opportunity. I am so happy right now. I could burst."

Olivia chuckled. "Oh, this is going to line my pockets, as I sit back and watch you girls make money for me." She slid her gaze to meet Deb, who gave her the thumbs up signal, and she knew she'd done a great thing.

†

Olivia was too wound up to go to sleep and sat on the couch clicking around on the internet. She was researching professional grooming equipment and calculating the costs in her head. She'd determined they could get top of the line tools for just shy of ten thousand, when she heard a quiet knock.

She set the laptop on her coffee table and opened her front door. Deb's brilliant smile greeted her. "Hey, don't you have to work early tomorrow?"

"I do, but I wanted to drop by and tell you how much I appreciate what you're doing for Siera. Damn, woman, you are making it extremely hard not to fall madly in love with you, and I haven't even tasted your delectable fruits."

Olivia frowned. "Come on in. I've been meaning to have a serious talk with you."

"Oh, that's never a good sign. The four most hated words in the English language, 'we need to talk.'"

Olivia sat heavily on the couch and Deb followed. She turned and met Deb's inquisitive gaze. "I've really loved spending time with you, Deb..." Olivia started.

"I hear a huge but coming."

Olivia sighed. "I don't have the capacity at this time to offer anything more than friendship. I know I've been clear about that before, but I'm afraid I've allowed myself to engage in the innocent flirtations and banter. The last thing I want to do is lead you on or hurt your feelings."

Deb looked down. "I know the score." When she lifted her eyes back up to meet Olivia's, they were filled with unshed tears.

"God, I'm so sorry. I wish things were different. I would be lying if I didn't admit I am attracted to you, but I really

cannot handle a relationship right now. Do you understand that? Will we be able to remain friends?" Olivia asked.

"If that's all that is on the table, I'll take it. Maybe someday things will change, but for right now, your friendship is important enough for me to work through my other feelings."

Olivia pulled Deb into an embrace and hugged her. "Thank you for understanding."

When Deb was released from Olivia's embrace she smiled. "Don't expect me to stop flirting though, because that is a fundamental part of my personality. You'll have to endure that along with my sincere offer of friendship."

Olivia chuckled. "Deal. I have to admit it feels kind of good, so I can easily accept that added condition."

"Just remember, you'll have to be the one to cross the barrier. I won't ever violate the boundary, but I can't help remaining hopeful that one day you will." Deb grinned.

CHAPTER SEVENTEEN

OCTOBER 2010

Siera sat next to their brand-new grooming table and used her hand to prop her head up. Business was slow, school was hard, and she wanted to admit defeat. In high school, she'd had a lot of extra help. Now that she was at Big Bend, she was hesitant to tell her mom she needed to seek out help from the tutors at school.

Bri had pulled up a chair and sat next to Siera. "It'll be okay, Siera. Aunt Olivia said it takes time to build a new business."

"I know. School is so much harder than I thought it would be. I can't help out a lot during the week. The only people that come in are the ones Olivia sends to us. I can't be an equal partner, when we can't fill our Saturday schedule," Siera complained.

"We will. I'll bet those flyers you handed out at the college and around town will get us some new business." Bri slung her arm around Siera's shoulder.

Siera hesitated to share her idea with Bri, but hope inspired her to take a chance. "Bri, I learned something in my business econ class today."

"Is it something that will help us?" Bri asked.

"Maybe. There's this thing called supply and demand. I was thinking. There's so much supply in Moses Lake—all the other established groomers—and not enough demand. I think we should cut our prices. We can make a big deal out of having the lowest cost, but the highest quality in town. We could put testimonials on the flyers," Siera explained.

Bri hugged Siera and planted a big kiss on her lips. "Oh Siera, that's brilliant. You're so smart." Bri took both of Siera's hands in her own and looked into her eyes. Siera saw such an intense emotion, a lot like when her dad looked at her mom. Bri's words were intense too. "Is it okay I love you, like Aunt Olivia loved Aunt Irene? I think it's like a best friend but more. Does that make sense?"

Siera's sadness lifted and floated away like a wisp of smoke. She was so happy Bri put into words her exact same feelings. "Oh Bri, I love you too. I want us to be girlfriends. Maybe someday, we can live together. Just the two of us. We can be a family."

Bri pulled Siera into her arms and kissed her again. "We're going to make this business successful, because you're so smart. Can you make up some new flyers on your computer? We can start handing them out at the dog park."

Olivia and Deb had opened the door to the back room and were holding their bike helmets in their hands. The cleats on their shoes tip tapped on the polished cement floor, announcing their arrival.

"Hey girls. Are you interested in going out for some lunch today? We thought we would stop by and see if you were busy," Olivia said.

Siera frowned. "No, we have another two hours before our next appointment. I was hoping for a drop in, after I put up my flyers."

Deb clip clopped over and put her hand on Siera's shoulder. "Aw honey, you have to be patient. New businesses take time to establish. You can't expect to be an overnight sensation."

"I know, that's what Bri said Olivia told her," Siera answered.

"Is that all that's bothering you?" Deb asked.

Siera shook her head. "I'm learning a lot in school. I got an idea today—from my business econ class. School is really hard. I'm not doing very well, especially in math. I got a C minus on my first test."

"If you're learning useful skills and tips for the business, that's all that matters. You don't need to get all A's for us to be proud of you or for you to be a success." Deb squeezed her shoulder.

"Thanks Aunt Deb. We're going to make new flyers and cut our prices. See, there's too much supply in Moses Lake. We gotta do something to differentiate our business from the competition."

"Oh, look at you. Deb, I think we're in the presence of the next Bill Gates and Paul Allen. Those Microsoft giants don't have anything on Siera and Bri." Olivia winked. "I am so proud of both of you. That is a very astute observation."

"Astute?" Siera asked.

"It means you done good, kid."

Siera grinned.

Bri kissed her cheek. "Isn't she smart? We'll be a success, because Siera knows all the important stuff about running a business."

"Wow, our very own Moses Lake business moguls, let's get something to eat while you tell us all about your brilliant business strategies." Olivia motioned for them to follow.

†

Bri missed spending the evenings at the park feeding the geese with Siera, but she wanted to support Siera going to college. When Siera said she loved her and wanted to be her girlfriend, Bri's heart soared. But for some reason, Siera thought it was better to continue to emphasize they were best friends in front of her mom.

When they spent time with Aunt Olivia and Deb, Siera seemed a lot more comfortable. They would cuddle together on the couch, holding hands and sharing popcorn. They were always invited to stay, whenever their aunts declared it was time for another movie night. That was happening at least once a week, usually after a bike ride, but now the days were getting shorter. Their evening rides were less frequent, and they still had to work around Deb's every other weekend work schedule.

Bri woke up that morning with a big smile on her face. She'd asked Siera if she wanted to spend Sunday together, after she finished her schoolwork. Siera had promised she would be done no later than noon. They were going to meet at the park and try to hand out some flyers they'd worked on after finishing up at the clinic.

The oranges were brilliant with the golds and reds on the changing trees. Bri was leisurely pedaling her bike to the park. Fall was one of her favorite times of the year, because

it wasn't too hot or cold. She liked to gather all the leaves on the ground and make a big pile to jump in. Then she would toss them in the air. Aunt Olivia taught her this was a fall tradition they should always remember to do, no matter how old they got, because it was fun. She wanted to include Siera in their tradition.

After she locked up her bike, she sat on the bench and watched for Siera. She didn't have to wait long before she saw Siera cruise around the bend with her dark, wavy hair flowing in the breeze. She loved to watch the joy on Siera's face as she pedaled into the park. Lately, Siera had seemed so down, and Bri desperately wanted to see her smile again, like she used to before all the pressures of school got in the way. Today, she saw the delight in Siera's broad smile and that made her very happy.

Too anxious to wait for Siera to lock up her bike, Bri jumped up and jogged to meet her. When Bri reached the bike rack, Siera had already locked up and had a fistful of flyers in her hand. Bri hugged her friend. Their lips joined together in a hello kiss. They'd been practicing their kissing, but knew the longer kisses were intended for private time. Private time always happened behind closed doors in Siera's or Bri's rooms.

"I'm so happy we get to spend the day together," Bri said.

"We spent the day together yesterday, at the clinic."

"I know, but that was work time. Sunday is play time." Bri grinned. "After we feed the geese and hand out our flyers, will you come home with me? I want to show you our fall tradition. It's fun."

"Okay. I'm glad it's a nice day." Siera shifted her eyes around the park and smiled. "There's a lot of people out and they have dogs," she said with excitement in her voice.

Bri grabbed Siera's hand. "We can feed the geese later. Let's hand out our flyers."

"Okay." Siera swung Bri's hand and smiled.

Bri knew some of the dogs and their owners from the clinic, but they'd managed to hand out flyers to a few potential new clients. Bri was encouraged when one of her favorite dogs and his owner overheard them give their spiel to a woman and her dog. He told the woman how much he liked how Bri took care of his dog and highly recommended their services.

†

Olivia was raking the kaleidoscope of colors, as the leaves fluttered around in her yard. She couldn't help the smile that overtook her face when she saw Deb pedal up her driveway. Deb had mentioned she might stop by, but they hadn't made definite plans. Spending time with Deb had become a frequent occurrence, and she looked forward to their time together. If only she could forget Irene...the loss was still too raw for her. No matter how tempting Deb was, she couldn't go there.

"Hey gorgeous. Looking good." Deb came to a stop and remained seated on her comfortable recumbent trike. "I think I'll sit here and watch you work, while those beautiful deltoid muscles tantalize me."

Olivia chuckled. "You are so good for my ego, but that isn't going to get you out of work. Come on and give me a hand. The girls should be back from the park in a few hours,

172

and I need help getting everything ready. You're just the person to assist me."

Deb groaned. "You're going to make me rake leaves, aren't you? I'll bet you're trying to get me back for that first bike ride we took. I'm gonna have spaghetti arms by tomorrow. I'll only agree to slave labor if you promise to help me with my pain. A little body massage, and I'm all yours."

"Deal, but don't try to turn it into something it's not," Olivia replied.

"Who me? You are such a killjoy." Deb pushed herself up from the bike and held out her hands. "Rake me."

Olivia handed Deb the rake and turned to retrieve her second rake from the garage. "I'll be right back, but you know what to do. Any special music requests? I'll open up the windows and blast out the tunes. We can dance and rake, then it won't seem like work."

"Surprise me, you know I'm easy." Deb grinned. "In more ways than one, if only you would take advantage of that."

Olivia chuckled. "Okay, I think I'll pull out my seventies disco music."

"Perfect."

†

There were ten small piles of leaves Olivia was trying to turn into one massive mound. When Deb figured out why Olivia was creating the large, leaf trampoline, she was all in. It had been years since she'd jumped on a pile of leaves and tossed them around. This was the side of Olivia Deb was falling in love with. She could be the responsible, supportive, loving friend, but her playful side was downright irresistible.

It took all her willpower not to toss Olivia on the pile of leaves and kiss her senseless.

Siera and Bri cycled up the driveway, as they were raking the final, small hill into the heap of color they'd collected in the middle of the lawn. The joy Deb saw on their faces was unmistakable. After putting their bikes away, the girls rushed out to the pile of leaves.

"Aunt Olivia, you remembered. I wanted to show Siera our tradition. Now I can," Bri said.

"Of course I did, honey. So, are we ready?" Olivia set her rake aside and motioned for Deb to do the same. The two rakes lay side by side, well away from the newly formed mountain of fallen leaves.

Bri took Siera's hand, then reached for Olivia, who was holding out both of her hands. Deb took that as her cue to clasp Olivia's hand, and the four women ran for the pile in an unbroken line. Their laughter filled the air, as they fell on the leaves and started giggling and tossing the iconic symbol of fall all over each other.

Siera and Bri rolled away together, and Deb smiled when she saw Bri brush her lips against Siera's. Siera grabbed Bri's hand and pulled her up, as they continued to chase one another with handfuls of leaves they used like confetti. Their laughter floated through the air, joining the leaves as they rained down, scattering all over the newly raked lawn.

Deb started covering Olivia with leaves, scooping them up by the handful. Without thinking, she rolled on top of Olivia. As Deb straddled her with another fistful of leaves, she looked into dilating pupils. She'd never wanted to close the gap so much as she did now, but she'd made the promise to Olivia she would not be the one to cross the line.

Olivia had a large red leaf stuck in her hair, as the others fluttered all around her. Deb's hand automatically went to Olivia's hair to pluck the interloper from her silky locks. When their eyes met, Deb could see the desire. She started to make her move, despite her promise.

She'd almost closed the gap, bringing her lips dangerously close, when she felt Olivia's body tense beneath her own. It had felt so natural to kiss Olivia. She'd assumed that was what Olivia wanted, but her body gave off an entirely different message from her eyes. Deb hovered on the precipice, not knowing which signal she should respond to. Olivia's words would make that decision for her.

"I can't. Oh God, I'm sorry, I can't," Olivia whispered.

Deb quickly rolled away and laid back in an attempt to gather her emotions. She was thankful Siera and Bri were frolicking on their own and not paying attention to the intensity of what had almost occurred before Olivia put the skids on her momentary lapse in judgment.

Deb pushed her body up and stood in front of Olivia, holding out her hand. "No apology needed, Olivia. If anyone needs to apologize, it's me. I know the score. I think it's time for that hot chocolate now, because I'm sure the traditional leaf bath is always followed by a steaming mug of chocolatey goodness. And don't be stingy, because I want mine with those mini marshmallows." Deb turned in the direction of where the girls were tossing leaves at each other and called out, "Are you girls ready for hot chocolate now?"

"Yeah," both girls responded and skipped toward the older women.

CHAPTER EIGHTEEN

JUNE 2012

Bri was scrubbing Sasha, Olivia's dog, while Siera walked over to the stereo receiver and turned up the volume. Siera knew that "Rolling in the Deep" was Bri's favorite song, and she glanced over to the tub to watch Bri sway her hips to Adele's music.

Sasha was squirming in the steel basin, but Bri's magic touch calmed her down. After she'd rinsed Sasha off, the dog shook her fur and water sprayed everywhere, soaking Siera's t-shirt.

"Sasha," Bri admonished. "You got Siera wet."

Siera noticed Sasha had also soaked Bri's t-shirt, and she could see Bri's breasts as the wet shirt clung to her body. More and more, Siera felt the urge to touch Bri. She wanted to do more than kiss, but she wasn't sure what, exactly, she should do. She only knew watching Bri with the swimsuit plastered against her body made her feel all funny inside her stomach.

Siera reached out and pushed Bri's golden, wet hair aside and started giggling. "We're both wet from Sasha."

Bri laughed. "Yeah we'll have to use the machine on us after drying Sasha."

"When are Aunt Deb and Olivia coming by today?" Siera asked.

"I think they're on a long bike ride. We'll have to keep Sasha with us all day. She's really well behaved. I told Aunt Olivia that would be fine."

Siera sighed. "I know I should be glad we're all booked up today. We've been super busy lately, but I miss being able to ride with them."

"I know. At least we can have a date tomorrow. It's Sunday. It's good we decided to never book appointments on Sunday. It's the only day we get to spend together. I would miss our special time. Will you come over and spend the night? We can ask Aunt Olivia and Deb if they want to have a movie night. Then we can have another slumber party. I like when we have our slumber parties. We can snuggle together." Bri led Sasha to the drying table and held her, while Siera plugged in the dryer.

"Oh, me too. I'll bring my homework. I'm sure Mom and Dad won't mind." Siera waved the dryer across Sasha, who rolled over and let the two girls dry her fur.

†

It was still warm when Bri and Siera had finished their last client of the day. The breeze they created as they cycled home had no effect on the stifling heat, and when they arrived at Olivia's house, the sweat caused their t-shirts to adhere to their skin.

Bri offered to get Siera something cold to drink before her shower. Siera thought she was the luckiest girl in the world, because Bri always thought of her comfort first. Siera wanted to suggest they could take a shower together, but she was afraid Bri might think that was wrong. She accepted her offer and shuffled off to get clean. She kept extra shorts and t-shirts in Bri's room for their sleepovers.

After Siera took her shower, she joined Deb and Olivia, who were cuddled on the couch together watching an old movie. Deb had her head in Olivia's lap, and Olivia was absently moving her fingers through Deb's hair. To Siera, it sure looked like they were a couple, like her and Bri, but they insisted they were friends. Siera thought maybe they did their kissing in private. Siera usually kissed Bri in private when they were around Siera's family, but for some reason, they were more open when it was only Deb and Olivia.

Olivia looked up when Siera walked into the room. "Hey Siera, I'm sorry it's so hot in here. The air conditioning is on the blink. Are you sure you want to stay here tonight? I asked Deb the same thing, but I guess a head rub and *Love Story* beats out her cool condo."

"It's so sad. Can we watch something that has a good ending? Bri will be down soon after her shower," Siera said.

"Of course, kiddo." Olivia brushed her hand along Deb's cheek. "Hey sleepyhead, have you crashed already? What should we watch that has a good ending?"

Deb removed her head from Olivia's lap, sat up, and yawned. "Man, I'm sorry, those three long shifts in a row kicked my butt. How about we watch, *When Harry Met Sally*? That has a good ending."

"Good choice. We can stop watching this any time, because you're right. It always makes me blubber like a

baby, and I'll imitate your aunt. You know, she's a really ugly crier," Olivia teased.

Deb smacked Olivia on the arm. "Ha, ha, you'll never let me live down the first day I met you. Definitely not one of my finer days."

"Oh, I don't know, Deb. You'd look gorgeous even if you were hiccup crying."

"Careful Olivia, you know if you give me an inch, I'm gonna take a mile." Deb winked.

Bri came bounding into the room. "Hey, what'd I miss?"

Siera whispered in Bri's ear, "Aunt Deb and Olivia were flirting with each other."

"Hey now, no secrets over there," Olivia chastised.

Bri and Siera giggled.

†

After the movie, Bri sat on the end of the bed. A shy smile blossomed on her beautiful face. "Um, it's really hot tonight. Aunt Olivia said they won't be able to come and fix the air conditioner until next week. I'm sorry I forgot. Maybe if we take off all our clothes it will be okay."

"Okay, but you gotta turn off the light. 'Cause I have an ugly, dumpy body," Siera answered. It was one of the things about herself she hated most. She was so short and carried extra weight in her stomach. Bri always made her feel good about herself, but still, sometimes she obsessed over her belly fat.

"You have a beautiful body, Siera. I love it and everything about you. Please don't say that about yourself. I'll turn off the light, because I know how shy you are sometimes." Bri reached over and turned out the light.

Siera could hear Bri rustling around while she took off her clothes.

Siera neatly folded her t-shirt and shorts and set them aside before crawling into the bed and moving close to Bri. They always snuggled together at night, so she didn't think anything of it when she moved her body against Bri's.

Bri's hand draped over her stomach, and she could feel her naked body up against her backside. Siera felt tingles up and down her spine, and she wanted to do more than kiss Bri. She wanted to touch her in other places, but she didn't know what she was doing.

Siera turned around and tentatively put her hand on Bri's naked breast and let her fingers brush lightly over her nipples. When they pebbled and changed shape, Siera was sure she'd done something wrong, but Bri broke the silence, "That feels nice, can I touch yours too?"

Siera nodded. The two girls continued to move their fingers across each other's breasts and stomach. When Bri continued her exploration, and stroked the soft hair in Siera's private area, Siera felt something building. Moisture began to collect. She knew she didn't have to go to the bathroom and it felt so nice. She decided she wouldn't say anything, because she wanted to feel Bri's gentle caress. It felt better than when Bri pushed her hand through Siera's wavy, dark hair.

"It's not as soft as the hair on your head. It still feels silky. Is it okay to do this?" Bri asked.

"It feels really nice. I want to feel your golden hair too. Aunt Deb told me sex is a beautiful thing between people who love each other. She said it usually involves touching a person's private area. Mom used to tell me I should never let someone touch me down there. I don't think she meant

someone who loves me. I guess it's like when she said I shouldn't talk to strangers when I was little. When I got older, it became okay to talk to strangers. Like when we first started our business. We had to do a lot of marketing. Things change when you become an adult and fall in love."

"I love you, Siera. I want you to touch me like I'm touching you," Bri said.

"I love you too. I wish I knew what we're supposed to do during sex. Every time I try to find out. I get a funny look. Even Aunt Deb squirms a little. She won't go into a lot of detail. She only repeats the same thing. 'Sex between two people who love each other is very special and private.'"

"Aunt Olivia bought that book about pet grooming for us. It had a lot of detail. I'll bet if we went on the internet, we could find a book about sex."

"We're two girls who love each other. We should look for a book on lesbian sex."

That night, Siera had the feeling they could take things further than they had, but didn't know exactly what further meant. Siera was too embarrassed to mention about the book on lesbian sex, and when Bri didn't bring it up again, she forgot all about it. Their business continued to expand and her schoolwork increased so much it seemed like Sundays were the only days they had much time to spend with one another. It was nice to snuggle and touch Bri, even if she didn't know exactly how to have lesbian sex. Siera figured they had plenty of time to figure it all out.

CHAPTER NINETEEN

APRIL 2013

Siera sneaked a glance at the young woman sitting next to her. A little, silver ball in her nose matched the one on her tongue. Siera had overheard the woman talking about her girlfriend one day and how she loved the way the ball felt on her clit. Siera wanted to ask her if she was a lesbian and what she should do if she wanted to make love to Bri, but Rain seemed so tough. Siera was afraid.

She'd seen Rain one time when she'd gone with Olivia to the animal shelter. She knew Rain volunteered there and was very gentle with the cats and dogs. Siera thought Rain was a good person, despite her outward appearance. She mentally chastised herself for making assumptions about someone because of the way they looked and dressed. Wasn't that what everyone did with her? Siera shifted her eyes again to Rain, who was slouched back in her chair.

"Why do you keep looking at me? What's your problem, Siera?" Rain asked.

"You...uh...you know my name?" Siera asked.

"Sure, I mean, this isn't a class of a hundred or anything. There's only twenty of us. Besides, I remember when you came to the shelter with Olivia. Olivia's cool. She volunteers her services, and that makes all the difference in the world to the shelter," Rain answered.

Siera was surprised Rain hadn't mentioned anything about being amazed that someone like her could be in college. It was like Down's didn't matter, and that was a rare occasion with Siera. She decided she wanted to learn about lesbian sex more than she was afraid to ask. "Are you a real lesbian?"

Rain laughed. "As opposed to a fake one? You got a problem with lesbians?"

"Oh no, I'm a lesbian too. My girlfriend's name is Bri. We own Pretty Paws together," Siera answered.

Rain lifted her eyebrow. "Is that so? You two should come to one of our parties. They get a little wild, but everyone's nice. They won't be cruel to you or anything."

"You mean because we're Down's?"

"Sorry, I guess that was kinda rude, huh? Look, I would like you two to come. I'll make sure everyone behaves and doesn't try to get you guys drunk or anything. My friends are harmless, but they do like everyone to have a good time. Sometimes they push too much alcohol."

"Can I ask you a question?" Siera asked.

"Sure," Rain answered.

"Bri and I have been together for almost three years. We want to have sex, but we don't really know how."

Rain smiled. "Do you kiss?"

"Oh yes. We like to kiss. We've slept together once without clothes. We touched each other's breasts. We didn't know what to do after that. Even Olivia and Aunt Deb get

183

uncomfortable if we ask specific questions. They're lesbians, you know. But they won't tell us exactly what to do. They just say making love is a beautiful thing. If two people love each other, there is nothing wrong with it. That isn't very helpful," Siera explained.

Rain chuckled. "I love your thirst for knowledge. I'll buy you a cup of coffee after class and give you a few pointers. Have you guys ever considered getting a book?"

Siera blushed. "I suggested that. We learned a lot about our business with a book. I thought maybe we could learn about sex from a book. Then I wasn't sure if I should bring it up again. We were naked together that one night. Bri didn't say anything about it after that. I thought maybe she didn't want to learn that way."

"First rule, Siera, is you gotta communicate with each other. If you want something, you gotta tell the other person what you want. Your partner isn't a mind reader. If something feels good, you have to tell them, otherwise they won't know to continue."

Siera nodded. "I guess honesty is the best policy. Even with sex, huh?"

"Now you're catching on."

The professor entered the classroom, but Siera was looking forward to having coffee with Rain. She knew this unlikely new friend would tell her about lesbian sex, and she got the impression Rain was really good at it.

†

Deb was bored. She had the day off and decided to visit Olivia at her clinic. Sometimes, Olivia would have new puppies or kittens that needed their first shots, and that always lifted Deb's spirits. Oh, who was she kidding? Deb

was in love with Olivia, and she'd invent any excuse she could to spend time with her unrequited love. She needed to talk with Olivia, because she wasn't sure what to do. She'd seen Siera having coffee with a very rough-looking girl a few days ago. Her spiky hair and face piercings didn't seem to fit the kind of person Siera would be friends with.

Deb barreled through the clinic doors and saw Evie typing on the computer. She could hear music in the back and thought Bri probably had a client. If Siera was helping Deb could ask about the rough woman. Siera didn't have classes on Friday, so there was a good chance she was helping Bri today.

"Hey Evie, any chance your boss can get away for lunch?" Deb asked.

"I can move around a few appointments. Let me do my magic. Lucky for you, her next appointment lives close by and is always flexible." Evie winked.

"You're a doll, Evie. Are you sure you're straight?" Deb joked.

"Absolutely, but you keep working on the boss. One day, she's gonna realize what a catch you are."

"A girl can dream," Deb answered.

Olivia peeked her head out of one of the rooms. "I thought I heard your voice. What's up, trouble? You flirting with Evie again?"

"Yeah, but she shut me down. So, I guess I'll have to direct all my flirtations to you. Is Siera back there?" Deb pointed to the back room.

Olivia nodded. "Uh huh, why?"

"I wanted to ask her about this girl I saw her having coffee with."

Olivia frowned. "What girl?"

"I don't know, but she looked a bit rough to me. Face piercings, spiky hair, tattoo sleeve."

Olivia smiled. "Oh, don't worry, I'm pretty sure that's Rain. She's in one of Siera's classes and volunteers at the animal shelter. She's a good kid. I wouldn't be too concerned."

"Okay. They seemed like an odd pairing. If you think the kid is okay, I'll trust your judgment. So, my gorgeous friend, can I take you to lunch?" Deb asked.

Olivia glanced at Evie. "Can she?"

"Yep, I'll call Mrs. Carlson. It's not an emergency. Buffy got into something she shouldn't have. I can schedule her for later today. You have an opening at three. I'll ask her to bring Buffy in then."

"Thanks Evie, you're a miracle worker. I could use a nice, leisurely lunch today. Let me wrap up with the new batch of kittens, and I'll be right out."

"Ooh, can I come love on them, please?" Deb asked.

Olivia motioned with her arm for Deb to follow. "Sure, come on in, but I'm warning you. They are cuteness personified. You'll want to take another home for Socks to play with."

"Not a chance. He's the king, and he won't tolerate sharing his space with anyone. He's a spoiled rotten little furball."

†

Siera was sitting on Bri's bed, her leg bouncing the laptop up and down. Bri could tell she wanted to say something, but she wasn't talking. Bri always knew when Siera was nervous or stressed. Sometimes Siera got worried

before a big test, so Bri wondered if that was making her anxious.

"You're almost done with school, Siera. Don't worry about those big tests. You'll do okay. You always do," Bri soothed.

Siera lifted her eyes to meet Bri's. "I'm not worried about my finals. Well, I am kinda worried. But that's not what I want to talk to you about."

"You can tell me anything, Siera. I love you. You're not gonna break up with me, are you? Are you going to be Rain's new girlfriend? She's pretty and smart." Bri's eyes filled with unshed tears.

Siera wrapped her arms around Bri. "No, you silly goose. Rain is my friend and she's...uh...she gave me some advice about something."

"Advice?"

"Yeah, remember a long time ago. I said maybe we could get a book to teach us about sex?"

"Uh huh." Bri smiled.

"Rain says it's important to talk about everything. She said you should tell your girlfriend what you like and what you want. I want to learn more about lesbian sex. Can we go on the internet and find a book?"

Bri nodded her head vigorously. "Let's do that right now. Will you do the search? You're better with computers."

Siera opened the search engine and typed *Lesbian Sex + Book*. "There's so many choices. How are we gonna pick one?"

"I don't know. Let's read all the descriptions and the ratings. If there are lots of positive ratings, it must be a good book to get."

"Good idea. This is gonna be so much fun picking one out," Siera said excitedly. "I shouldn't have been afraid to talk to you. I shoulda known you would want to get a book. I'm sorry Bri. I'm going to always talk to you about everything."

"Me too. I promise," Bri replied. "Hey, Siera…"

She looked up from the computer. "Yeah?"

"How are we gonna pay for it? Do you have your card?"

"Yeah."

"Cool. I'll give you half."

"Okay."

Bri liked that Siera knew it was important for her to pay half and didn't argue.

CHAPTER TWENTY

June 2013

Deb leaned on the nurse's desk in the emergency department. She'd offered to take a pediatric patient to her unit. "Can I talk to Kathleen before I take the patient to her room?" Deb asked the unit clerk. "My niece is graduating, and I wanted to confirm the plans for the graduation party."

"Oh, I know. She is so excited and proud of Siera. She talks nonstop about how Siera's all set to go to Washington State, as soon as she decides to apply."

Deb frowned. "Siera and Bri's business is doing extremely well, and I'm pretty sure she doesn't want to get a Bachelor's degree. That's Kathleen's dream, not Siera's. I thought she'd let that go."

"Oh, don't say anything to her. I don't want to cause any trouble," the clerk said.

Deb heard the swoosh of the emergency department doors and turned to watch a ghost from her past step inside the air-conditioned waiting area.

Deb's stomach turned sour, and she felt her heart pound in her chest. She clutched the edge of the desk, as she imagined her face had taken on a deathly glow.

"Hi Deb, how have you been?" her ex-girlfriend asked.

"Carrie, what are you doing back in Moses Lake? I thought you'd moved to Spokane?" Deb's voice quivered.

"I'm interviewing for a day shift position. Can we not have this conversation here? Would you please consider having dinner with me? I've already moved back to town. Now all I need is for your sister to agree to give me the job."

"Oh, you'll get the job, unless I kill my sister before she has a chance to offer it to you," Deb sniped.

"Don't blame Kathleen, I asked Codee, in HR, to set up the interview. I specifically told Codee not to tell Kathleen who it was with. I wanted to present my case in person, without her dismissing me out of the chute."

Deb remembered when they had noticed the beautiful human resources executive, Codee. It seemed every lesbian in the hospital had a schoolgirl crush on her. She was pleasant enough, but definitely gave the hands-off vibe. Deb wondered, briefly, about Carrie's decision to go straight to the top to discuss her application, rather than going through Sharlie, Codee's assistant. That irritated her for some unknown reason. *What do I care if she makes a play for Codee?* Deb thought bitterly.

"She would never have done that. She has far too much integrity to let our shit get in the way. You're a great nurse. I know she'd be happy to see you return," Deb said.

"Dinner?" Carrie pushed.

"I'll think about it. Call me tomorrow. I need a little time, okay?"

"Okay," Carrie replied quietly.

Deb turned to the clerk. "Um, can you call me when the patient is ready? I'll talk to my sister tonight." Deb spun on her heels and nearly ran out of the department. She needed to pull herself together and call her best friend.

When she returned to her unit, her supervisor gently took her arm. "Hey, I just heard. Listen, I called in Mila to cover for you. She was happy to come in. Go home, get a drink, call your friend, whatever you need to do. Come back tomorrow with your head squarely screwed in place and ready to give your all to the patients."

"News travels fast," Deb replied bitterly.

"People care, don't take this the wrong way."

"I'm sorry. Shock doesn't begin to cover what I'm feeling right now," Deb whispered.

"I know. It's okay, we got this covered."

†

Olivia wished she didn't have to deal with Mr. Simpson and the aggressive Rover without Bri's calming influence, but at least the jerk owner had agreed to muzzle him. Every time she thought of his name, she rolled her eyes. *Rover, how original.*

The Motown music next door brought a smile to her lips. The girls always turned on the music and danced around while they bathed and groomed their customers. Bri insisted music soothed the savage beast. Olivia wasn't sure if it was the music or Siera and Bri's special skills with animals. Siera had proved to be as talented as Bri, and Olivia hadn't been lucky enough to find anyone that could replace either of the girls, even though her new assistant was a vet tech.

Uma, her new assistant, slid open the wood door, and Olivia frowned at the expression on her face. "Please, don't tell me Rover is missing the required muzzle."

"No, no, it's not that. Deb is here, and she looks terrible. Something is seriously wrong. Do you want me to have Evie re-schedule Rover?" Uma asked.

"Yeah, that's probably a good idea. If he's pissed about it, even better. I'd just as soon he takes Rover to a new vet anyway." Olivia grinned.

"Why don't you refuse to see him?" Uma asked.

Olivia sighed. "Because I promised Bri, and I'd never break my promise to her. She has a soft spot for the nasty little bastard."

"Mr. Simpson or Rover?"

Olivia chuckled. "Rover of course. She insists he's a sweet dog beneath all the aggression, and he only acts out because Mr. Simpson is, as you insinuated, the real nasty little bastard."

Olivia followed Uma to the front reception area. She took one look at Deb and ushered her into her office.

"Oh, hon, what's going on?" Olivia pulled Deb into a tight embrace.

"My ex is back in town interviewing with Kathleen right this very moment. She'll get the job, and I'll have the pleasure of running into her every time I work." Deb extricated herself from Olivia. She sat in the extra chair with her head in her hands and began to cry softly. "Fuck, it's been six years. Why does it still hurt?"

Olivia walked over to her and let her hand brush up and down Deb's back. She wasn't sure how she felt about this revelation. She had an easy friendship with Deb. Panic began to set in, as she imagined Deb getting back with her ex and

leaving Olivia out in the cold. She wasn't yet ready to put a label to her feelings. "Did you two talk?"

Deb raised her head, revealing her bleary eyes. She nodded. "A little. She asked me to go to dinner with her. I'm not too embarrassed to admit I'm hesitant to listen to what she has to say. She looked at me like she used to, with that same love in her eyes. Before we broke up, we were good together. I thought she was my forever partner. She had other ideas and ran to Spokane when I wanted to make things official."

"She's a fool for turning you down. So, are you going to go?" Olivia held her breath waiting for Deb's answer.

"I told her I had to think about it, but yeah, I think so. I'm like a moth to a flame. I can't help myself. Besides, I'm dying to hear what she has to say. Can I call you afterward?"

"Of course you can. How about I sidetrack you for now and ask about the graduation party plans?"

"I ran out before I had a chance to talk to Kathleen." Deb frowned. "Look, I know we are confident Siera knows what she wants, but convincing Kathleen is going to take a village. You, me, Jeremy, and Toby need to be a united front. She is going to shit a brick when she finds out we all went in on a down payment for a small house for them. I can't believe you got your sister to pitch in. You had the papers drawn up, right?"

"I did. In less than a month, the two of them will be the sole partners to Pretty Paws and will have full independence. I know it's merely symbolic, because from the very start, I've had little impact other than teaching them how to groom cats and dogs. The success is all attributed to their hard work and talents. Siera not only has an amazing way with the animals, but she has a very good head for business. Her

classes at Big Bend simply filled in some of the learning gaps. I am so damn proud of them."

"Do you think the two of them finally took their relationship to the…um…next level? They sure look cozy sometimes?"

Olivia shrugged. "I try not to stomp on their privacy."

"I don't think my sister is ready for that, even after three years. I'm envisioning her head exploding. She can't imagine Siera as a sexual being."

"Don't tell her this, but I did see, *The Whole Lesbian Sex Book* hidden in Bri's nightstand a couple of weeks ago. I was looking for something and hadn't intended on finding it." Olivia chuckled. "I couldn't help myself and leafed through it. Let me tell you, it is very thorough."

"Really? I'm coming over. I want to read this book." Deb grabbed Olivia's hand and gave her a quick squeeze. "Thanks, you just diverted my melancholy mood. You always seem to do that for me."

"Anytime, my friend, anytime. I only hope you don't toss me to the curb if you and Carrie get back together."

"Never. Not going to happen."

Olivia felt somewhat reassured by Deb's words, but there was a big part of her that already felt the hole Deb would leave if they stopped spending as much time with one another. Over the past three years, they'd gotten very close. Every once in a while, she had to physically stop herself from crossing the threshold she'd established on their relationship. At times, the desire to close the gap and kiss Deb was overwhelming, then Irene's fuzzy face would pop in her head and Olivia would pull back. Each time, she knew Deb had sensed what nearly happened, when the sad smile emerged on her beautiful face.

Today, right this minute, was one of those times. She wanted to drag Deb back to her house and lay claim to her like some overbearing redneck. She would take her into her bedroom and do all the things she dreamed up in her occasional waking fantasies. Lately, they'd gotten unbearably hot, and she felt an acute need to close the gap.

She wanted to shout at Deb, *Don't do it. Don't get back with your ex, just give me a little more time, and I'll cross the line.* Instead, she offered Deb her own sad smile.

"Come on, I'll close early. Let me take you out to dinner. We can let the girls have a little alone time," Olivia tossed out. "After dinner, we can watch *Fire* with the girls and eat Ben & Jerry's ice cream until we pop."

"You got yourself a date. Hey, I can hear today's music choice is Motown. I'm going to head in the back and soak up some of their positive energy for the rest of the afternoon."

"I'll come back with you until my next appointment shows. I have a little free time now." Olivia grinned.

"You cancelled Mr. Simpson. I can tell from your evil grin," Deb noted.

"Busted. You know me so well."

That was another thing about Deb, she did know her better than any other person. In some ways, Deb knew her better than Irene ever had, because she never felt like she had to censor her thoughts or opinions on anything. Deb simply accepted everything about her. The good, the bad, and the ugly.

"Come on, let's go back, and start shakin' our booty with the girls."

†

Kathleen felt the buzz of her phone in her pocket, as she balanced her keys and the bags of groceries in her hands. After setting everything down, she pulled her phone out and grimaced.

> *Forewarning might have been nice. Olivia and I are coming over tomorrow to discuss graduation plans, since I left early today. You better have a conciliatory meal for us*

> *Sorry, I swear I didn't know*

> *Did u hire her?*

> *I did, is that okay?*

There was no immediate response and Kathleen let loose. "Shit, shit, shit. I am so fucked."

> *Yeah. You owe the swear jar now:)*

Jeremy strolled into the kitchen. "What's wrong, hon?"
"I hired Carrie today."
"You what?"

"Don't give me any shit, she's an excellent nurse. What other option did I have?"

"Deb know?"

"Yeah, they're coming over tomorrow for dinner and to go over graduation plans."

"Oh…"

Kathleen narrowed her eyes at Jeremy. "Okay, spill. I know that look. You're keeping something under wraps. I'm not going to like it, am I?"

"When do you think Olivia will finally give in to her obvious feelings for Deb?" Jeremy diverted.

Kathleen knew Jeremy had tossed out a stall tactic but decided to let him have his little secret. He loved her, so how bad could it be?

"Good damn question, maybe Carrie resurfacing isn't such a bad thing after all."

"Hmmm. The little green monster has been known to be an effective mobilizer for uncovering people's true feelings. I like it. Maybe we should poke that fire."

"We should stay out of it. Shouldn't we?" Kathleen grinned.

"No, we should not. Deb has been alone far too long. She even gave up her little flings. It isn't natural to go without sex for that long."

"Spoken like a true guy."

"Don't tell me you'd be fine without sex for three years."

"Good point."

"Is Siera coming home tonight?"

"No, she texted that Olivia suggested the four of them have a movie night. Siera's crashing there tonight. I think it will be good for Deb to have the distraction."

"Yeah, that's a good idea. Has Siera said anything more about wanting to get her driver's license? I could teach her to drive."

"No way. Deb offered, and I think that's a good idea. Another distraction for her."

"Why? I'm a good driver."

"No, you are not. You have a lead foot and ride up everyone's ass."

"You know you're probably up to at least five dollars now. Family vacation in Yellowstone, here we come. I love having the swear jar."

CHAPTER TWENTY-ONE

Siera followed Bri into the garage, and they helped each other lift their trikes and secure them to the hooks Olivia had installed for them. It kept the bikes out of the way and allowed more room for the truck and for Deb to park her car when she came over.

Now that she'd finished school and graduation was around the corner, Siera had hinted at getting her own place with Bri and reminded her mom she wanted to learn to drive. She'd argued that the pet sitting and dog walking part of their business was suffering, because their range of travel was limited. Deb had agreed to teach her, and Olivia said she would take Bri out to give her driving lessons. Siera had her eye on a used truck she wanted to ask her dad to check over. Every dollar they earned, Siera meticulously recorded in her spreadsheet. She knew they could afford the truck. She'd learned they could easily write it off on their taxes, which made it a good business decision all the way around. They had a healthy amount of money in their business account

now, because they'd put almost every penny away since the business started.

Siera kept bringing the subject up about moving out, but her mom wasn't listening. She kept stating that until Siera finished school they were happy to support her. Her mom wanted her to apply to Washington State University and transfer to their business program, but Siera had struggled enough with school. She didn't think getting a Bachelor's degree was important. It took her an extra year to finish at Big Bend, because she didn't want to leave most of the burden to Bri to keep their business going. It was hard to work and go to school. It didn't leave a lot of time for fun. Their business was already successful, and she wanted to spend more time having fun with Bri.

Sasha greeted them at the door, wagging her tail, and Bri ruffled her fur.

Siera bent to kiss her nose and then stood up facing Bri. "Can we put Sasha in the mudroom and go to your room?"

"Uh huh. Let me give her some dinner. When Aunt Olivia and Deb come home they can let her out."

Bri quickly filled Sasha's bowl and brought it into the mudroom, where she set it down. Sasha began devouring the meal. Siera followed with a bowl of fresh water that she set down next to the food bowl. Bri closed the door, grabbed Siera's hand, and led her into her bedroom. She giggled when she pulled out the book hidden in the nightstand.

"Did you read it?" Siera asked.

"Some of it. There were parts I didn't think we would want to try. They seemed kind of icky and might hurt. I thought sex was supposed to feel good. It doesn't make sense to me," Bri answered as she sat down on the bed and pulled Siera next to her.

"Will you show me which pages I should read?"
Bri nodded.

Siera watched Bri flip to one of the pages in the book. Siera mouthed the words, as she read over Bri's shoulder and recognized the complicated word from her earlier conversation with Rain. "I have a hard time saying this word. Rain said this is her favorite. I didn't know you could kiss private parts. She assured me we have to try it. She invited us to a party a few months ago. I think we should go and meet some other lesbians."

Bri smiled. "Okay, that sounds fun."

Sierra looked at the picture in the book again. "Um, do you want to try this?"

"Uh huh, but maybe we should start by touching each other down there," Siera said. She flipped to another page in the book and pointed. "We can do this."

"Okay. That sounds like a good way to start. Aunt Olivia told me she is taking Deb out to dinner. Deb needed someone to talk to. Aunt Olivia wanted to cheer her up. They won't be back here until later. We have time to try some things out."

"I think we should get naked again. I like lying next to you when we're naked." Siera blushed.

"Okay, we can both take our clothes off and climb in bed. I think that's where you're supposed to do it."

"Don't watch me, okay? I have belly fat and you don't." Siera lifted her eyes to meet Bri's before standing up.

"I think you're beautiful. I love everything about you. Don't say that kind of stuff." Bri stood up next to Siera and ran her hand through Siera's thick silky hair. She pressed her lips against Siera's. "I love you. I want to show you how much. Aunt Olivia calls this making love. That's what we're gonna do right now." Bri lifted her t-shirt over her head and

201

folded it carefully, placing it on her dresser. She removed her shorts, underwear, and socks and added them to the pile.

Siera turned around when she removed her clothes, holding them against her body before setting them next to Bri's, then dashing to the bed. She clambered under the light, summer sheet and bedspread.

Bri crawled next to Siera and turned to her side. She rested a hand on Siera's cheek and Siera sighed in contentment.

Their lips joined and repeated a ritual they'd engaged in since they first started dating. At first their kisses were light and tentative. As they explored what felt good, they started experimenting with their tongues and lightly sucking on each other's lips. Sometimes, Siera would study the way people in love kissed in the movies. She'd attempt to duplicate their technique until she felt that tingling in her private area, or when she heard Bri respond. Bri would make a sound like when she was really enjoying an ice cream cone or a piece of pizza. That's when Siera knew she was kissing the way she was supposed to.

Bri was usually the first one to kiss her neck or breasts. When Siera discovered how good that felt, she'd started to reciprocate. Tonight, she decided to take the lead and brought her mouth to Bri's breast as she stroked the sides. She got the response she was hoping for when Bri moaned.

Her hand traveled down Bri's stomach, and she twirled her fingers around the soft golden hair below Bri's belly button. Rain had told her when your partner got wet down there, you were doing it right. Siera felt the moisture, as she moved her hand lower between the other lips on Bri's body. Bri lifted her bottom off the bed.

"It feels funny, but good. Can you keep moving your fingers down there?"

Siera ran her fingers up and down the area that was wet, and Bri continued to move with her. Bri started breathing heavy.

"I feel like something is about to happen, don't stop Siera."

Bri looked so beautiful moving next to her. Siera continued to move her fingers up and down.

"Oh, oh, oh, it's like my muscles are doing a dance." Bri put her hand on top of Siera's to stop her movement. "Oh Siera. That was amazing. Now it's really sensitive. I want to touch you now. You have to feel what I felt."

"Okay."

Bri pressed her lips to Siera's and hugged her close. "Thank you, Siera. Will you tell me when I am touching the right places?"

Siera nodded.

Bri lightly brushed her hand down Siera's breasts and began stroking up and down her stomach before weaving her fingers into Siera's dark curls. Siera felt the tingle build. She brought her hand on top of Bri's and bravely moved it down to where her own wetness seeped out. When Bri hit a particularly sensitive spot that sent shivers of pleasure through her body, Siera's own bottom began to move in a rhythm that enhanced the feeling. Siera understood what Bri had described earlier, as that building sensation grew and she didn't want Bri to stop.

"That's the right spot, Bri. Gosh, you're right. It's like nothing I've ever felt before. It is so wonderful. Just like you."

The feeling kept building, until Siera felt a wave of sensation flow over her body. It was the most glorious feeling, and she cried out as Bri slowed her caress.

"It's wonderful, isn't it? I am so happy I met you, Siera. Being in love is about the best thing in the world. Making love is even better," Bri said.

"I think we should read more in the book and try some new things."

"Me too," Bri agreed.

†

Olivia kept sneaking side glances at Deb, as she drove to the restaurant. She wanted to gauge where Deb was at regarding her decision about a dinner date with her ex. Olivia groaned inside when she thought of Deb on a romantic date with another woman. That image definitely did not sit well with her. The more she thought about it, the more she realized she didn't want Deb to get back with Carrie. Somehow, over the course of the last three years, she'd developed strong feelings for Deb. The fact that she hadn't taken that next step hadn't mattered until now. Olivia knew she had some serious soul searching to do. She wondered what Deb would think about her proposing a redefinition of their relationship. It scared her to consider that possibility, but the alternative terrified her.

"What? Do I have something gross on my face? You keep looking at me," Deb blurted out.

"Sorry. I'm trying to wrap my head around the possibility I might lose my best friend to an ex I haven't approved of. I want to meet her."

"You'll like her. Everyone does."

"No, I won't," Olivia answered.

"Why not? You haven't met her yet."

"She broke your heart. I already hate her," Olivia declared.

"Spoken like a true best friend."

"Maybe I don't want to be your best friend anymore," Olivia confessed.

"What are you talking about?"

"Maybe I want to cross that line I drew in the sand three years ago. You said you'd never be the one to cross it."

"Seriously? Now you want to cross the line, after my ex strolls back into town?"

"Sorry. Can you erase that from your head and forget I ever said anything?" Olivia gripped the steering wheel, as she made the turn into the restaurant.

"No, Olivia, I can't, but I also can't deal with that right at this moment. You know you just delivered a heaped spoonful of confusion and angst. We're going to talk about this, but not tonight. I need a lighthearted night, and you're going to stick to how we've been for the last three years. I'm going to continue to flirt, and you're going to laugh it off and not take me seriously. We're going to snuggle together on the couch and watch that movie for the hundredth time, as I fall asleep in your arms. That's what we do. Don't change the rules on me now."

"All right. Change of plans, let's get something to go and head back to my house so we can make this an early night. You'll probably be tossing and turning all night long now, because I'm an idiot." Olivia put the truck in park and paused before opening the door.

"Yes, you are, but I love you anyway. Good thing we have the girls to buffer the awkwardness, which I will only

allow for thirty minutes," Deb said, as she pulled on the handle of the truck door and got out.

Olivia chuckled. "God, you can be so bossy and precise."

†

By the time Deb and Olivia arrived at Olivia's house with to-go containers in hand, they'd returned to their normal friendly banter. Each was carefully making an effort to brush the confession under the rug. Deb wasn't about to admit how Olivia's declaration had landed on her. She'd fallen in love with Olivia a long time ago but would never come out with that admission, because she was sure Olivia did not return her feelings. The unrequited love was painful enough, but the prospect of not having Olivia in her life was beyond what she was willing to endure.

Carrie had been gone a very long time, but when she stood there in the emergency department, all those unresolved feelings came rushing back to Deb. She honestly did not know what she would do if Carrie wanted to give their relationship another chance. Now, Olivia was dangling another possibility in front of her. One that she'd longed for. Life was simply not fair.

Everything was quiet in the house, except for Sasha, who was whining in the mud room. Deb wondered where Bri and Siera were. They were normally back at the house by now.

"I'll let Sasha out. Why don't you see if the girls are hanging out in Bri's room? We can get the movie started soon and pull out the Ben & Jerry's for dessert," Olivia said.

Deb started walking to Bri's bedroom and noted the door was closed. For a moment, she wondered whether she should

open the door and possibly violate their privacy. She discarded the notion she'd be interrupting anything major. As she turned the doorknob and opened the door, she called out, "Hey girls, we brought...oh shit, sorry."

Deb glimpsed enough to realize both Siera and Bri were naked together in bed, and she surmised from their harried fumbling that she'd interrupted a very intimate moment. She quickly closed the door and nearly ran into the living room to keep Olivia from making the same mistake.

"Um, give the girls a few moments and don't interrogate them, okay?"

"What?"

"I'm pretty sure I interrupted a very intimate moment. Neither one of them had a stitch of clothing on, and by the frantic rustling of the covers, I'd venture to guess they were on an exploration of each other's bodies," Deb explained.

"Oh shit. Do you think we should intervene? We've been allowing them free rein for quite some time. Sex is kind of a big deal. Are you sure they're ready for that?" Olivia asked.

"God, now you sound like my sister. They clearly love each other, and I think they're a perfect match. Besides, you found the book. What did you think they've been doing—playing tiddlywinks?"

"What about your sister? She's going to blow a gasket. She already thinks Siera should start separating herself a little from her attachment to Bri, because it will be too painful when she attends WSU in the fall."

"You know as well as I do Siera has no intention of continuing her schooling. Why the hell should she? Shit, they probably make as much money on their business as I do working as a staff nurse."

"I know, but who's gonna give your sister that updated memo?" Olivia asked.

"We are. Remember? United front."

"Maybe you can introduce the topic and then kind of ease into our suspicions that the two of them are, maybe, a bit more serious with one another than Kathleen is willing to envision," Olivia suggested.

"Oh no you don't, you are not going to leave me the task of telling my sister her daughter is finally having sex with her girlfriend."

"Jeremy?"

"Um, I don't think so. He wants to continue to have sex with his own wife. If he lays that bomb on her, she'll shoot the messenger, and her aim is very precise," Deb answered.

"Well, somebody has to fill her in." Olivia sat heavily on one of the kitchen stools.

"Why don't we concentrate on breaking the news about the house and no WSU in the fall, before we move onto the next phase of attempting to convince my stubborn sister her dreams and Siera's dreams aren't quite the same thing?"

Deb turned her head and grinned when the two young women emerged from Bri's bedroom with their hair completely in disarray. They both had shy smiles, as they tentatively approached.

Deb couldn't help herself as she asked, "Did you have a nice nap, girls?"

Olivia snickered. "Are you girls still up for watching *Fire* with your old, decrepit aunts?"

"Yeah. I love that movie. I gotta get up early tomorrow. We scheduled some appointments before graduation," Siera said.

"How come you didn't take off the whole day?" Deb asked.

"Mrs. Carlson said it was an emergency. Buffy rolled into something rancid. I told her we could clean her up, if she brought her in at seven," Siera replied.

"I can run you over to the clinic in the morning, if you want. Do you mind if I crash here tonight?" Deb asked. "I made sure they scheduled me off for Siera's commencement ceremony," she added.

"You don't need to do that. I can take her. I'll head into the clinic early. I only scheduled appointments until eleven. I'll come back and pick you up; that way you can sleep in. We'll have ourselves a big slumber party. How does that sound?" Olivia asked.

"Awesome," Siera and Bri replied.

CHAPTER TWENTY-TWO

The warmth of the sun tickled Deb's cheek, as she opened her eyes and reached above her head to stretch. The first time Olivia had led her to the guest bedroom and tucked her in, she'd asked why Olivia kept the blinds partially open. Deb didn't mind the sun waking her early in the morning; she was simply curious. Olivia had explained when Tom and Jerry were kittens, Jerry got his head stuck between the blinds. Olivia had to cut one of the strings to keep him from choking to death. If she didn't keep them open, just a little, so they could look out at the birds, she was afraid they'd strangle themselves. Deb could see it happening, because on several occasions when she crashed at Olivia's house, she'd woken up to the young cats playing with the blinds and looking outside with rapt attention to the chirping birds. This morning, they weren't in her room and only the sun had woken her.

As she stretched, she remembered Olivia waking her up the night before. Deb had fallen asleep wrapped in Olivia's arms on the couch, again, while watching *L Word* reruns. She could still feel the warmth of Olivia's lips, as they brushed across her forehead when she'd said goodnight. Olivia probably thought she was already asleep, but Deb noticed her lingering in the doorway before padding off to her own bedroom.

Deb stared at the ceiling, as she wondered what she was going to do about Carrie. She hadn't called her back yet to arrange dinner. With the excitement of Siera's graduation today, along with Olivia's blunt declaration, life had gotten very complicated. She knew she owed it to both Carrie and herself to listen to what Carrie had to say. Deb wasn't sure what she was hoping for. She knew she was in love with Olivia, but she was a little pissed it had taken her three years to indicate any interest in something more than a friendship and only after hearing Carrie was back in town. Maybe Deb should have started dating someone seriously, to prompt the green monster's arrival earlier.

She glanced at the clock on the nightstand. It was still early, so she rolled over and closed her eyes in an attempt to fall back to sleep. She heard the girls stirring in Bri's room and smiled. Now that she realized Siera and Bri had begun to explore their own physical relationship with one another, she longed for that missing piece in her life. Since meeting Olivia, she'd gone on a few dates but hadn't returned to her previous pattern of short-term flings with women she knew she'd never develop serious feelings for. She missed the intimacy. Yet, if she analyzed her relationship with Olivia, they had that intimacy in every single way except for that one very important aspect. She'd managed to take care of the

need on her own, but it wasn't the same as sharing with another person. She knew if she got back with Carrie, that wouldn't be an issue. They'd always been compatible in the bedroom.

Deb rolled over again and concentrated on getting a few more hours of sleep, so she would have enough energy for the busy day. She'd promised to help her sister with the party decorations and was planning on going over to the house at nine. That would give them plenty of time to decorate and get the food ready. Finally, she drifted back to sleep. When she woke again, the house was quiet.

†

Bri watched Siera walk on stage to collect her diploma. The whole family was hooting and hollering, and she joined in along with her aunt. She'd brought her camera and kept taking pictures, though she knew she was too far away to get a clear shot.

Kathleen brought her fancy digital camera that also took high-definition videos and filmed the whole thing. Toby kept tugging on his shirt collar and making funny faces at his dad, and Bri was laughing at his antics.

"Cut that out, Toby," Kathleen chastised.

"It's hotter than the bowels of hell today. You guys get to wear sundresses, but Dad and I are melting in these damn dress shirts and ties. It's not fair," Toby complained. "The least you can do is let me joke around a bit."

"Fair? Don't get me started on how many hours of labor I endured, not to mention bras, nylons, and having to shave our legs every day in the summer," Kathleen lectured. "Your sister will be meeting us soon, so hold your damn horses."

"You're not wearing nylons, and nobody said you have to wear bras. Bring back the seventies when you guys burned them. I wouldn't mind seeing Amy without a bra." Toby wiggled his eyebrows.

Kathleen leaned across and smacked Toby in the chest. "Can you please behave for five more minutes, then we can return home for the graduation party. I don't give two shits what you change into then."

†

Kathleen was rushing around the kitchen pulling out bowls and pots, setting out the potatoes to dice up and roast on the grill. Other vegetables intended for grilling were already on the counter, and she began to slice them into large enough pieces for Jeremy, the grill master.

Siera had dragged Bri to her room, and Kathleen assumed Toby had gone to change out of his dress clothes. She'd sent Jeremy to the store for last-minute groceries she'd forgotten. He grumbled about needing to change out of his good clothes, but agreed to go right away to the store.

She wasn't sure whether it was a good idea to invite Carrie, especially after sensing something had shifted between Olivia and Deb. It was so subtle she'd almost missed it, and now she was wondering if she'd made a big mistake.

On so many occasions, she'd wanted to take Olivia aside and have a come-to-Jesus meeting, knowing Deb was in love with the kindhearted woman. Every passing month made it more difficult for Olivia to finally admit she cared for Deb as more than a friend, but Kathleen had no doubt that was exactly how Olivia was feeling, whether she would admit that to herself or not.

Two quick knocks on the garage door, and Deb and Olivia entered the kitchen.

"Okay the cavalry is here now, what can we do to help?" Deb asked.

"Yeah, put us to work," Olivia added.

"Can one of you wash and cut up the potatoes?" Kathleen asked.

"Sure, I can do that. Where are the girls?" Deb asked.

"They went to Siera's room. I think maybe they're changing. I'm not sure what they're doing," Kathleen responded.

Deb glanced at Olivia and smirked. Olivia chuckled.

Kathleen furrowed her brow, as she noted the look that passed between Olivia and Deb. "What's so funny?"

"Nothing. You need to give Olivia a job, you know, idle hands." Deb poked Olivia in the ribs.

"Okay. If you wouldn't mind, can you start cutting up the bell peppers? Just put them in this bowl." Kathleen pointed to a large bowl sitting on the island.

Kathleen decided she might as well break the news to Deb rather than surprise her later. "Um listen, Deb, I need to tell you something. I hope it's not a problem. I was talking in the ED the other day, about Siera's graduation and how proud I am of her…"

"Yeah that's not a big surprise, you always talk about Siera." Deb picked up the bowl of potatoes, took them to the sink, and began washing each one and setting them in the colander.

"Well, when Carrie was interviewing with me, I sorta invited her to the party," Kathleen confessed.

"You what?"

"Now Deb," Kathleen began. "Carrie was very close to the family before you two broke up. It seemed like the polite thing to do."

Olivia frowned, but didn't say a word.

"Fuck the polite thing to do. I am not ready to be around her yet. Could you have at least given me a chance to get used to the idea? God damn, Kathleen, first you hire her and now this. I'm your sister for Christ's sake." Deb threw the potato in the sink and stomped out of the kitchen, slamming the door behind her.

Kathleen looked at Olivia with a pained expression. She knew it was going to be awkward, but she hadn't quite expected that reaction.

Olivia patted Kathleen's shoulder. "I'll go."

†

Olivia found Deb on the back patio sitting in one of the lawn chairs with her head in her hands. She squatted down in front, touching Deb's knees.

"Kathleen makes me so damn mad, and I can't believe I let this upset me after so many years. She left, so what, people split up all the time," Deb said. "It's not like I haven't moved on. I can't figure out if these are tears of frustration or pain, but I know what the catalyst was."

Deb looked up and her tear-stained cheeks nearly broke Olivia's heart. She wanted to take away the pain and confusion, and before she realized what was happening, she touched her lips to Deb's.

Deb's eyes grew wide, and she put her finger to Olivia's mouth.

"Oh shit, I'm sorry Deb. I'm not helping, am I? What can I do for you? You know if it was in my power, I would remove every single stitch of pain."

Deb swiped away a tear. "I wanted a couple more days to prepare myself. That isn't too much to ask, is it?"

"No hon, it isn't."

"Today is about Siera and her accomplishment not some dyke drama," Deb said.

"Um, Deb, have you looked at yourself? Definitely not in the dyke category, and although I've never met Carrie, I'm guessing she wouldn't fit that stereotype either."

Deb lifted her eyes and met Olivia's. "Why did you kiss me?"

"Bad timing, huh?"

"Ya think? Now answer the question. You've never been afraid to lay things on the line before."

Olivia sighed. "No, I haven't. I did start to fess up to my feelings yesterday, but you aren't ready to absorb anything yet. It was wrong of me to kiss you. I guess it felt right, though I know it wasn't. Look, I'm not going to push you to figure things out, but for the record, I've officially crossed the line and now the ball is in your court. Take some time and go to dinner with Carrie, or spend a bit of time with her. If, after you do that, you're ready to explore what we might evolve into, then I'll still be here. Now, let's talk about your current dilemma. What do you need from me right this minute?"

"I need you to be by my side, like you always are, and be ready to whisk me away if things get too weird in there." Deb jerked her thumb at the glass doors that led into the house.

"You got it. We can stay an appropriate amount of time at the party and leave early if you want. Bri and Siera are surprisingly intuitive, more than people give them credit for. They'll understand. I'm sure of it."

"Okay, I'm ready to go back inside, but I'm not apologizing to my insensitive sister."

Olivia grinned. "Nor should you. I almost feel compelled to pull her aside and read her the riot act myself."

Deb stood up, grabbing Olivia's hands, and hugged her. "Be sure to give me a play by play of that conversation."

"You got it."

†

After kissing a little and caressing each other's bodies for a few minutes, Siera and Bri changed into shorts and tank tops. They emerged from Siera's bedroom and went out to the back patio to hang out, while waiting for the rest of the guests to arrive. They'd both asked if Kathleen needed help, but she'd shooed them away to enjoy the sunshine.

Toby joined them after promptly changing into his own casual clothing. He'd invited his on-again, off-again, girlfriend, Amy. Siera thought he deserved every time Amy broke up with him, because he would always do something stupid. Boys were so immature sometimes. She'd told him that, one day, Amy wasn't going to take him back, and he would deserve it. Siera loved her brother, but he was full of himself and that always got him in trouble.

Jeremy was cleaning the outside of the grill, trying to make it sparkle. Kathleen had told him she wanted everything perfect, and his domain was the outside. Siera had heard her tell him he was getting on her last nerve and had

better scoot outside to make sure everything looked nice before she decided to trade him in for a younger model.

Siera knew it was an idle threat, because she'd never seen two people more in love with one another, except for maybe her Aunt Deb and Olivia. One day, she thought they'd finally realize what was so obvious to her. There was no doubt she loved Bri as much as her mom loved her dad. The state of Washington had legalized marriage in December, and she knew she wanted to marry Bri one day. But first, they had to spread their wings and venture out on their own.

Every time she tried to bring up the subject, her mom wouldn't listen. Her mom kept talking about Siera attending WSU and making different living arrangements and then moving to Pullman, Washington. Siera was planning on putting her foot down today and telling her mom she wanted to find a place with Bri and live with her. She hadn't figured out how and when she would ask Bri to marry her, but she planned on doing that soon. She wanted to ask Aunt Deb and Olivia's advice on that.

When her aunt and Olivia came to the back patio and set out the napkins and silverware, Siera could tell right away something was wrong. Deb's eyes were all red and puffy, like she'd been crying. Siera jumped up, and wrapped her arms around her aunt and squeezed.

Bri looked at her, and Siera could tell she was wondering what was going on.

"Aw thanks sweetie, I needed that," Deb said.

Olivia put her hand on Deb's back and rubbed up and down.

Bri followed Siera's lead, offering Deb her own hug.

"You two are the best medicine for me. I love you guys," Deb murmured.

"Are you okay, Aunt Deb? Did something happen. Was Mom mean to you?"

"I'm okay sweetie. No, your mom was not mean to me, at least not directly."

"Mom doesn't always think before she speaks."

"Oh, honey you got that right," Deb answered.

"But Aunt Deb, I know she means well."

"She does," Deb answered. "So, are you excited for your graduation party? I saw a pretty delicious-looking cake in the fridge."

Siera nodded. She was happy when she saw her aunt smile, but the smile vanished. Siera turned around and saw Carrie walking across the grass. She hadn't seen Carrie for a long time and wondered what she was doing at her graduation party.

Her mom came bustling out. "Hi Carrie, I'm glad you could come."

"Thanks for inviting me." Carrie turned to Deb and narrowed her gaze. "Hello Deb, it's good to see you. Who's your friend?"

Siera looked back and forth between Carrie and Olivia. It reminded her of the times when she would see two alpha dogs size one another up at the clinic. She grinned when she saw Olivia's subtle touch to Deb's arm before she held out her hand.

"Hi, I'm Olivia, Bri's aunt and a close friend of the family. Bri and Siera own Pretty Paws together and run the business out of my clinic."

"I'm Carrie, an old friend of the family. Deb and I used to be together."

"I know who you are," Olivia said.

Bri scooted closer to Siera, brought her mouth to Siera's ear, and whispered, "I don't think Carrie and Olivia like each other. They act like they're competing."

Siera giggled. "Uh huh."

"Uh huh, what?" Kathleen asked.

"Nothing, Mom," Siera answered.

A few more guests arrived, including Uncle Frank. The party progressed to a lively affair. Uncle Frank brought a woman who had big hair, but Siera didn't think it was her natural color. The woman had the biggest breasts Siera had ever seen on a woman. Siera tried to avoid both Uncle Frank and Carrie, but Uncle Frank made a beeline for her when he arrived and put his arm around her shoulder. He said he had something important to talk to her and Bri about and dragged them off to the bench on the edge of their property.

Siera knew Uncle Frank was family, but she always felt uncomfortable around him.

"Sweetheart, I am so proud of you. You too, Bri. I understand you two have a very successful business now, so I want to help you expand it. I had my lawyer draw up some papers. All you two need to do is sign them, and I'll be another partner. I can take care of all the things too complicated for you," Frank said.

"Olivia already helps us with things. She's our silent partner," Siera answered.

"Oh, I know honey, but Olivia is too busy to help you really make the business pop. That's where I can come in."

Siera saw Olivia glance her way, and she was glad when she walked over with Deb.

"Hey Frank, it's good to see you again." Olivia narrowed her eyes. "It looks entirely too serious over here. You know it's a celebration, right?"

"Uncle Frank wants us to sign some papers so he can be another partner in our business," Siera said.

"Really? Is that right, Frank?" Olivia asked.

Siera noticed Olivia had her mad face. Uncle Frank was about to get a lecture.

"I got connections that can make your business grow into something big, really big. Maybe turn it into a kind of franchise."

"Hmmm, let's take a look at those papers you want them to sign. As the third partner in the business, I believe I'll need to agree to this as well." Olivia scanned the papers and frowned when she shuffled to the third page.

"Well, I thought maybe you'd want to bow out and let me take over. You know, running a busy clinic is probably all you can handle, so I'd be doing you a favor, too. You can stop worrying your pretty little head and let me take care of the complicated business matters," Frank explained.

Olivia clenched her jaw and took a big breath. "Siera and Bri do you want to go into a partnership with your uncle?"

Siera shook her head. Bri's eyes were wide and she squeaked, "No."

"Frank, you heard the girls. For the record, they don't need a third partner. If they ever want to venture out on their own, I plan to bow out gracefully. If I ever hear about you approaching them again, you won't like my reaction. I think I should tell your brother about your idea. He might have an opinion, especially after he sees these papers." Olivia folded the papers and stuck them in her pocket. She crossed her arms across her chest and glared at Frank.

Frank held his hands up. "Hey, I was trying to help."

Jeremy walked over to the group and raised his eyebrow. "Frank, what's going on?"

Frank looked at his shoes and mumbled, "Nothing, a little business proposition. You know how proud I am of your daughter."

"Olivia, why don't you tell me what the hell is going on?" Jeremy asked.

When her mom joined the group, and scrunched up her face, Siera almost felt sorry for Uncle Frank.

"Yeah, I'd like to hear exactly what you're up to, Frank," Kathleen said.

"Frank offered to be Bri and Siera's third partner. He drew up some papers for them to sign, giving himself a fifty-percent cut in exchange for his marketing and accounting services."

"How in the world did you come out of the same womb as Jeremy? That's it, get out, you slimy bastard. I swear, if you ever try to take advantage of Siera again, I will rip you a new one," Kathleen said. "Jeremy, I'm sorry, but this is the final straw. I don't want your brother coming around."

"I think you'd better leave and take your date with you. Let me add, the only reason you are still standing right now is you're my brother. I swear I'll do more than rip you a new one if you ever try something like this again. Did you really think you'd be able to get away with it? I need you to leave right now, before I do something we'll both regret," Jeremy ordered.

After the drama with her uncle, Siera decided to spend the remaining time with Bri, Olivia, and Deb, who had moved to a more remote corner of the back yard. When they finally decided to open up the graduation presents, Siera was

relaxing in one of the lawn chairs and holding Bri's hand
while they shared a large slice of cake.

†

Olivia was happy when Deb interacted with Carrie
politely but chose to avoid spending any time with her alone.
Although Carrie kept trying to corner her, Deb adeptly
avoided her overtures. That made Olivia smile. She was
perturbed Carrie refused to leave and stayed to the bitter end.
It left them no choice but to include her in on their surprise
gift for Siera and Bri.

After the confrontation with Frank, Olivia was hoping
the night wouldn't result in any more drama, but she wasn't
naïve enough to believe the surprise wouldn't create waves.
She was still seething about that slimy bastard, Frank, and
was perplexed as to how in the world he was related to
Jeremy. She could easily see Jeremy as a respected, future in-
law, if Bri and Siera decided to make the ultimate
commitment to one another. Olivia had no doubt that would
happen one day.

After Kathleen served the cake, she pulled everyone
together and set the presents in front of Siera. Olivia had to
admit it was nice of Carrie to bring a gift. Kathleen must
have told her about Siera's business, because Carrie had put
together a basket full of organic pet shampoos and other
specialty items.

Olivia was excited to see Siera's reaction when she
opened the envelope. The flyer showcased the house, and the
papers would complete the transaction, if Siera and Bri
decided they wanted to take the leap. Olivia had cashed in
her favor with Tara, the bank executive who ran the
mortgage department. The woman had a very sweet mastiff

named Barney, and Olivia had opened her clinic for the Sunday emergency, when Barney ran in front of a car and ended up with multiple injuries.

Tara had taken care of everything, collecting Bri and Siera's financial information to show a consistent income that more than supported the mortgage for the property. Jeremy, Deb, Maribel, Greg, and Olivia had made an offer on the house and contributed both the down payment and the additional fees to set up the loan. They had all agreed to present the gift at the party, where Kathleen could not react too negatively with others present. Olivia was sure Jeremy would catch hell later, and she was happy he was willing to take one for the team.

Olivia glared at Carrie, while Siera picked up the envelope with her name scrawled in big letters. Olivia transferred her attention to Siera and watched her slip her finger under the flap, open the envelope, and pull out the papers.

Siera tilted her head to the side. The real estate flyer showed the small, sage-colored house framed with beautiful flowers and trees, and trimmed in cream paint.

Deb rushed to get all the words out, "It's the house for sale close to the park you and Bri like to go to. It's small, but has a large room that can easily be converted for your grooming business. We made an offer on your behalf and put a ten percent down payment on it. You both qualify for a first homeowner's loan that only requires ten percent down. That's our gift to you. It's from Olivia, your mom and dad, Bri's parents, and me. I remembered when you made a comment about the house and said you wished you could live in a house like that with Bri. You and Bri are all approved for the loan, and you can run the business in your new house.

224

If you don't like it, you can say no. We won't lose much in the earnest money we put up."

Siera launched out of her chair and threw her arms around Deb, hugging her so tight she grunted. Siera quickly made the rounds to her mother, father, and Olivia.

"I feel like I've won the lottery. Thank you, thank you, thank you. Can we really afford this?" Siera asked.

"You can more than afford this, and we might have to renegotiate the terms of our business partnership. You won't need me any longer, after you set up the room in your new house—unless you want to expand your business and set up a second location. Then you would have to hire more staff," Olivia said.

"Will you help us, Aunt Olivia, you know...hire some people?" Bri asked, as she offered her own hugs to everyone.

Kathleen was scowling, but didn't say a word. When she glanced at Jeremy, he shrugged his shoulders.

"Wow, that's quite a gift," Carrie noted. "Are you sure that's a good idea, putting pressure on the girls to make a monthly house payment when they have to depend on a successful business? Small businesses file for bankruptcy all the time."

"Bri and Siera have an extremely successful business. With what they have in their savings account, they could pay the mortgage for several years without taking in one more dollar. You need to shut your mouth about things you know absolutely nothing about," Deb snapped.

"I thought Siera was going to WSU and that might put too much pressure on Bri. Is Olivia going to pick up the slack as a silent partner?" Carrie asked.

"I don't want to go to WSU," Siera said.

"Now, honey, I know you're a little burned out. I expected you to take a year off while you spend time on your little hobby, but then you can apply and get your Bachelor's. After you get your degree, you can get a real job," Kathleen patiently explained.

Jeremy glared at Kathleen. "Honey, we are so proud of you and your success. If you don't want to continue your schooling, you don't need to. You have a successful business with Bri, and your mother and I have the utmost confidence you both will continue to succeed, whether you continue your partnership with Olivia or not."

"Well of course we are proud of Siera, but she has so much more potential," Kathleen said.

A tear ran down Siera's cheek. "Mom, will you please listen? I don't want to go to WSU. I want to live with Bri and get married."

"You what?" Kathleen exclaimed.

Carrie shifted in her seat.

Jeremy grabbed his wife's arm. "Honey, come inside with me. I need to talk to you, *alone*." He pulled her from her chair and practically dragged her into the house.

"Carrie, I think the party is over. Time for you to go. Look, I know we need to talk, and I promise I'll call you, but I think we need to figure some family things out right now," Deb said.

"How come Olivia isn't leaving?" Carrie frowned.

"Because Olivia is part of this whole thing as another partner. Please, just go," Deb pleaded.

"Okay, but can we at least have dinner? I need to talk to you," Carrie said.

"I'll call you later," Deb promised.

Olivia watched the events unfold and laid her hand on Bri's shoulder. She stood off to the side, apparently shell-shocked.

"Come on girls, let's go back to my house. You can both crash there and we'll talk. Deb, do you want to come on over and stay?" Olivia asked.

"Yes. I think that's a grand idea," Deb responded.

"Won't Mom be mad?" Siera asked.

"Don't you worry about your mom. Your dad will make sure it's all okay, and I'll call her tomorrow."

"Thanks, Aunt Deb. I love you," Siera said.

"I love you too," Deb responded.

CHAPTER TWENTY-THREE

Kathleen was so angry she could barely talk to her husband. "How could you do that? You ambushed me."

"No, I did what I thought was the right thing to do. Siera doesn't want to go to WSU, and you're too damn stubborn to see what's right in front of your eyes. Siera and Bri are in love, and they have a wildly successful business. Did you realize they have over sixty thousand dollars saved? They are currently turning customers away," Jeremy replied.

"Did you hear your daughter? She said she wanted to marry Bri. It's not that I think Bri isn't a sweet girl, but for God's sake, this is getting out of hand."

"What exactly do you have a problem with? Your daughter's success and desired independence? Or the fact she wants to get married to someone she loves, like any other normal young woman?" Jeremy asked.

"She's too young. She doesn't know what's best for her," Kathleen insisted.

"She's almost twenty-three, not sixteen. She's far more mature and able to decide what's best for herself than most young women her age that I know. After the first six months, when Olivia might have helped the girls a little with the business, they did everything on their own. I'm pretty sure they know what they're doing. Hon, listen to yourself." Jeremy grabbed his wife's hands and led her to the couch, gently guiding her to sit with him. "Remember, years ago, when you said I was right? Well things haven't changed. You're back to treating her like all those people who underestimate Siera. Don't jump on that train. Don't you want her to be happy? Because you should have seen her face, hon, she's happy. Can't you be happy for her? Let her have her dream. Don't make her live yours."

Kathleen sighed. "Of course I want her to be happy. Can you imagine how much shit narrow-minded bigots will throw at Siera and Bri when they learn they're married? Doesn't she have enough crap to overcome regarding the prejudgments about people with Down syndrome?"

"No offense, hon, but you're kinda the pot calling the kettle black. From the very beginning, for whatever reason, you've tossed out objections to Siera and Bri as a couple."

"Do you think they're...um...physical with one another?" Kathleen asked.

Jeremy shrugged. "I don't know, maybe. They kiss each other. I suspect there has been some experimentation."

"Oh God." Kathleen groaned. "I don't know why I have an issue with that, but isn't it normal for a mother to have a hard time imagining their little girl as a sexually active being?"

"I suppose so, but hon, I also think a little bit of your issues has to do with narrow views about both homosexuality

and kids with Down's. Don't fall into those traps. I'll bet if you open the door, Siera will confide in you and tell you everything she's thinking and feeling." Jeremy squeezed his wife's hands. "You know how sensitive she is to people. She can tell when you disapprove of something. Call her up tomorrow, and let her know you support her one hundred percent. I'll bet she tells you her hopes and dreams, and you two will work your way back to the closeness you used to have."

A tear escaped Kathleen's eyes. "I'm the cause for the distance, aren't I?"

Jeremy nodded. "She loves you, hon, but you've got to let her live her own life."

"God, I hate it when you're right."

Jeremy chuckled. "Wow, twice in one decade. Not that I want to kick you when you're down, but you'd better call your sister while you're at it. I don't think you're her favorite person right now, either. I know you wanted to poke the fire a little and conjure up the green monster, but what the hell were you thinking inviting Carrie to the party?"

"You thought it was a good idea to encourage a little jealousy, so don't play Mr. Innocent with me now. I was trying to get Olivia to finally recognize her feelings for Deb. In this instance, I think I was right. Did you see how Olivia reacted to Carrie? Something has shifted, I'm sure of it."

"Okay, maybe you're right on this one. I sure hope so," Jeremy responded.

†

Bri slung her arm around Siera and kissed her. Although she knew Siera was sad about what that woman, Carrie, had said and how her mom had reacted, Bri was happy Siera

wanted to get married. Bri couldn't think of anyone she wanted to marry more. She'd been wanting to talk to her aunt about how she could ask Siera.

"Did you really mean what you said—you want to get married?" Bri asked.

Siera nodded. "I wanted to think of a special way to ask you. I don't have a ring yet. I was going to ask Aunt Deb to help me."

"I don't think your mom wants us to get married."

Siera looked down. "I know."

"Do you think your dad will be able to change her mind?" Bri asked.

Siera shrugged. "Maybe." She giggled. "I'll bet Aunt Deb will say something. She can be scary sometimes. She's got a temper, you know."

"Aunt Olivia is like that too. Especially when people are mean to me. Boy, you should see her when someone makes her mad. I don't think she likes your aunt's friend, Carrie. I don't think I like her either. Is that wrong?" Bri asked.

"Carrie was nice to me. She wasn't comfortable hanging out with me like Olivia. I never felt like we were friends or anything like that."

"I know what you mean. Aunt Olivia and Deb treat us like we're normal," Bri said.

"Are you excited about going to sign those papers tomorrow?" Siera asked.

"Yeah. I can't wait for when we can live together all the time. I like when Aunt Olivia invites you to stay and have a slumber party. When we have our house, we'll be able to sleep together every night. We can read more of that book and try some new things."

"I'd like that." Siera smiled.

†

Olivia took the chance Deb wouldn't push her away. She took her hand, as they ventured outside for an evening stroll. The girls had retreated to Bri's room, and she could hear them murmuring behind closed doors. She knew that, tomorrow, she would need to talk with Bri about Siera's declaration. She suspected knowing Siera wanted them to get married was a very welcome announcement, but sensed her niece was trying to figure out a way to have a heart-to-heart with her. She wasn't sure if it was about their newly discovered sexual intimacy or about topics like marriage and family. Olivia would be there for her niece and answer every question with brutal honesty.

Over the past two years, she had methodically been preparing Maribel and Greg for this inevitable conclusion. She knew Bri and Siera wanted to live together. Siera's declaration wasn't a surprise to her. She thought that, maybe, her sister and brother-in-law were more prepared than Kathleen for the news. On the few occasions they had visited, Maribel had seen for herself how much Bri had blossomed. Maribel had asked about Olivia's relationship with Deb, and Olivia had insisted they were only friends. Her sister hadn't said anything, but her smile suggested she didn't quite believe it.

"So, when are you planning to call Carrie and go out to dinner?" Olivia asked.

Deb smiled. "Why? Are you jealous? I saw the daggers you two were shooting each other today. I think I like the idea of two women dueling over me." She laughed.

"She's a tool. Who does she think she is, butting into family stuff?" Olivia asked.

"Um, I think I pretty much took care of that. I blame Kathleen more than Carrie. She was merely spouting the shit my sister has been spewing. They used to work together, so I'm sure Kathleen had already filled her head with her viewpoint on what Siera should choose for her future."

"Mmm hmm, I'm not so sure. I do believe there was a bit of a dig at me in her comment. I don't think Carrie is too happy about my involvement with the girls and their business. No doubt, she is trying to figure out where I fit into your life." Olivia stopped walking and looked into Deb's eyes.

"Well, join the crowd. I'm also trying to figure out where I fit into your world."

Olivia brought her lips to Deb's forehead. "We're not having this conversation until after you figure out where you stand with Carrie. Have your dinner with her, and then we'll talk. I promise to tell you everything I've been ruminating over since that she-devil walked back into your life."

Deb chuckled. "She-devil. Geez, Olivia, don't hold back. Tell me what you really think. Ruminating, huh? I think I'd better have this dinner soon, I'd hate to have you ruminate too long."

Olivia squeezed Deb's hand. "I care about you."

"I know."

"So, tomorrow morning, I think we should talk to the girls before we take them to sign the papers. If they have sex questions, we'll have to get over any discomfort we have with the talk. Although, I think they went ahead and took it upon themselves to get the information on their own. I am a little concerned about how thorough that book is regarding lesbian sex. I think it goes into graphic detail and includes

BDSM and anal sex. I'm not so sure they should be experimenting into the more fringe elements."

Deb raised her eyebrow. "Hmm, vanilla huh?"

"What, no!"

"Ooh, do tell. What fringe are you into?"

"Oh no, we are not having this conversation," Olivia said.

"You opened the door." Deb grinned.

"So...um...you mean you're...oh God, never mind. Let's save this conversation for another time, if and only if, it is relevant to...um...the evolution of our relationship."

Deb chuckled. "God you're cute when you blush. Just for the record, a little bit of role play and light bondage can be quite fun."

"Indeed, it can," Olivia bravely declared. "Will you call me after your dinner date?"

"I will."

†

Siera and Bri stumbled into the kitchen. Olivia was flipping pancakes, while Deb sipped her coffee. Bri thought they looked comfortable together. She liked how Deb made her aunt smile.

"Good morning girls. Are you ready to sign those papers?" Olivia asked.

Siera bounced on the balls of her feet. "I'm so excited. When can we move in?"

"I think you can close on the house in another three weeks, but you also have to find a contractor to convert that large room. I thought it would make the perfect place for grooming, but it needs to be plumbed."

Bri frowned. "Will that cost a lot? Do we have enough saved?"

Olivia waved her hand in the air. "You have plenty, and I believe it'll be a good investment. But if you want to continue to work out of my clinic, we can keep our current setup."

Bri looked at Siera who nodded. "How about if we kept both locations?"

"I want to hire people like us to do the grooming at the clinic. We can give somebody a chance. It's hard to get a job when you have a disability or look like us," Siera said.

Olivia glanced at Deb. "Okay, but you two are pretty special. We need to make sure the person has the skills to work with animals, even the ones who are afraid and nervous."

"Aunt Olivia, Siera is really good at stuff like that. It's like she has this superpower for screening people. You can trust her judgment," Bri exclaimed.

"You're right. I trust you two to make the right decision. I can help with all the paperwork. It gets more complicated when you hire someone and have to pay them. Did you learn about that in your classes, Siera?" Olivia asked.

Siera frowned. "No, we didn't learn a lot about that. Would you Olivia? Then you can still be a partner. We can expand our business. I like the idea of running it out of our house—being independent like that. I also like you being another partner. Are you disappointed we don't want to go completely on our own?"

"Of course not. I would love to stay involved. I'll try not to butt in too much, because that will surely mess up your mojo," Olivia said.

"Mojo?" Siera asked.

"Yep the magic you've got going with Pretty Paws," Olivia answered.

"We wanted to talk to you two about something else." Deb looked at Olivia, who gave her a slight nod.

"Olivia found the book in your nightstand. She wasn't trying to invade your privacy, but…" Deb started.

"I'm sorry. When you've asked questions in the past— you know, about sex—I must have given you the idea I wasn't comfortable answering them. I'm sorry for that. We want you to know you can ask us anything," Olivia added.

"Do you and Aunt Deb have sex?" Siera asked.

Deb spit out her coffee and looked up at Olivia.

"Uh… No, we don't," Olivia's voice stuttered.

"Why not?"

"Um, it's complicated. Look, sometimes adults don't have all the answers, especially when it comes to their own personal situations. I was thinking more along the lines of you two having questions about your own feelings for each other and…you know…"

"We got the book. It's been really helpful. There are some things we don't want to try. Do you think that's bad? If we really love each other maybe we should try everything?" Bri asked.

"No, no, no. Different people like different things. You can love each other and not want to do everything that is in the book," Olivia explained.

"Okay, that's good. We didn't understand why it would feel good to do things that would hurt," Bri said.

"Remember when I went on that first bike ride with you and Deb, and it was especially long? I was definitely in pain, but I still wanted to go riding with Deb, because I liked spending time with her. I know a bike ride is different then

what the book shows, but it's the only thing I can think of to explain those things. People like to try different things sometimes. There are some folks who hate bike riding or exercise, because it doesn't feel all that good to them. Others like it. It's okay for everyone to decide what they do and don't like. Nobody is going to judge you and Siera, and you'll have to figure out on your own what you like."

"Okay, Aunt Olivia. You don't have to talk to us about sex. It's okay. We like figuring it out on our own. I want to talk to you later about something else. It's a surprise. Would that be okay?" Bri asked.

"Of course, sweetie," Olivia answered.

"Me too, I want to ask your opinion, Aunt Deb. Even though I think I kinda blew it," Siera said.

Bri pulled Siera close and wrapped her arm around Siera's waist. "Don't be sad, Siera, it was a good surprise. I don't mind that you blurted out how you want to marry me. I want that too."

"Okay, here's the plan. After you two sign the papers, we'll split up and have some special aunt time then we'll help you with your secret plans." Olivia winked. "I'm happy for you both."

Maybe Bri's plans to ask Siera to marry her wouldn't be a complete surprise, but that didn't matter. As long as she found the perfect ring, she'd make it as romantic as she could. She was excited, because she knew the ideal time was right around the corner. All their dreams were coming true. Everything would be perfect. Bri hoped Siera's mom would be happy for them too.

†

237

Olivia watched Deb run her hands through her wet hair. Deb was sexy. There was no debate about that. Olivia was kicking herself for waiting so long to realize and declare her feelings. Now that Carrie was back in the picture, she might lose Deb due to her lethargy. She'd taken things for granted and thought she had plenty of time to work out her emotions. How was it possible three years had passed, and she'd never forced herself to consider the possibility of them as a couple? She'd gotten lazy and fallen into an easy routine—one that included Deb as a central part of her world.

"Comparing BDSM with your out-of-shape ass from our first bike ride, really? Is that the best you could think of?" Deb started laughing.

"Ha, ha, smartass. I didn't see you stepping in to help me out," Olivia said.

"Why should I? Your analogy was nothing less than inspired. So, did you seriously want to continue to bike with me, despite all the pain of that very first ride?" Deb asked.

"It's a first date we'll never forget. We can tell that story to our grandchildren."

"Oh, look at you, trying out the flirtation thing. Not bad. It's not as clever as my attempts, but it was very sweet. I give it an eight on a ten-point scale."

"So, you're going to dinner tonight, huh?"

"Nice segue. Yes, I agreed to meet her for dinner tonight. She's taking me to Michael's on the Lake."

"Fancy, hope she chokes on a fishbone," Olivia murmured too low for Deb to hear.

"What was that?" Deb asked.

"Oh nothing. I hope you have a good time. Michael's is nice. They have good food. Not really my style of restaurant,

or yours, but to each their own. I suppose she's trying to impress you. Does it?"

"Does it what?" Deb asked.

"Impress you," Olivia answered.

Deb laughed. "No, I prefer slapping some veggie burgers on the grill and kicking back with Ben & Jerry's. You know that."

Olivia chuckled. "Yeah, I do."

"I told you I would call afterwards, and I will. We'll talk then," Deb said.

"I know. I can't help showing a few of my cards."

"Well, hallelujah. After three years, you've finally plucked those from your vest."

"I know. Believe me, I couldn't be sorrier for waiting so long," Olivia whispered.

CHAPTER TWENTY-FOUR

Deb looked around the dimmed room and the candles that cast a golden light behind Carrie. She wasn't sure why Carrie had picked this restaurant. It almost felt like they were returning to the scene of her previous crime. The one where she had the audacity to ask Carrie to marry her. That should have been her first clue things would not go well, but she shook away those maudlin thoughts. Carrie looked good, but then she always was a stunning woman. Deb had done the happy dance when she first heard Carrie was a lesbian. They were both so young in nursing school. Deb hadn't gotten the courage to ask her out until five years later, after they started working at the same hospital.

"You look good. You never age. How do you do that?" Deb asked.

Carrie offered her a small smile. "You're still the most beautiful woman I've ever laid my eyes on. I can't believe I didn't ask you out when we first met. I knew you were interested, but I guess I thought you were too serious for me.

You were so focused on school at the time. I'm glad you lightened up a bit."

"Why'd you leave?" Deb blurted out.

"I was scared. I've had a lot of time to think. Frankly, since I left, I haven't met anyone I click with. I never stopped loving you, Deb."

"You hurt me."

"I know I did. I had my reasons. Stupid reasons, really. So, who is this Olivia to you?"

"We're not sleeping together, if that's what you think," Deb answered.

"You looked awfully cozy."

"She's my best friend, and I love her."

"Are you in love with her? Have I waited too long?" Carrie asked.

Deb did not want to discuss her situation with Olivia. She was there to find out what went wrong with their relationship. She could deal with her feelings about Olivia later, after she understood how things had gone sideways.

"You still haven't told me why you didn't want to make a commitment. Everything was going fine. The minute I started talking about registering as domestic partners and having kids, you ran." Deb looked straight at Carrie and waited for her response.

"I know. I had some irrational thoughts. I admit my reasoning wasn't entirely sound, especially since I'm a nurse and know better. I couldn't see me pregnant, and you know that you getting pregnant wasn't a good idea, either. I know we could have taken an amniocentesis test, but I didn't want to have that conversation with you, knowing how you feel about Siera. She's a great kid and all that, but…"

"Are you seriously saying that genetics played a role?"

"I told you I wasn't being rational, and no, I'm not saying that now. What I'm saying is if we were faced with that decision, I knew you wouldn't want to abort. I would have. I've been telling myself that ever since we split up. I know the odds of either one of us having a Down's Syndrome child are so small, so I was being irrational."

"It's Down syndrome, not Down's. That is how little you know." Deb paused. "You're serious, aren't you?"

"See, that is why I didn't want to have this discussion. I knew you wouldn't react well to my opinion on this," Carrie replied.

"Are you fucking kidding me? You basically said Kathleen should have had the test and when she found out, she should have aborted. Siera is a great kid, and I'm proud to be her aunt."

"Being an aunt is easy. Besides, Siera's on the higher end of the functional scale. You can't say it hasn't been a challenge for Kathleen."

"Oh yeah, it's been a challenge for her all right, mainly due to narrow-minded, bigoted individuals like you who take one look at Siera's physical appearance and make all kinds of assumptions. You know what, Carrie, in case you aren't clear on this, there is no hope for us, especially now that I know your opinion about Siera and Bri. And in answer to your question about Olivia, yes, I fell in love with her almost immediately. She is a kind, loving, intelligent, open woman who understands how wonderful Siera and Bri really are. Neither of us would change one single thing about them."

"I'm sorry, Deb. I did not want to hurt your feelings, and I do know how wonderful they both are. You all have every right to be proud of them. I wouldn't wish for a gay child for

the very same reasons. It's too damn hard. I don't want that for my child, is that so difficult to understand?"

"Yeah, Carrie, it is. Look, I'm not saying you're a horrible person, but our fundamental beliefs about some very important issues are far too different to overcome. I do hope the world evolves a bit more, because it is those beliefs that make it so much more difficult for kids who are a little different, and that's just sad. I will always care about you, but I can't be with you. You made the right decision when you left," Deb answered.

"I guess that says it all. I had to try. At least I've been completely honest with you. I suppose I should wish you luck with Olivia. I do care enough about you to want you to be happy. If Olivia is the one to do that for you, then I hope it works. From my observation, she's in love with you. If you tell her how you feel about her, I'm sure it will work out for you."

"Well that's big of you to wish me luck. I guess I got my closure. You know, even if we never end up together, my relationship with Olivia will be ten times the depth of any relationship you and I could have had. I suppose I never realized how shallow you are."

"I was simply being honest," Carrie defended.

"I suppose that's true. I do respect your honesty. I just happen to believe your truth is shallow and narrow-minded. Good luck finding that perfection you seek, because Carrie, it doesn't exist."

†

Olivia couldn't help herself, she was pacing while waiting for Deb's call. Maybe she should step aside if there was a chance Deb and Carrie could make a go of it. But why

did Carrie leave in the first place? There was no way she would ever have made that mistake. Oh, who was she kidding? She'd been making a far greater mistake for the last three years by keeping Deb at arm's length. Well, she vowed to change that tonight, if things didn't work out with Carrie. She wasn't going to let one more day pass without telling Deb she'd fallen in love with her.

It was already nine o'clock. That wasn't a good sign. Deb promised she would call after dinner, but maybe she'd gone back to Carrie's place or Carrie had followed her back to her condo. Either scenario did not bode well for Olivia.

She was glad Bri had decided to spend the night with Siera at Kathleen's house, because if she still had a chance with Deb, she wanted to ask her to come over so they could have that talk.

Olivia hoped Jeremy had managed to convince Kathleen their graduation gift was a good thing. Olivia had also spilled the beans to Jeremy about finding the book and confirming her suspicions that Bri and Siera had ventured into an intimate relationship with one another. That would be something else Jeremy might have to convince his wife on. Sometimes, it took Kathleen a little time to get used to something that didn't exactly fit in her neat plans for Siera's future. Ultimately, Kathleen loved her daughter. Olivia didn't have concerns about her ability to come around.

Bri had asked Olivia to help pick out a ring, and Deb had let it slip that Siera had done the same thing with her. She didn't think either one was completely in the dark about the other's intent; they simply weren't privy to the specific details.

Olivia and Deb had both suggested the same thing. Since Siera and Bri met at the park, it would be the perfect place to

declare their love and ask that important question. They'd each come to that conclusion on their own, already, without much prompting from her or Deb.

The light knock interrupted her thoughts. When she opened the door, she saw Deb standing on the other side with a beautiful smile on her face. It was past the time to hold back. Olivia pulled Deb close and brought their lips together, exploring Deb's soft, generous mouth. The kiss started slow and increased in intensity, as she had pushed her tongue inside without experiencing a single bit of resistance from Deb, who matched her passion. Olivia couldn't tell who moaned first, as she pulled Deb inside.

Olivia's heart was pounding nearly out of her chest when they broke apart. "God, I've wanted to do that for so long. I didn't realize how badly I wanted to kiss you like that until a few days ago. I'm an idiot."

Deb touched Olivia's lips with her index finger. "Shhh. We should talk first, but let me give you the Reader's Digest version. Carrie and I are not getting back together, and I'm so glad you've crossed the line, because I'm going to interpret that as my cue to stomp all over your line and take this further, much further. Where's that book? Do you think the girls would care if we borrowed it for tonight?" Deb joked.

"Oh, it may be true it's been over four years since I've been intimate with anyone, but I think it's pretty much like riding a bike. I'm sure we'll figure it out. I want this, Deb. I want us."

"That's enough for me. I need to devour you first. We can talk more later on." Deb kicked off her sandals.

Olivia grabbed Deb's hand and tugged her along. "Time to take this to my bedroom. The girls are gone tonight, so if

you feel compelled to make a lot of noise, go for it. I like a vocal partner."

"Mmm, good to know. I'm very vocal, so no worries there."

When they reached Olivia's bedroom, she gently pushed Deb on her bed and climbed on top. She began by nibbling on Deb's bottom lip and then working her way down, kissing Deb's neck and stroking her hand down Deb's collarbone. This was one of her favorite places on a woman. As Olivia reached the top button of Deb's shirt, she began to slowly reveal olive-toned skin and a lacy, nude-colored bra. She kissed the part of Deb's breast that peeked out above the lace and ran her finger down the crevice. Once the shirt was completely open, she pushed it off Deb's shoulders and reached behind to undo her bra and let her breasts fall out.

"I seem to be at a disadvantage here. Quid pro quo. If you take something off of me, you need to lose an article of your clothing. I vote for the shirt," Deb said.

Olivia lifted her t-shirt over her head and quickly removed her sports bra. "That's fair, now we're even."

Olivia moved her hands down Deb's body, stroking her stomach, and hovered at the top of the dress pants that hung low on her hips. She ran her fingers along the band, teasing as the tips brushed along the edge of lace panties. Back and forth, she caressed Deb's silky-smooth skin in excruciatingly slow movements.

Deb reached down to undo the top button, and Olivia brushed her hand aside. "You're going to make me crazy, aren't you?" Deb asked.

"Mmm hmm, patience," Olivia answered and popped it open. Pulling on the zipper revealed matching lace

underwear. She splayed open her fingers and grazed them over the top of the soft silk.

Deb squirmed underneath her feathery touch. "I think maybe you should remove my pants, lest they become too wrinkled."

"Uh huh, and do your panties wrinkle as well?" Olivia asked.

"Oh yes, they do." Deb lifted her bottom, and Olivia tugged until she'd pulled them off. She moved from the bed, carefully folded them, and placed them on the top of the dresser.

By the time Olivia returned, Deb had wriggled out of her silk underwear. Olivia gathered them to add to the folded stack.

Olivia's breath hitched, as she looked at Deb's naked form laid out. Her arousal went through the stratosphere. Deb was a beautiful woman, and Olivia wanted to devour every inch of her glorious body.

Deb's finger swirled in the air. "I do believe you owe me two pieces of clothing."

Olivia smiled and shimmied out of her shorts. Like a cat, she crawled over the top of Deb and began her worship. Starting on her lips, Olivia sucked, nibbled, and licked, prompting a loud vocalization from Deb. Olivia moved on top of Deb, as their naked bodies connected.

"Oh my God, you feel so good," Deb exclaimed.

Deb tried to flip Olivia over, but Olivia captured her hands and brought them above her head in a gentle restraint.

"Let me love on you the way I've imagined in my head. I can hardly believe my nighttime fantasies are about to come true," Olivia whispered.

Deb's eyes opened wide. "You've dreamed about this?"

"Many times," Olivia admitted.

Olivia moved her lips down Deb's beautiful curves, pausing on her breast and gently biting down, as the small bud pebbled in response. She stroked the sides of Deb's breasts as she sucked each nipple. Her hands traveled down over Deb's taut stomach, and she kissed her navel. When her fingers reached the apex of Deb's dark, neatly trimmed patch of curly hair, she stopped her reverence and looked into Deb's aroused eyes. "So beautiful."

"Please, don't stop," Deb pleaded.

Olivia moved her fingers through the patch of hair and felt the moisture, as she stroked Deb's swollen labia.

Deb began to move under her.

Olivia separated Deb's lips and brought her mouth to the top of her hood, as she slowly licked the most sensitive part of Deb's body.

Deb groaned. "Go inside, fill me up."

With her index and middle fingers, Olivia penetrated Deb's opening. Deb's body bucked, as she matched Olivia's movements, stroke for stroke.

Olivia was sure if anyone else were in the house they would certainly hear Deb's loud moans and encouragements to continue. Deb's vocal outpouring created an immediate response in Olivia, as her own arousal increased exponentially.

"Mmm, yes, almost there, don't stop, oh God, please don't stop what you're doing."

Olivia's fingers curled up inside of Deb's vagina, as she felt the soft spongy area where she knew Deb's G-spot was located. Ten seconds later, she felt the contractions pulse against her fingers.

A loud, long moan reached Olivia's ears, as she felt Deb's orgasm. She slowed her touch and extended the contractions until she had pulled out every second of pleasure.

"Holy shit, I think you went from not touching your racing bike to winning the Tour de France," Deb declared.

Olivia chuckled before placing a gentle kiss on her lips. "Nothing better than hopping back on a bike."

"You got that right. My turn."

Before Olivia had a chance to react, Deb had flipped her on her back. "You're a lot stronger than you look."

"Slow or fast?" Deb asked.

"Well, considering I'm about ready to explode. Fast please."

"Slow it is." Deb shot Olivia an evil grin.

As Deb moved across her body, Olivia groaned.

CHAPTER TWENTY-FIVE

Kathleen woke up to find Jeremy's long arms wrapped around her body. She was thankful Jeremy liked to spoon, especially in the morning right before they woke up. The girls were already long gone. It was Saturday—one of their busiest days. She cringed, as she remembered the comment she'd made about their business being a hobby and Siera securing a real job after earning her Bachelor's degree. On some level, she knew she'd overstepped, but the horse was already out of the barn. After Carrie had made her comments, Kathleen had added to the insensitivity. Thank goodness, Jeremy was so level headed. She felt blessed she had a forgiving daughter. Bri was equally good-natured, when Kathleen had called and begged Siera to bring Bri over to spend the night. She'd needed to make amends, and she'd done that.

Kathleen had to admit Bri and Siera adored one another, and their business was going strong. It wasn't like they were moving across the country. In reality, the house wasn't very

far away at all—just down the road. She wasn't losing her daughter at all. However, it did scare her when Siera declared her intent to marry Bri. Marriage was an entirely different issue that Kathleen hadn't quite worked through yet. Jeremy had mentioned he wanted to talk with her today about something else, and she knew by the way he hedged she wasn't going to like what he had to share.

As Kathleen slipped out of bed, Jeremy opened his eyes and smiled.

"Any chance you can get the coffee started? I'll be up in a few minutes and can make us some breakfast," Jeremy offered.

"Deal," Kathleen answered.

Jeremy always made the coffee too strong and she would complain loudly. So they'd eased into a routine where she would make the coffee, and he would cook up the steel-cut oats. On occasion, they would have blueberry pancakes. Kathleen always made those, because Jeremy wasn't as meticulous about placing the blueberries evenly on the batter while they cooked.

Jeremy yawned and scratched his behind, as he walked into the kitchen.

"Real attractive, hon," Kathleen exclaimed and shot him a disgusted look.

"What?"

"Do all men scratch their ass in the morning and rearrange their family jewels in the evening without any concern for who might be watching?"

"Yes, yes we do. It's a rite of passage we teach our offspring. Toby took to it like a fish in water." Jeremy grinned.

"Just wash your hands, please, before making the oats."

ff4

Annette Mori

Kathleen finished making the coffee, poured two cups, and set them on the kitchen table. She sat there sipping her coffee and watching her husband in the quiet solitude of the morning, while she started to slowly wake up.

Jeremy set a bowl of oats in front of Kathleen. Honey was already on the table, and Kathleen spooned a generous amount on her cereal. Jeremy squeezed coconut nectar on his.

"Okay, honey, time to come clean. I've had my first cup of coffee. Tell me whatever it is you believe I'll go ballistic over," Kathleen said.

"Olivia found a lesbian sex book in Bri's nightstand, and she's convinced Bri and Siera are having an intimate relationship with one another, beyond kissing," Jeremy blurted out.

"What? How could Olivia allow that to happen? Are they having sex in Siera's bedroom too? I thought their relationship was innocent, and now you're telling me they're having sex right under our noses, in *my* house," Kathleen yelled.

"*Our* house, and I think you forget Siera is almost twenty-three and perfectly capable of making adult decisions."

"Stop, just stop. You know as well as I do that Siera is innocent. I don't give a shit about that old argument I should treat her like any other normal adult, because she isn't. Bri is taking advantage of her innocence, and you idiots are all encouraging it," Kathleen raged.

"Are you actually listening to yourself? You do realize Bri is a sweet, loving, young woman who loves our daughter. I, for one, will be damn proud to welcome her to the family. You will not interfere. I know it takes you some time to get

252

used to things, but I swear Kathleen, if you interfere in your daughter's happiness, I will never forgive you. Like you never forgave my initial reaction to Siera. I was wrong then, and you are wrong now."

"Are you actually suggesting I should be happy about Siera's declaration she wants to marry Bri and have sex with her?" Kathleen asked.

"Yes, I am. You take whatever time you need, but when those two girls become officially engaged, and they will, we will celebrate with them and throw the best damn wedding this town has ever seen. If you can't come to terms with this, then you better fucking keep your mouth shut. I'll not lose my daughter over your narrow-minded, knee-jerk reaction to something you, of all people, should know better." Jeremy's chair screeched across the wood floor and punctuated his position, as he stalked out of the room.

"At least my sister isn't a low-life, slime bag like your brother," Kathleen yelled to the empty room.

†

Deb had her hand propped up on her head, as she watched Olivia's golden hair fan over the pillow. Olivia had a slight smile, as she continued to sleep. Deb reached across with her free hand and caressed Olivia's cheek. They'd made love several times, but Deb had restrained herself from telling Olivia she'd fallen madly in love with her three years ago and wanted to explore a future with her. She could see herself asking Olivia to marry her and having at least two kids. Olivia was everything she'd always wanted in a loving partner.

Olivia's silver-blue eyes popped open. "Are you watching me sleep?"

"Mmm hmm. I could get used to waking up next to you every morning." Deb bent to kiss Olivia. "In a bed and not on the couch," she amended.

Olivia chuckled. "It certainly is more comfortable than my couch when you fall asleep on movie nights."

"And much nicer than your guest room," Deb added.

Olivia's phone buzzed on her nightstand. She quirked her eyebrow, as she saw the screen and recognized Jeremy's number. Placing it on her forehead she said, "I predict this is the warning call from Jeremy. He talked to Kathleen this morning and is now calling to provide the grim update. You'd better hightail it to your sister's so we can double team her before she does something rash she will regret."

"Shit. Why do I have to play cleanup?"

"Because you're good at it." Olivia pressed the button. "Hey, Jeremy…. Yep, that's what we thought…. No, Deb's right here…. Seriously, I am not dignifying that with an answer." Olivia waved her hand at Deb, who raised her eyebrow. "I'm sending her over right now." Olivia sighed. "Sure, come on over, and no, you aren't getting any details. We need to deal with this emergency and not get sidetracked. I swear guys are worse than women." Olivia chuckled as she ended the call.

Deb smiled. "You can tell Jeremy. He means well. He's been rooting for me."

"You talked about us?"

Deb pushed the covers aside and jumped out of bed. "Sure." She frowned, as she looked at the neat pile of clothes on the dresser. "Well, it looks like I'll be wearing my good clothes when I visit my sister." Her face brightened. "Hey, maybe that will distract her from the bomb Jeremy detonated."

"Don't count on it. Not that I don't want to spend an enjoyable morning in bed with you, doing scrumptious things to that smoking body of yours, but I think you'd better hurry. Hurricane Kathleen might head over to the clinic before you have a chance to stop her."

"I know, I know, I'm on it." Deb slipped on her pants, leaving the underwear, and buttoned her shirt after putting on her bra. She quickly kissed Olivia. "Wish me luck."

"Oh honey, you're going to need more than luck, but you got it, babe."

"You know, I already feel lucky. I finally got you in the sack. Today is my lucky day. I will make sure she doesn't blow her stack and let shit fly everywhere."

Olivia smacked Deb's rear. "Got me in the sack, huh? I do believe I made the first move."

"Mmm hmm and what a move that was. I'm coming back, and we're going to have our own serious conversation." Deb pulled Olivia into an embrace and gave her a proper kiss before running out the door.

The kiss left Olivia breathless, and she knew today was the day to admit she'd fallen in love with the vivacious woman.

†

Kathleen had never seen Jeremy so angry. Clearly, he was still upset that their biggest fights usually prompted her to throw up his initial reaction to Siera. It always hit a raw nerve. She knew that, like she realized it was definitely a below-the-belt hit. Ironically, he'd stomped out of the house before she had regurgitated that old argument. He'd been the first to mention it this time. Kathleen was pissed, and his

words did not penetrate her stubbornness, regardless of his dramatic exit.

She grabbed her keys and stomped out the door, ready to go to the clinic to stop the nonsense. Yes, Siera was almost twenty-three, but certainly, her maturity level was more along the lines of a sixteen-year-old. What mother would let their sixteen-year-old have sex with her girlfriend? She was right about this no matter what Jeremy, Olivia, or Deb said about it. Sometimes, you had to fight for what was right. It wasn't about Siera being a lesbian, though she wasn't necessarily convinced about that either. It was about all the added complications sex and marriage would bring to the couple, who were far too young to consider the consequences, even if they were one hundred percent sure about their sexual preference.

Deb's car screeched into her driveway and blocked her from leaving. Kathleen unclipped her seat belt, jumped out, and slammed her car door, as she stomped toward Deb. She motioned for Deb to open her window. "Get out of my way, Deb, and stay the fuck out of this. I know Jeremy sent you."

"Yes, he did, and you're going to thank both of us later."

"I swear, I'm going to punch you in the throat if you don't move." Kathleen put her hands on her hips.

"Sheez. You definitely got Mom's temper. Give me five minutes. If you still want to zoom to the clinic, make an ass out of yourself, and do irreparable damage, I won't stop you, but I will say I told you so after the fact."

Kathleen turned her wrist over and glanced at her watch. "You've got four minutes and fifty seconds left."

"Uh. My five minutes starts when you plop your ass down in your kitchen after pouring me a cup of coffee. I need a clear head, and I haven't had my coffee yet."

"Fine." Kathleen pivoted on her heel and stomped back inside.

†

Deb puffed out her cheeks, blew out the air, and followed her sister into the house. She sat at the table and gathered her strength. For a second, her mind wandered to her night with Olivia and she smiled.

"What the hell are you smiling about?" Kathleen sniped.

"I'll tell you after I've saved you from running off half-cocked. Let me ask you this, Kathleen."

"What?"

"Do you love your daughter?"

"Of course I do. What the hell kind of question is that?"

"Good, because I was beginning to think you stopped loving her. Right about now, it seems you're about to do something that demonstrates the exact opposite."

Kathleen crossed her arms across her chest. "I am not."

"Coffee, please," Deb responded.

Kathleen poured coffee into a cup and set it and the cream and sugar in front of Deb. "Why is it that any time I try to do anything to protect my daughter, everyone tosses that lame argument in my face?"

"I'm going to ignore that for a second." Deb fixed her coffee, pouring cream and dishing a spoonful of sugar into the cup. After taking a sip, she continued. "Ahhhh. Do you think Siera is happy right now?"

"Yes," Kathleen answered hesitantly.

"Was she happy three years ago, before she met Bri?" Deb asked.

"Oh, for Christ's sake, what does that have to do with the price of tea in China?"

257

"Absolutely everything. Siera knows how she feels about Bri. Give her some fucking credit and stop being such a goddamned prude. So, they're having sex and expressing their love physically for one another. She can't get pregnant, so what are you really worried about?" Deb asked.

Kathleen slumped in her chair. "What will people think about me, if I let this happen and do nothing?"

"Let what happen? Let them freely express their love like any other normal couple, let them get married, again like any other normal couple? Since when do you care what people think?"

"They'll be picked on. People can be so cruel," Kathleen defended.

"Yes, they can, and they have been. Siera has faced that her whole life, and now that she has other people in her life to love and support her, she feels better about herself. She absolutely glows around Bri. Please, Kathleen, don't do anything to take that away from her or give her the message that her love for Bri is somehow wrong. You know how sensitive she is to how others perceive her. She needs your support, not your disapproval. You'll lose her, if you don't accept her. She'll gravitate toward Olivia, and I'm here to tell you straight up we will be there for her if you reject her."

"I'm already afraid of losing her. She's always confided everything to me, and now I'm the last to know about this recent development. My little bird is leaving the nest, and I'm not ready."

Deb stood and put her hand on her sister's shoulder. "Let us help you get ready, because Siera will fly back now and again. She'll want the help and support from her mother, not her aunts. Just so you know, Siera picked out a ring for Bri, and she will ask Bri to marry her. The only reason she asked

258

me to help her pick out the ring and think of a romantic way to ask was because you let her know you weren't on board. Keep expressing that disapproval, and you'll push her away for good. Since you have more panache than I do, please don't make me have to step in to help her pick out her wedding dress."

"You'd probably pick out a tux to make it easier."

Deb chuckled. "It's a good idea."

"Siera likes dresses."

"So, do I need to call the rest of the cavalry to get you to listen to reason, or has our little talk resulted in a successful mission?" Deb asked.

Kathleen looked at her watch. "You're losing your touch. It took ten minutes." She stood up and Deb accepted a heartfelt hug.

"I love you, Sis. I knew there was some logical reason for your reaction. When I have kids and start to hover, I know you'll return the favor," Deb said.

"Okay, can we move to a new subject? Can I ask what's going on with you, because I definitely detect a spring in your step?"

"I spent the night with Olivia," Deb admitted.

"So what, you crash at her place all the time."

"No, I mean we finally did the horizontal mambo."

"Gosh, Deb, I know you care about Olivia. Why so crass?"

"You're right. We made love last night; it wasn't sex. I love her, and I'm petrified she doesn't return the depth of my feelings. Although, I have to say, I really felt the emotion last night, and I don't think I was the only one."

"Did you tell her you love her?"

"God no, it's too soon for that."

"No, it isn't. You two have been in love with each other for three years. It's about damn time you both fessed up," Kathleen said.

"You invited Carrie to the party to prompt a response from Olivia, didn't you?"

Kathleen shrugged. "Jealousy works."

"Kathleen, I don't even know where to start with how wrong that logic is. At the same time, I have to admit to being grateful things have turned out the way they did. I went to dinner with Carrie last night and learned the reason why she left."

"Really, why?"

"You don't want to know, and I am not going to tell you, because I just got you calmed down. Please, Kathleen, let it go. I'm happy and that's all that matters."

"All right. I do like Olivia. I think you two are good for each other. I approve."

Deb chuckled. "Well that's good, but I don't need your approval. Just like Siera doesn't need your approval either. Your support is a whole other story."

"Enough said. I got the sharp point of your tongue earlier. Let me rephrase. You have my support, and so will Siera. Point, set, and match. You all win. God, now I have to tell Jeremy he was right again. He'll be an insufferable ass."

"One that you love. By the way, will you finally give the big lug a break and forgive him for the errors of his youth? He embraced everything about Siera a long time ago, and he loves her. Allow him his humanness. Everyone makes mistakes; the important thing is to learn from them. It was a knee-jerk reaction of a man in his twenties. You know women mature faster than men."

"You're right, and my apology is long overdue. Thanks, Sis."

"Anytime."

CHAPTER TWENTY-SIX

Siera stuck her hand in her shorts pocket, making sure the ring was still there. Her hand began to sweat. She was nervous. She'd practiced her speech in the mirror, after her shower that morning. Aunt Deb had told her to talk from her heart, and she was sure the only possible answer to the important question was *yes*.

They came to their bench—the one they always sat on when they fed the geese and the one where she'd first seen Bri the day they'd met over three years ago.

Bri seemed nervous, and Siera was worried. Maybe Bri already guessed the question, but wasn't ready to get married. *Is Bri worried she'll hurt my feelings?* That didn't make sense. Hadn't Bri already said she wanted them to marry?

They sat on the bench, and a group of geese waddled close, expecting their birdseed. Bri must have had something

important on her mind. "I forgot to bring their food," Bri said.

"It's okay, I don't think they'll starve."

"I have a question to ask you, Siera. I'm not very good with words. Aunt Olivia said I shouldn't worry. She said I'd know what to say when we sat down, but I'm nervous."

"You can ask me anything. I'd do anything for you, Bri. I love you."

Bri picked up her backpack, unzipped the front pocket, and took out a small white box. She opened the box and showed Siera a simple gold ring with a pink stone in the center. Pink was Siera's favorite color.

"Siera, I love you very much. I want us to be together forever. It's legal for two girls to get married. Will you marry me?" Bri asked.

Siera smiled at Bri and pulled her own ring box from her shorts pocket. When she opened the royal blue box, a rose gold ring with a blue opal sparkled in the sunshine. "I'll marry you if you marry me. I love you too. I had this whole speech I tried to memorize. I can't remember all the words now."

Bri threw her arms around Siera. "I'm so happy. We can make living together official." Bri giggled. "Now, we won't be living in sin. It's not a diamond. Aunt Olivia said I didn't have to buy you a diamond. Nowadays, people get each other different stones—depending on their favorite colors. The woman in the store said it's tourmaline. I asked her to show me a ring with a pink stone."

"I love it. It's perfect. Do you like your ring?" Siera asked.

"Oh yes, blue is my favorite color."

"I know. It matches your eyes," Siera said.

"Should we go back and show Aunt Olivia and Deb?" Bri asked.

"Yeah, I can't wait to show them my ring."

"Will your mom be mad?"

Siera frowned. "I don't know. Aunt Deb said not to worry about Mom. She had it handled. She said I should do whatever my heart told me was right."

"I love your Aunt Deb," Bri said.

"Me too, but I love my mom, too."

"I know, it'll all work out. Don't be sad, Siera, I love you." Bri put her arm around Siera when she stood up, and they began walking to their bikes.

"I love you too, Bri. I have since the first day I saw you."

†

After talking some sense into her sister, Deb rushed home to take a shower, change her clothes, and check on Socks. She'd called Olivia and asked if she wanted to take a short bike ride before the girls returned. Olivia wanted an update on the conversation with Kathleen. Deb promised to bring her up to date but reassured her everything was fine. Jeremy had stopped by Olivia's for a short while, then gone for a drive to calm down. Olivia remarked she'd never seen him that upset, but he had assured her some time alone to settle down was what he needed.

Deb knew they still had to have a serious talk about where Olivia saw their relationship going. She was hoping they were on the same page, because she knew Olivia could break her heart even more than Carrie had. Hoping for a positive outcome, Deb brought clothes to change into after their bike ride. She already had an extra toothbrush for the

multiple occasions when she'd crashed at Olivia's house; it wasn't uncommon to take a shower there in the morning. Maybe Olivia would float the idea of living together. A girl could dream.

Neither of them wanted to broach the subject of their budding relationship while they enjoyed a pleasant bike ride, and the procrastination extended after they'd finished their outing.

Things took a pleasant turn, when Olivia playfully offered to share the shower, so they could conserve water. They made love again. After playtime, they didn't want to ruin the afterglow of their newly found love by defining anything, but it was just a matter of time before they needed to open that door.

When the girls came home, a familiar sight met their eyes—Deb had her head on Olivia's shoulder, as they lay settled in front of the television, watching an old movie. The excited girls bounced into the room.

Both of them started talking at once.

"Aunt Deb, Olivia, we're engaged," Siera exclaimed at the same time Bri blurted out, "I asked Siera to marry me. She asked too. We're official now."

Olivia stroked Deb's shoulder before standing up and accepting hugs from the two girls. "Congratulations. I am so happy for both of you."

Deb was the next person to experience their exuberance, as they turned to step into her open arms. "Ditto. Come on, Olivia, we're taking the girls to dinner to celebrate. Siera, have you called your parents yet to tell them the good news?"

Siera looked down at her feet. "No, I'm afraid Mom will be mad."

Deb pulled her back into another embrace. "Oh honey, I don't think you have to worry about that. I talked to your mom today. I promise she'll be happy for you. Do you want me to call and invite her and your dad?"

Siera nodded.

"What about Toby? When does he get home?"

"He doesn't usually come home until later. Probably close to six thirty," Siera answered.

"Well, let's call him and tell him to meet us at the restaurant. He can order while we're having dessert. I'm sure they won't mind us hanging out a little longer. After all, it's a celebration."

"Thanks, Aunt Deb," Siera said.

"You're welcome, sweetie."

"Bri, I know your mom and dad won't be able to make it to the celebration tonight, but we'd better give them a call and let them know the good news. Do you want to make the call or would you like me to talk to your mom first?" Olivia asked.

Bri frowned. "Do you think they'll be mad?"

"They might be a little surprised..." Olivia paused. "Why don't you let me talk to them for you? Honestly, I think they'll be very happy for you."

Bri wrapped her arms around Olivia's waist again. "Oh, thank you, Aunt Olivia. Mom listens to you. Sometimes she treats me like a child. I'm not a child. I wish she could see for herself how much I've grown up."

"Oh honey, all parents do that. It's in their DNA. It's because they love you so much, and they want you to be safe, happy, and healthy," Olivia answered.

"I know. Siera's mom is like that too. It's 'cause she loves Siera, right? Not because she doesn't like me," Bri said.

Olivia put her arm around Bri. "Sweetheart, Kathleen likes you. What's not to like? You're a great kid."

Bri stomped her foot. "I'm not a kid."

"Oh, my bad, you're a wonderful young woman. Jeremy and Kathleen, and Deb, all love you. Don't worry about a thing. Your mom and dad will welcome Siera into the family with open arms. How about if I invite them up for an extended visit? With your business and my clinic, it probably isn't feasible to take a long vacation, but I'll bet your parents will want to visit to get to know Siera a little bit better."

"Oh, will you do that, Aunt Olivia? That would be great," Bri answered.

"Sure, honey."

Siera shuffled her feet. "I really love Bri and want her parents to like me. I can promise them I'll be good to her."

"They're gonna love you," Deb assured. "They met you before, so it's not like they don't know you at all."

"You two need to stop worrying, because this is a celebration. The most important thing is the two of you love each other. Everyone can see how happy you both are," Olivia said.

†

Kathleen was sitting on the couch, debating whether she should call Jeremy to let him know the storm had passed. She was starting to worry. Normally when Jeremy left in a huff, he came back after a few hours. It was nearly dinnertime, and he still wasn't home.

Kathleen was relieved when she heard the whir of the garage door. She waited patiently until he walked all the way into the room. "You were right, and I love you for standing up to me. I want you to know, though Deb was the one to finally get through to me, I did hear you. I know this is twenty-three years too late, but I need you to know that, in almost every possible way, I consider you the better parent. I forgave you for your initial reaction a long time ago. It's a low blow whenever I bring that up in an argument, and I'm sorry for that. You love Siera without strings attached, and you always consider her feelings above anything else. Sometimes, my vision for Siera's future gets in the way of her ultimate happiness. Now, I would appreciate it very much if you wouldn't dance around taunting me about how you're always right."

Jeremy laughed and sat next to his wife, gathering her in his arms. "I think I need a little more incentive, or I'll be wiggling my fine ass in two seconds. What'll I get for not chanting, I was right, I was right, I was right? Let me give you a hint, it involves getting hot and sweaty."

"That could be fun. Done. In fact, the girls are still out and about, and Toby won't be home for at least another hour or two." Kathleen wiggled her eyebrows.

Kathleen's smartphone blared loudly and interrupted their prelude to make up sex. She picked up her phone and glanced at the screen. "It's Deb. I better answer it."

"She'll call back," Jeremy argued.

"I'll be quick." Kathleen pressed the answer button. "Hey, what's up?… I guess, after our little talk earlier today, I'm not surprised.… Don't worry, I've come to terms with this, and you know I am happy for them. We'd love to join the party.… Yeah, Toby can join us later.… Oh my God, I

get to plan a wedding. It doesn't get any better than that.... Yeah, yeah, yeah, I know it's their wedding, but the mother of the bride does have an important role—you have to give me that."

Jeremy was jumping up and down, pumping his fist in the air. "Did Siera finally ask Bri?"

Kathleen waved her hand. "Shh, I'm trying to get the details.... No Jeremy is acting like a goofball.... Okay, we're on our way, and Siera and Bri can give us all the details."

Kathleen ended the call, and Jeremy wrapped her in a bear hug while he lifted her in the air and swung her around.

"I'm gonna look dashing in a tux," Jeremy exclaimed.

Kathleen took his face in her hands and planted a big kiss on his lips. "Yes, you definitely are. We need to head to Olivia's, and then we'll decide where to go for dinner. I can't wait to start planning the big event. Siera really does love Bri, doesn't she?"

"She does, hon, every bit as much as I love you. They were made for each other, like you are the lid to my pot."

CHAPTER TWENTY-SEVEN

Deb studied the smiling faces surrounding her at the table. Bri and Siera were beaming with joy, and it was infectious. Kathleen and Jeremy looked like they'd reached a whole new level of love and understanding. The one-two punch earlier in the day must have caused Kathleen to do some serious soul searching, and it had paid off.

Toby slung his arm around his sister and kissed her cheek, telling her how happy he was for her and Bri. He genuinely loved both girls. Although he was younger than either of them, he behaved like their older brother. He was equally protective of Bri and had always treated her like another sister.

Deb was sitting next to Olivia and imagined her own elation was evident by her perpetual smile. Olivia would glance at her every few minutes and squeeze the hand she held under the table.

Toby plopped on the seat next to Deb. "Hey, Aunt Deb, why the shit-eating grin? Did you and Olivia finally muff dive on each other?"

Kathleen reached across the table and smacked her son. "I swear. Where the hell did your filter run off to?"

"Okay, how about, when did you two decide to play, *Hello Kitty*?" Toby lifted his hand and Deb met his in a fist bump.

Toby was not the only one who laughed, Olivia put her hand in front of her mouth trying to control herself.

"Jeremy, would you please talk to your son?" Kathleen huffed.

"What? Olivia's laughing, and Deb just fist bumped him. I'm pretty sure they're not offended," Jeremy answered. "So…any chance we'll get an answer to his question?"

"We're working on establishing the boundaries to our relationship, but yes things have shifted," Olivia answered. "Your aunt is very special to me."

Deb was anxious to corner Olivia after the celebration to get a clearer definition on how special she was to Olivia. She let herself imagine Olivia might have fallen in love with her over the years. It would be a dream come true. For a minute, she reveled in that fantasy. Maybe, over time, the relationship would develop and she would be celebrating with her family over their engagement. The sudden realization of her own hopes scared her. She'd been there before, and it hadn't worked out. Olivia was not Carrie. She had to remember that. The sooner she laid her cards on the table, the better. She needed to know where this was going, because she could not survive a repeat of her five-year relationship with Carrie to end up broken hearted again.

"Are you okay?" Olivia whispered.

"Yes, can we talk later tonight?" Deb asked.

"I was hoping you would stay with me tonight," Olivia replied hesitantly.

"I'd love to."

Olivia's smile lit up her face, and Deb basked in the warmth of the love poured out in that simple smile. Everything felt right, as if tectonic plates that remained frustratingly out of sync for three years had finally shifted into place. It certainly felt like an earthquake when Olivia rocked Deb's world the previous night. She grinned in remembrance.

"Stop thinking dirty thoughts until I can get you all alone again and take advantage of those delicious reflections," Olivia joked.

"What was that?" Kathleen asked.

"Nothing," Deb answered. "At least nothing we'll admit to."

†

Kathleen had seen how pure the love was between Bri and Siera. It was as if the fog had lifted and she could finally see what was clearly in front of her face and had been for a very long time. Kathleen wasn't a prude, and having *seen the light*, she was okay with Siera and Bri spending the night together. Kathleen had made the suggestion that the two of them come back to the house and stay the night. She had watched her sister at dinner. It was time to do something nice for her, considering how she'd been the one to get through to her about Siera.

It surprised Kathleen to realize she didn't mind if the girls did more exploration behind closed doors in her house.

She didn't want to think about the specifics of what might be occurring. What mother wanted to imagine her child having sex? Jeremy had smiled at her invitation, letting her know how proud he was of her ability to do a one-eighty. Of course, Siera's bedroom was a fair distance from the master. Kathleen was thankful, because imagining her daughter was having sex and hearing it were two completely different things.

After the girls retreated to Siera's bedroom, Jeremy grabbed her hand and dragged her to their own private love nest. He pushed her against the door and mashed their lips together. Breathing heavily, he ran his hands along her back and across her ass.

"Do you know how hot you are right now? I've been patiently waiting all night long to get you all alone. I am so fucking proud of you that you invited Siera and Bri back to the house," Jeremy exclaimed.

"So, did you catch the looks between Deb and Olivia? Do you think they were playing *Hello Kitty* tonight before dinner? Or what did Toby say again?" Kathleen laughed.

Jeremy joined her laughter. "Something about muff diving, and before you climb all over my ass, he did not get that from me. I'm absolutely positive they are at that 'can't hardly keep their hands off each other' point in their relationship. You might get your wish about having ultimate control over the wedding plans. They'll be far too distracted."

"Is Olivia finally ready to let Deb love her? I'd hate for Deb to get hurt again. Do you think I should have a talk with her?"

"Oh no, no, no, no. You stay out of it. Besides, you'll be far too busy playing overbearing mother as you completely

take over the planning of the wedding. Don't you think that's a sufficient amount of interference to satisfy your need for control?"

Kathleen smacked Jeremy in the chest. "That better be a joke. You're not worried about Deb getting hurt again?"

"No, I'm not. Remember, I'm the one who pegged Olivia as a lesbian from the very start, even though you were skeptical. From what I've observed, she's crazy about Deb and has finally experienced her 'ah ha' moment. I will admit that inviting Carrie to the party was an act of brilliance and probably responsible for prompting her moment of clarity," Jeremy responded.

"I do like being right. I was right. I was right. I was right," Kathleen chanted.

"If I agree, can we get back to my expert attempt at seduction—before it was so rudely interrupted by your need to poke your nose in your sister's business?" Jeremy asked.

Kathleen smacked him in the chest again. "Keep up your joking, and you'll find your pillow and blanket tossed on the couch and the bedroom door locked. The only kisses you'll get are from the cats."

Jeremy pulled Kathleen tight and began kissing her. "God, I love you."

Kathleen melted into his embrace, as she let him lead her to the bed and begin to remove her clothes.

†

Olivia held Deb's hand and kept the connection as they entered Olivia's house. When Olivia started to lead her into the bedroom, Deb stopped and gently nudged her toward the living room. She needed to know where the relationship was

heading. If they weren't traveling in the same direction, Deb vowed to set the boundaries, no matter how difficult that might be. She would go back to being friends before she would agree to an occasional roll in the hay minus any commitment.

"Can we talk first, please?"

Olivia nodded. "Yeah, we should talk. I guess it's long overdue."

"I'm going to lay things on the line. I want more than a spontaneous night of passion here and there. I did enough casual after Carrie dumped me. I'm at the age where I want to build a life. I need commitment." Deb led Olivia to the couch, and they sat down next to each other.

Olivia's nose crinkled in confusion. "We did share the same experience last night, didn't we? Last night wasn't only sex for me, Deb. We made love. I don't share myself like that with anyone. You knew you were the first person I let in since Irene. How could you possibly think I'd want something different?"

Deb couldn't help the tear that leaked out. "I couldn't stop myself from falling. I knew you weren't interested in a relationship, but I fell in love with you anyway. Now that you've opened the door, I can't help hoping…" she choked on her words.

Olivia pulled her into an embrace and rubbed her back as she murmured, "Oh Deb, I'm so sorry, I should have told you last night. Despite all my efforts to stay away from love, you wormed your way in. You, silly woman, have to know how besotted I am with you. I love you, Deb, and I was just too damn stubborn to admit it until now."

Deb's bleary eyes met Olivia's own watery blue ones. "You mean that? Because I won't let you take back the words after you confirm it."

"Every single word, Deb, every single word. I love you, and I want to make a life with you. Do you think we can date for a little bit before, you know, rings and all that? I don't want to take any attention away from our two lovebirds. Let's get them married first, okay?"

"That sounds like a good plan, but I don't know if I'll want to wake up alone ever again. This morning felt so right. I've been crashing here for three years now, but today when I woke up next to you, I thought to myself I'd like to do this every morning for the rest of our lives. I hope that doesn't scare you away, because it's how I feel. Any ideas on how we deal with that?"

"Nope, it doesn't scare me away. There's a simple solution. We can either go back and forth between my house and your condo, or you can sell your condo and move in with me." Olivia grinned.

Deb took a big breath. "Do you think maybe we can look around for a house we can pick out together? Not today, but sometime in the future."

Olivia turned her head and glanced at the picture of Irene and her that Deb was staring at. "Oh honey, of course. My epiphany is so new, but that doesn't make it any less true. I promise not to let a lingering memory of someone I loved very much put a wedge in our love."

"I'm not asking you to forget Irene. I'm asking that we have the chance to create new memories in a home we pick out together. You know you can talk about her."

"I know I can. Thank you."

"I guess, in many ways, losing Irene in a car crash was harder than if it had been a long, lingering illness. I suppose both tragedies have their own challenges. You never got to say goodbye, did you?"

Olivia's eyes shifted down. "No, I didn't. At first, when the police officer came to the door, I couldn't wrap my head around what had happened. She was so young. I haven't been able to spread her ashes yet, and it's been six years since she died. I'm a horrible person."

Deb pulled Olivia back into her arms. She comforted Olivia, who laid her head on Deb's shoulder. "No, you're not."

"It was her last wish for her ashes to be spread on Mt. Baker, and I've methodically avoided the whole area. It's time. I know that."

"I suspect you'll want to do this on your own, but you let me know what you need. I'll be there for you." Deb kept stroking her back.

"You know, Irene would have loved you. Your vibrancy and the way you embrace life and all it has to offer is so damn enticing. It was very hard not to fall for you. Irene always lived life to the fullest, like you, but I want you to know I haven't fallen in love with you as a replacement for Irene. You are so different. You have this vulnerability and compassion Irene never had. It's not that Irene lacked empathy, she just wasn't ruled as much by her heart. Sometimes, her logical approach to the world would drive me nuts." Olivia paused. "I think maybe I would like you to come with me, or at least drive with me. I can take a hike by myself and finally say goodbye."

"You tell me when you'd like to go. If I'm scheduled to work, I'll take those days off. Please, don't ever feel like you can't talk about Irene, okay?"

"Thank you. I do love you."

"I know and I love you too," Deb answered. "Oh, don't forget we're going to need plenty of room, because it's a package deal. We can't forget about Socks. I feel bad about the amount of time I spend at your place, and believe me Socks lets me know he is displeased by that."

"You know I love that little fuzzball. I remember when you picked him out on the first day we met. Of course he'll live with us. Three cats and a dog is still within reasonable limits. No one will say we're crazy cat ladies, yet. Hey, what about him being the king and not playing well with others?"

"He'll adjust. Kids should grow up with lots of animals," Deb remarked.

Olivia quirked her eyebrow. "Kids?"

"Don't panic, but yes I see kids in our future."

"Okay." Olivia's slow smile and one-word answer was enough for Deb. She'd found her match. It was a bonus Olivia hadn't pulled away when Deb made mention of kids. Everything was going to work out perfectly; she just knew it.

CHAPTER TWENTY-EIGHT

Siera wasn't able to keep the smile from her face as she walked beside Jeremy, who kept pace with Bri and her father. Siera thought Bri was the most beautiful bride she'd ever seen. She watched the sunlight reflect off of Bri's golden hair, as it fell across her shoulders. They each held a beautiful bouquet of lilac roses.

Her mom had suggested they walk down the aisle together with their fathers escorting them, and both fathers were beaming with pride. At first, Siera had been nervous when Bri's parents came to visit and stayed with Olivia for three weeks. She'd tried her best to make a good impression, and Olivia kept assuring her all she needed to do was be herself.

She liked Bri's parents, but not as much as she loved Olivia, because Olivia had never made her feel inferior. Maribel and Greg were very stiff and formal when she'd first met them, but over the years, they'd started to loosen up. Siera knew Olivia kept talking to them about the marriage,

and she'd tried not to listen in, but she'd heard their hesitation.

Olivia's raised voice surprised Siera, because Olivia seldom got mad.

"If you screw up your daughter's chance for happiness with your regressive beliefs, you can kiss off any future relationship with her. Bri is marrying Siera, whether you like it or not. They don't need your blessing, but if you love your daughter, you'll give it. I don't want to hear any stupid shit about Bri not being like everyone else, because that's nonsense."

Siera didn't want to continue listening to the conversation. Bri was in the shower, so Siera joined her to keep her from overhearing the fight. She knew their words might hurt her. So, she snuck inside the shower. They giggled the whole time the water rained down on them. It was the first time she'd done that and it was so much fun. They decided it was a lot more pleasurable to shower together than separate.

The next day, Siera felt genuine affection from Bri's mom for the very first time. After that conversation, there was a noticeable difference in how Maribel treated Bri. Siera suspected Olivia had finally managed to convince her it was okay.

When they asked Olivia and Deb to stand up as their maids of honor, both of them cried. They assured Siera and Bri the tears were for happiness.

Everyone was standing and snapping pictures. When they joined Deb and Olivia at the altar, they each accepted a kiss on the cheek from their dads, who joined their hands

together and retreated to their seats. Siera looked over her shoulder and saw both sets of parents in the front row. Her mom and Bri's mom were dabbing their eyes, but Siera knew it was like when Deb and Olivia had cried—they were tears of joy. She smiled at her mom and dad, and Jeremy gave her the thumbs up sign. Toby had both his thumbs up and was sitting next to Amy, who was holding her cell phone up taking pictures.

Siera had asked Deb to help her with her vows. Deb told her she should say what was in her heart—the words would come. She said the best vows were spontaneous, so Siera stood there at the church altar and poured her heart out.

"Bri's been my best friend from the first moment I saw her in the park. It didn't take long for me to know I loved her. I wanted to kiss her. I get to do that soon—after the minister says we're married." Siera smiled. "I promise, I will love you always. We are better together than apart. I don't know what else to say, besides I love you. I really want to be your wife." Siera grinned.

"You did fine," Deb whispered.

"I don't have pretty words. Can I just say, I love you and I really want to get married?"

Siera nodded.

"That'll do," the minister said.

Siera and Bri skipped and giggled down the aisle. When they reached the outside, people started tossing bird seed on them. Siera shook her head and was glad the birds would have something to eat. She knew Bri would be glad for that as well. She overheard Deb whisper to Olivia, "Be prepared, because I'm pushing everyone out of the way when they throw those bouquets. I will be the one to catch them, unless you want one, then I might let you have it."

281

"I want one. Let's join forces and muscle everyone away from our prize. We've got this." Olivia slung her arm over Deb's shoulder.

Siera was ecstatic. She knew it was just a matter of time before her aunt and her other best friend would get married. She hoped they would ask Bri and her to return the favor to be their maids of honor. She would like that.

When she saw Olivia and Deb kiss, she knew she wouldn't have to wait long for another wedding in the Kaufman family.

†

Deb grabbed the small purse she had set on the ground next to the head table. She grinned at Olivia and plucked two Tootsie Pops from her bag.

Olivia laughed when Deb handed her the cherry-flavored sucker. "Are you sure your sister isn't going to have a meltdown when the wedding pictures reveal us sitting in our Sunday best with white sticks protruding from our mouths?"

Deb waved her hand in the air. "Since you pushed me out of the way to get the flowers, I say we have a little contest on who has the most patience. First one to bite loses. Besides, I want to know how many licks before you end up biting into the creamy center." Deb wiggled her eyebrows.

"I'm not participating until I know the prize."

"Loser has to be the one to propose," Deb tentatively stated.

"What if I've already got the perfect proposal in mind and consider that the winning treasure?"

"You do?"

Olivia pulled off the wrapper and popped the lollipop in her mouth. "Mmmhmm."

"Tell me how you plan to do it," Deb ordered.

Olivia pulled the sucker out and it made a loud *plop*. "Nope. It'll ruin the surprise. Clearly, you have no patience and will never win the competition." She pointed to the unwrapped sucker in Deb's hand. "Hey, start licking."

Deb chuckled while she unwrapped her treat. "All right, how about the loser has to re-enact the same number of licks on__"

"That's not a losing proposition either. You are sweeter tasting than this candy."

"Well then, you come up with the prize." Deb took a long slow lick of her sucker and shot Olivia a smoky look.

"All these suggestions are giving me very inappropriate ideas, while in broad daylight. I'm taking this down a different track. How about the loser has to clean the trikes, including those big ass chains?"

"Done. So, does the proposal have anything to do with the trikes?" Deb asked.

"Stop trying to weasel the details out of me, and don't even think about pumping Bri and Siera."

Crunch. Deb bit into her Tootsie Pop and grinned.

"You lose," Olivia teased.

"No, I'm the biggest winner on the planet, because I got the woman I love to admit a proposal is on the horizon. Just don't take too long, neither one of us is getting any younger, you know."

Crunch. "Mmm chocolatey, creamy goodness, almost as tasty as you. Come on baby, let's blow this Tootsie Pop stand, and I'll tell you how many licks until I reach your creamy center."

"Oh, I love how my stash of suckers always gets you in the mood." Deb grabbed Olivia's hand, and they made a hasty exit, giggling all the way to Olivia's truck.

ABOUT THE AUTHOR

ANNETTE MORI

Annette is an award-winning author, published by **Affinity Rainbow Publications**, who lives in the beautiful Pacific Northwest with her wife and their five furry kids. With ten published novels and one Goldie Award for her fourth novel, Locked Inside, she finally feels like a real author. Annette is as much a reader as a writer and is always looking for the next lesfic novel to cue up. She came up with the One Fan at a Time tagline, because it rolled off the tongue much better than One Reader at a Time. After pondering who she was at her core, it was all about connecting to each reader on a personal level. Annette would be the first to admit she doesn't do well with the masses. If someone picks up her book and it touches them, she believes she has achieved what she wants with her writing by reaching each reader. It is who she is at her core. Drop her a line, she loves to hear from readers: annettemori0859@gmail.com.

Sign up for her mailing list.
Check out her YouTube channel.
Visit the Affinity Rainbow Publications website for her books and many other outstanding authors: https://www.affinityebooks.com

OTHER BOOKS FROM AFFINITY

Say You Won't Go by JM Dragon & Erin O'Reilly
Logan Perry spent part of an inheritance traveling to various states, unconsciously looking for something to focus her life on. Taryn Donovan has no self-esteem and hates the waitressing job that barely keeps her in food. Can an unexpected weekend encounter turn out to be something more fulfilling? Find out in this sexually charged romance.

Playing with Matches by Lacey Schmidt
Dr Augusta Stuart has devoted her adult life to supporting the mental health of disadvantaged children and moves to a new clinic in San Antonio. Her friend sets her up on a date with Callia Alexana. prickly debates are somehow as unexpectedly fascinating as playing with matches, and Gus is forced to consider what preconceptions she is willing to burn to find true love.

Changing Perspectives by Jen Silver
Art director, Dani Barker, lives life on the edge and finance director Camila Callaghan thinks it's necessary to stay in the closet to maintain her position. When Dani and Camila meet,

they both sense an attraction, A change of perspective for both women is needed if they are to act on it.

Death is Only the Beginning by JM Dragon
What would you do if you were in a fatal accident with a stranger and ended up in heaven with them? Only to find out it wasn't an accident, it was murder. Follow the ghostly adventures of these two acrimonious strangers, who help two women find love and find closure for their predicament.

Shotgun Rider by Ali Spooner
Kim and Laney, sweethearts for fifty years go on a road trip to their childhood home state of North Carolina. They follow trails they made as younger women, and relive cherished memories of their lives together. A haunting story, of romance, and lifelong friendship.

For the Love of a Woman by S. Anne Gardner
In a world where oil is supreme, passion rules reason and there is always the threat of civil war. In this jungle of power Raisa Andieta resides as one of its masters. Her only desire is to rule it alone. Carolyn Stenbeck is just trying to keep her marriage together. Her only desire is to be able to escape and never look back. When Raisa and Carolyn meet, it is like fuel and fire…A storm is brewing. Civil War is in the air, and passion like the coming storm begins to erupt.

Dress Blues by Dannie Marsden
Lucinda (Luce) Velazquez had it all; a job she loved, a woman she loved, and a bright future ahead of her. In a flash of light surrounded by the sound of twisting metal, her life

changes dramatically. Her inability to share her deepest thoughts and fears threaten all that she holds dear. Can she allow her lover and others in or will she lose it all?

The Bee Charmer by Ali Spooner
The Bee Charmer by Ali Spooner
After the death of her father, Nat St. Croix needs to decide on which direction her life should take. Does she continue her life alone, as a trapper and trader, or does she start over and try to fit into a town surrounded by strangers? Will the call of the wild and all that is familiar or, will the call of love capture Nat's heart?

We're Not in Kansas Anymore by Annette Mori
Silver Lining, a successful lesbian romance writer, is just starting to come out of the dark tunnel after her wife's untimely death when she has the crazy idea to sponsor a contest. Silver has more than an unwelcome stalker to overcome as she struggles with the guilt over her attraction to Jasmine and the lingering memories of her dead wife. In this prequel to, The Review, learn where it all started.

The Organization by Annette Mori & Erin O'Reilly
The feisty, fiery women from Asset Management are back for another heart-stopping adventure! This time, their sites are set on a new mob boss Leonid Petrov. Val is tagged as the go-to member to infiltrate Leonid's inner circle. Tasked with keeping Leonid's impossible new wife, Gina, safe, Val encounters more problems than solutions. Will wild card Gina be Val's Achilles heel and lead to her demise, or will it fill her with a strength she didn't know she had?

Jeager's by JM Dragon
When your world turns upside down and all your safe secure yearnings are thrown to the wind what happens? What would you do? University lecturer Dr. Kirsten Van De Pelt shortly due to retire early from her academic life is about to find the answers to those questions when Corley Anders, a TV star, enters her life. Will Kirsten take an opportunity of a lifetime or simply settle for the safety net that has been her life.

Running From Love by Jen Silver
Sam Wade returns home from a business trip to discover her wife, Beth left her for another woman, Lydia. To take her mind off the breakup, Sam accepts an assignment to learn to play golf at the newly opened Temperley Cliffs Golf Resort in Cornwall not knowing that is where Beth and Lydia plan to go too. There is more than one way to run from love; from never having to make a commitment and say those magical three words, "I love you." Find out what happens when they find themselves together—sport, betrayal, jealousy, and love form an unforgettable fusion of emotions.

Specter of Fear by Erin O'Reilly
Anne and Bailey are in love and planning a future together. Only the letters that Anne keeps getting are filling her with fear and doubt. Could the love they share really be a sham? Or is there something more behind the letters? Is the sender of the letters after Anne, Bailey or both women? Find out in this suspenseful tale...or is it a real story?

Affinity
Rainbow Publications

eBooks, Print, Free eBooks

Visit our website for more publications available online.

www.affinityrainbowpublications.com

Published by Affinity Rainbow Publications
A Division of Affinity eBook Press NZ LTD
Canterbury, New Zealand

Registered Company 2517228